I0608035

Modified Horizon

By
Ran Vant

Modified Horizon
A Shear Plane Book

This is fiction. The characters, names, events, places, and other elements of the novel are fictitious or used fictitiously.

Book One
Version: 20200607

ISBN: 978-1-952977-01-5

0. Light and Shadow

A single shaft of light cut down through the dusty workshop air, creating a world of shadow. The shadow was silent. It had been quiet for a long time. But soon the silence would be broken.

A hint of voices emerged out of the stillness. Laughter grew louder in the distance.

"Where on earth are you taking us, Es?"

"Just a few steps farther."

"This better be good, dragging us all the way out here."

"Oh, it will be. Trust me."

A latch on a solid steel door lifted. The voices became loud and clear.

"I do have classes tomorrow. I can't be out all night."

"Relax, William. We all do."

"Yeah, but I have to-"

Jamie cut William off as she got her first glimpse into the secret workshop. "What *is* this place?"

The four university students walked into the dark fabrication shop.

"It's kinda creepy in here, Es."

Es walked over to a panel on the wall, and did what she had become used to doing: she threw the light switch, illuminating the center of the room and the sleek winged machine that waited there.

But she wasn't looking at the winged machine; she was watching her friends to see their reactions.

William, Jamie, and Felix stood for a moment stunned, taking it in. Felix stood with his mouth agape. Es watched them with pride. This was just the beginning. Wait until they heard about the rest. She had been patient, she had kept the secrets, she had worked hard. The anticipation had been like buying the perfect gift months in advance of that special day when it would be given. Now came the joy of revelation. Finally she could begin to tell them about it, about what they could accomplish together. And she could also tell them that they would not need to do it alone.

Jamie jumped up and down. "I can't believe it! Look at that, Es! It's amazing!" Jamie had read the old books, so she knew exactly what she was looking at. But this was the first time she had ever seen a real life exemplar.

"What is it?" William asked, the only non-engineer of the group.

"A sled, you moron!" Jamie ran over to it.

"Pardon me, Miss Know-It-All. I've never seen one before," William said. "How was I supposed to know?" Why should he know about banned technology? Why should anyone?

"*Nobody* around here has seen one before. That's the point. Nobody and nothing has been allowed to fly for ages," Felix said.

"It probably doesn't even work," William commented.

"Oh, it will fly, no doubt about that. This baby is capable of climbing up to the heavens. And she packs a punch, too," Es said. She should know; she helped build it. The models, the testing, proved it. No doubt about it: it would fly.

"How'd you do it?" Jamie said, already trying to crawl into the cockpit to get a good look at the controls.

"That's what I wanted to talk to you about," Es said. "The gens have been calling the shots for far too long. I mean, who do they think they are? I met some people, some people who don't just talk about bringing down those genetically modified freaks. These people are actually working on how to do it. The gens seem to think that they are becoming gods, if not gods already. We aim to show them that they still can die just like the rest of us."

William scoffed. He may not have studied old flying machine engineering books, but William had read a lot of other things. And he knew that what he was hearing was dangerous. "You know how many people have thought that way before, Es? You see them around? No? You don't see them around because they are gone, because they are dead. People who talk like you are talking don't last long. People who build planes and rockets and sleds die. That's the way it is. Whether the gens are gods or not doesn't matter. Nobody else is around who thinks the way Es is talking, cause the gens are good at killing them."

"Dude, Billy-boy, relax for once in your life!" Jamie's muffled voice came from the cockpit.

"No, we are around, William," Es corrected him in a gentler tone than Jamie had. "You just don't have the eyes to see us, William. We're here. We're growing stronger every day. There's more of us than you think. But we need more good people. People with an education in the relevant fields. People like you."

Jamie scrambled out from the cockpit. Was she seriously being recruited? By Es? Jamie needed to hear this as clearly as possible. This was too awesome.

William was not so enthusiastic. "Are you kidding me? You're crazy, Es! You can't bring down the gens. You should be reading fewer engineering books and more history books. You think a couple little flying sleds with guns are going to tilt the scales of power against the gens one little bit?" You didn't need to be an engineer to see that a sled was no match for a gen army.

"Sleds alone? Of course not," Es said.

"What else, then?" William asked. It would take a miracle weapon to even begin to dent the gens. And how many people had tried even so-called miracle weapons and failed? So what did Es think she had up her sleeve?

"Don't be ridiculous, Billy," Jamie admonished. "You think you get to know all the secrets up front? You just find out one of your best friends is secretly working with the Organization and now you expect her to spill the beans on everything? Come on! But use your imagination. If Es here can build this with a little help, without us even knowing, think what a whole bunch of us could do. The sky's the limit."

"I've learned how to build sleds and more. You can be trained for-"

Es stopped as she heard two distinct bumps on the roof directly above the aero sled.

The others looked up.

The ceiling exploded downward and a shower of glass and metal rained down. A black winged figured dropped through the hole in the ceiling, landing heavily on the sled, causing the flying machine to buckle under the force of the figure's impact.

The black figure's wings spread wide. "For the crime of developing the forbidden technology of flight, you are sentenced to death." The figure raised its gauntleted fist: Es fell to the ground, lifeless.

Then the armored creature pointed its gauntleted fists straight down at the aerial combat sled beneath its feet and melted it into slag and smoldering plastics. The black figure rode the melting sled to the floor.

It is said that creatures, when confronted with danger, have two natural responses: fight or flight. But the dark figure knew from experience that there was a third natural reaction, for he had seen it time and time again among the primitive humans. After the one named Es fell, the others did not fight or flee. They froze, paralyzed with fear, unable to act or speak. Jamie whimpered, on the verge of collapsing into a heap of uncontrolled emotion. William shook with fear. Felix stood with eyes wide, watching. The winged creature knew that the cowering humans before him who were still alive had no special knowledge, had not developed or possessed forbidden technology, and would serve a more useful purpose alive than dead. They would serve as witnesses to what happened to those that tried to defy the Ancients.

"Remember," the dark winged figure said as it prepared to leave: "The sky belongs to us."

Prologue

There is always change. Yet some remain the same, only different.

I have changed much since I took my first breath upon the earth. Still, there is a part of me that I feel has been the same since the beginning. I feel that I have been continuous, but no doubt many would not recognize me now. Nor would many who know me now have recognized me then. My ideas, my appearance, my desires, my dreams – all have changed. Am I the same person then?

You rarely know when change is going to happen, that moment when the world shifts, and you see everything from a whole new perspective. Sometimes the change happens quickly. Sometimes it is a gradual process, evolving over time. Sometimes you look back and you know the change happened, but you are hard pressed to find the moment, to say when or how it happened. You simply know that it did.

Then there are those rare moments, those times when you can see the change about to happen. Sometimes the change is lurking in the shadows; you know something is out there, but you aren't quite sure when it will strike, only that it likely will. Other times the change is a storm on the horizon, building, wind shifts announcing to those who can read the signs that the sunshine is soon coming to an end. You can prepare for some change, even fight it on occasion. Other times, it is like the tide: inevitable, unstoppable.

Of course, the tides have risen and fallen for nearly an eternity. Storms have come and gone countless times. Creatures have leapt from and back into the shadows since long before they crawled from the sea.

And you. You have failed, you have succeeded. I have succeeded, I have failed. Is there anything new under the sun?

New, or old, I intend to tell you a story. And as I find with most stories, it is hard to know this story's true beginning, and therefore it is hard to know where I should start. Perhaps that is because all stories are part of one bigger story, and there has only been one true beginning. Or perhaps only a few witness each new beginning, and this makes the start blurred to the rest of us. Perhaps the story is a coil, a circle with never a beginning nor an end. Perhaps it is something else entirely. Though I have seen much, I do not know the answer.

Whether they are at the beginning or at the end, or more likely somewhere in between, I want to tell you about the one called Michael and the one called Clara. Each of us has reasons; sometimes different reasons at different times. I have my purposes; you have yours. But in order for you to understand, I will need to go back further.

For generations, human society had been based on the idea that every person had the ability to succeed, to improve one's condition, even to rise to the top. The *idea* was one of equality of potential and of opportunity. These were the concepts that made the world go round, that powered the masses, that fueled economies, that improved standards of living, that gave hope. Despite the occasional setback, the idea contained a simple equation that stated that hard work would pay off, that effort would yield gains; Try, and eventually things would work out; Work hard, and one day you'll make it. This idea made life better for billions where other ideas had failed.

The equation, however, changed. Hope in equality did not spring eternal. One might argue it began with the drugs or with the chips. One might argue it began long before. But whether or not they were the genesis of events, the drugs and chips mattered. Some of the first drugs subtly improved memory. Others improved stamina and alertness. Then came those that dramatically reduced the time needed for sleep – some found they need no sleep at all. Later, the drugs radically increased brain connectivity. New breakthroughs were made. Life got better.

The chips were simple enough back then. Accountants, businesspeople, and engineers found math bio-chips useful. Why bother with clumsy user interfaces and slow speed, when a bio-chip in the brain or under the skin could do the work flawlessly and with little effort, almost intuitively? Language and communication chips offered the promise of even closer human societies. Life got better.

Life got better. For some.

The drugs and the bio-chips came to be known as "the modification technologies," "modology," or, in shorthand, "mod." It could have been that the modification technologies were simply an extension of what humanity had always done. Throughout recorded history, and likely even before, humans were always changing their environment to better suit their needs and wants. And they were always changing themselves. They changed what they ate. They changed how they worked. They changed what they thought. Why not change a little more? It could have been merely a subtle continuation, but it wasn't. Modology wasn't simply a gradual extension of what humanity had always done. It was a sudden revolution, and a revolution not accepted by all.

Perhaps the most alluring part of the mod revolution was the extension of life. Having obtained the fruit from the tree of knowledge long ago, they now sought to seize the fruit from the tree of life. But who could blame them? Would you turn down 10 more years of healthy life if it were offered to you in a pill? Would you turn down 50 more years? Or 100? Why not try to live forever? Who could blame them?

Well, many people found that they could blame those who sought immortality, and they did. They blamed them out of jealousy or out of moral outrage. They blamed them out of concern for the less fortunate or out of concern for the future. They blamed them for many reasons. The modification technologies were expensive and not all could afford them. Others could afford them, but opposed the technologies on moral grounds. What was the true cost? Should thousands work almost as slaves so one can try to live forever? What right did these people have to play god? Couldn't they see what the modification technologies were doing to economies and social systems? Did some people have the right to try to live forever at the expense of the rest?

They called those who used the modification technologies "modified humans" or just "mods." Those who rejected modology were first called "traditionalists," or sometimes "true humans," but they were soon known simply as "truds," a shortened version of "traditional" coined by a modified who looked upon them as people who allowed themselves to be walked over, little more than evolution's residual sludge. And then there soon arose a third major grouping: the "genetically modified" or "gens."

The gens did not merely adopt the modification technologies; the genetically modified were changed before conception, genetically engineered to be superior. First, parents might have simply selected the sex of their child, then the eye color. But why not give them perfect vision, too? Or how about a better memory? Or the ability to think faster? Better looks? More athletic? A better way to naturally interface with the chips? Why not? It could be done. All of it. For a price.

Some argued that the Conflict would not have happened had the modification technologies been introduced slowly or if everyone had had equal access to the technologies. Some argued that the Conflict could have been prevented if the robots and machines had been built sooner, if the robots could have engaged in autonomous production with the fruits of their labors going to the masses; Others argued the robots and machines would have only made things worse. There were a host of theories about what might have happened. But the modification technologies came fast. The robots were not ready. It did not stop with the riots. The Conflict happened. And at that point, the past could not be undone.

In the Conflict, truds battled against the mods and gens. It started small, but grew quickly. The idea of equal opportunity gave way to something else: the idea that equal outcomes were possible by force. Hope in opportunity was lost.

How could a traditionalist compete on the job with a modified human, let alone a genetically modified one? Truds with 20 years of education and 20 years of experience would be replaced by a mod who could afford a bio-chip or a gen who was only 12 and could do the work by instinct. Businesses run by truds were out competed by those run by mods. If you believed modification technologies were wrong, you could not compete: not for education, not for jobs, not for money, not for hope. Capitalism began to crumble as the modifieds began to dominate. The mods and gens lived like kings.

Those without access to the technologies, the truds, lived nearly the life of serfs.

Some modifieds did indeed "dominate" in the worst sense of the word. They were still born human after all. They were still people with the same human flaws that had always been present throughout history. Or were they?

But the traditionalists were not finished yet. In the Conflict between truds and mods, the truds still had the numbers, and with the numbers, power. The traditionalists would not be dominated. In their minds, earth was for humans, not for modifieds, not for crimes against nature, not for artificial creatures concocted in a laboratory, not for those who played in the realms reserved for God. The truds would not be ruled over like animals. Force would be used to bring down those who dominated, and freedom would be restored. So the traditionalists seized the earth firmly before it could be taken from them. Or rather, they tried.

It is true that in some places the Conflict was not violent. The mods and gens were allowed to walk away to the west. Indeed, sometimes the truds walked east. But these were the exceptions. Mods were slain in the street, gen labs were ransacked, while elsewhere truds were cut down by an enemy that could think and move faster.

The mods and gens had many advantages, but the truds had two of their own: leaders and numbers. The modifieds were independent and difficult to govern and lead. The traditionalists had effective leaders, and with that and the power of numbers willing to follow them, they managed to push the mods and gens to a corner of the west. At the water, the truds were slowed. Then the Conflict subsided for a time, for the truds could not advance any further against the mods and gens. The truds declared that all those who wished to use the modification technologies must move west.

Some of those made it west. Many did not.

Thereafter, the modification technologies were forbidden in the east, and travel to the west, where the modifieds lived, was not allowed.

Time passed.

The difference between mod and gens lessened to the point that both were simply called "gens." But the beliefs of the gens and truds hardened and the gulf between them grew wider.

Now there was a gen who had once (before the Conflict) wielded great power and wealth. He had lived far in the east and could not forget what he had experienced and witnessed on his trek west during the Conflict. He could not forget, nor could he forgive, even though most of the truds who had been alive during the Conflict had by then been long dead. To him, truds were inferior, backward creatures. So he gathered other gens to him, and together they secretly built an army of machines, unknown to both the truds and most of the gens.

When the gen-man thought the time right, he invaded the trud lands in the east and sought once more to exercise dominion over them. The attack of the machines, the start of the Machine War, was so swift that the truds in that region fell quickly. But many other gens were aghast at what had happened to the truds in that region and conspired to stop the gen-man who they believed was power hungry. After a time, they exercised their plan and through much effort he was overthrown. The great machine army was withdrawn from the trud lands.

But the damage had been done. The Machine War rekindled the truds' fear that they would be forever dominated by the gens, that they were never safe. The fear was rekindled and with the fear, a plan. And it grew slowly, like a hidden ember.

Those who had led the truds during the Conflict had died, and with those trud leaders had died the goal of exterminating the gens. The truds had begun to grow accustomed to the idea that a land of gens would always exist in the west. But with the Machine War the cry of mod extermination was born again. The truds had secretly developed powerful new weapons of their own, and now they sought to use them.

These new weapons released nothing that would poison the earth for an age, unlike the weapons of old. There would be no fallout to contaminate the earth. After the attack, the land could be resettled immediately. The weapons destroyed not only life, but all circuitry in the machines, and with the machines gone, the gens were vulnerable. The weapons would rid the world of the gens who played at god and their protective army of machines. And the weapons would not destroy their trud masters, if the attack was perfect. It nearly was.

The weapons came in waves. First, the ones smuggled in. Then, the missiles and drones. Finally, the soldiers and agents. Cities of gens were wiped out in an instant. Then the towns. Then the countryside. And then the gen remainders were hunted down, one by one. It was called the Annihilation.

But the truds had forgotten something. Or rather, they had never known about it. It was another city. And it was under the sea. There, under the roiling waves, in the last city of the original gens, they took refuge. There, under the boiling water, they conceived a plan that would lead to their salvation. Or so they hoped.

Like most creatures, the gens feared death. But there is a curious thing about those who live long lives. When one can imagine living forever, one becomes even more fearful of death, not less. Death becomes something unnatural and foreign and all the more tragic. The gens were no different, and they strove to ensure they would not be wiped from the face of the earth by the truds.

There were now few gens left, and they had been alive a long time. They did not want to risk dying in an effort of liberation, but they also did not want to live in fear of the day the truds discovered their hidden Atlantis. So the gens took council and began growing an army. An army without vulnerable circuits. An army of liberation. An army that would not be afraid to die. An army for themselves.

And thus in time the gens emerged to take lands of their own and conquered the trud armies of the east. The gens at that time did not wish to dominate the truds, but neither could they allow the truds to build weapons that might destroy them. Therefore, it was necessary to police the trud lands to suppress the old technologies and to ensure that no new technologies were allowed to arise that might threaten the gens and their eternal life. The truds would often see the gens' agents flying in the sky, protecting the gens and destroying technologies or regions deemed a threat. The truds came to look at the sky in fear.

Many trud generations passed in this state. An uneasy tension grew along with rumors of a plan for the gens to be done with the truds forever, a plan called 'the Event.' And then it was time to change again.

Which brings us to the one called Michael Lightbringer and a girl named Clara.

1. Lightbringer

He looked out across the plain, far below. The target was down there, hidden among the smooth buildings of steel and glass. The target was down there, and they would destroy it. The fortress hovered seven thousand feet above the small city below.

"It's time," he said into the microphone hidden beneath the black metal of his mask. He took a step toward the edge and jumped from the floating fortress. His black armored body fell like a rock towards the earth beneath, his chin leading the way. Above and to his right, his silver-armored mate matched his descent. A bit farther behind and to his left, two more companions hung in the sky.

Like birds of prey diving, they plunged towards the city. The smooth buildings drew closer and their large size became apparent. He knew exactly where he was going: it was beneath the smaller angular building to the north of the river. His eyes scanned the ground, following the ribbon of blue. There. It would be underground. The contraband almost always was. They foolishly thought they were safer there, under the earth.

The four armored bodies hurled through the air until the tops of the tallest buildings were rising above them. Then, one by one, from each armored body's back sprung metal wings, switchblades opening to slice the air. The wings angled to catch the resistance, rapidly slowing their descent, until each guardian's legs swung down to gently greet the ground. With another switchblade action, the wings were once more concealed in the small oblong pods on their backs.

A few pedestrians scattered as he aimed his fist at a point on the ground directly next to the wall of the small angular building. A nearly invisible beam instantaneously flew forth from his black gauntleted fist. The only evidence of the beam was a distortion of the air, like heat rising from concrete on a hot summer day, and the exploding bits of concrete that bounced off the four armored beings.

A gaping hole stood open but for a moment before the four jumped through in rapid succession. It was as they had been told. Before them stood a lab with boiling beakers, spinning centrifuges, and several people lying about the room, thrown down by the creation of the improvised doorway. One man tried to reach for a rail gun, but the red-armored one turned his gantlet beam on the man first, and now only a sad pile remained. The silver-armored one grabbed some vials from a vault while the others melted everything of value in the lab. Everything of value but the people. With the exception of the one who reached for a gun, they let them be this time. Those were sometimes the orders. The yellow one did, however, inject each person with a tracer. It would enable them to be easily identified later and associated with this illegal lab, if the need arose.

He slowly scanned the room, and then uttered the only word of the mission, "Solid." First the black one, then the silver, left through the same hole in the concrete that led to the street above. The dark red and yellow ones were not far behind.

The black figure led the four skyward, back to their floating castle in the sky.

2. Father and Daughter

The little red-headed, blue-eyed girl clutched the emerald green pendant that hung from her neck with one hand and gripped her father's hand with the other. They stood side by side, looking across the tall grasses and rolling hills. In the near distance, a tall man walked towards them. Farther back, beyond the man walking towards them, a massive and muscular man sat calmly by an old oak tree. The man under the tree seemed to ignore the father and the girl and instead visually scanned the horizon while a black bird in the tree crowed. The little girl felt as if they might be the only four people left in the world.

"Clara, we've finally made it. You've been a trooper. You've walked a long, long way. But our journey finally ends today. That, over there, is my friend, Alaric," he said, pointing with his free hand at the man confidently striding towards them, a smile on his yellow-bearded face. "He was mom's friend, too. I think you'll like him." He looked down at the girl. Clara stared at the dirt. The father knelt next to her and lifted her chin up. He brushed her red locks to the side to look into her blue eyes. "We'll be safe here for a long time. I promise. They won't find us here, okay?"

Clara managed a weak smile and nodded. She'd heard promises before.

"So, are you ready?" She nodded again reluctantly and the father stood to greet the approaching man, letting go of his daughter's hand.

The approaching man with the yellow beard spoke first. "Lothar, we're glad you made it."

"Alaric, I thought I'd never see your scruffy face again."

"Who are you calling scruffy, Red Beard?" Alaric said, commenting on his old friend's growing stubble after the long journey.

The two embraced and slapped each other on the back.

"I see you've brought your daughter. You must be Clara."

Clara didn't answer.

"Since her mother…" Lothar trailed off. "She hasn't felt like talking much recently. We're just going to give it some time."

"I understand," Alaric replied. Turning to Clara, he leaned over to look at her eye to eye, hands resting on his knees. "Clara, we're glad to have you here." Clara grabbed her dad's hand again. "They call me Alaric here. Well, I know you're not in the mood for talking, but think a little bit about your new name." Alaric patted the pockets in his jacket, before locating the proper one. "When you're ready, write it down on this." He held out a scrap of paper and an ancient stubby pencil. She stared at it a moment before releasing her tight grip on her necklace. Then, looking up at her father for a reassuring nod, she released his hand and reached for the paper and pencil. "I'm sure your father has filled you in, but you need to be very careful not to use your real name or your dad's real name anymore, not with anyone, not even your father, okay?" He tousled her red hair and stood up straight again.

Alaric looked at Lothar with his eyebrows raised. It was a difficult thing to put your life in the hands of a little girl.

"Don't worry, Alaric, she knows. We've gone over everything just as your instructions stated. She's a smart kid. When I told her you'd greet me by the name of 'Lothar,' she couldn't help but crack a smile."

Alaric thought he saw her crack a smile even then, though it disappeared in an instant.

Lothar cracked a smile himself. After all this time, after traveling an arduous path, he was once again with a friend. That was at least something. He knew he couldn't protect her alone.

"Well, we should probably get moving right away," Alaric said. He motioned over at the tree where the muscle-bound Conan was waiting under its shade out of earshot. Conan stood, threw his massive rail gun over his wide shoulder, and walked to join the others.

Alaric pointed to the west. "Our settlement is over that way, another couple miles. You'll be amazed how you can't see it until you're on top of it. Try not to walk in a single file line. We want to do our best to avoid cutting a permanent trail. The grass can only handle a few footsteps spread out." He started walking while Lothar and Clara followed slightly behind and to either side. Conan followed behind at a distance, rail gun in hand, head on a swivel.

"Much Fanatic trouble?" Lothar asked, noting Conan's continuous scanning of the territory.

"Not recently. It's been quiet of late. As the ominous cliché goes, one might even say 'it's been too quiet.'" Alaric chuckled to himself. Not too long ago, he would have thought it impossible for the world to be too quiet. "We've been sending scouts farther afield, but there's no sign of any atics – Nearby, anyway. But we're always careful, Conan especially."

"Well, they're still certainly out there somewhere."

"That's for sure," Alaric agreed as they made the final trek toward their new home.

**

They had stopped to rest. Lothar scratched his balding short blond hair before bringing his hand down to the red-beard-stubble on his chin. He studied the pencil scratches on the paper.

"You sure about this?"

She nodded.

"Well, it's a lovely name," he said.

She smiled genuinely.

"Katherine Diana Penelope." Lothar said as he read the name aloud. He had expected perhaps *Sarah*, after a favorite character in one of her books, or *Diana*, or *Penelope*… But not most of those character names piled together, one on top of another. "Katherine Diana Penelope," Lothar repeated, trying to commit his daughter's new, excessively long, name to memory. Maybe he let her read too many books, he thought with an internal smile. Or maybe he needed to teach her to be a little more decisive. Oh well, she could have picked worse. And the names certainly had a noble history. They were certainly better than *Lothar.* "May I call you just Katherine for short, from time to time?"

She nodded, smiling broadly.

Lothar took the piece of paper, folded it, and put it in the pocket over his heart. "Well then, today, Katherine, we get to be born again. Now, Miss Katherine Diana... Penelope, may I have your hand?" Lothar took his daughter's hand, and together they crossed over the little rise, and saw their new home before them.

**

"That's Pete," Alaric said with a sweeping arc of his hand. "We're glad to be able to welcome you to this, our humble settlement."

"Pete?" Lothar asked.

Alaric responded, "That's what we call the settlement out here. Its original name was 'prairie dog town' after the first dirt caves. But that name offered clues as to its location, so we shortened it to its initials, 'PDT.' It wasn't long until before 'PDT' ran into 'Petie' and then simply 'Pete.' I'll introduce you to 'Chuck' and 'Mary', that is, the wood camp and the emergency retreat, later."

Clara surveyed her new home that would go along with her new name, Katherine, and her new life. The settlement was nestled into the gently sloping walls of a shallow draw. Several small buildings emerged from the earth like scattered half-buried rocks left by glaciers in another age. Live grasses grew from the roofs such that only the front vertical surfaces were barely visible, and those were painted to a close approximation of the colors and patterns of the grasses.

At the bottom of the draw, a small spring fed a tiny creek that ran through the fields. As she would soon learn, it ran towards a larger stream some quarter of a mile away. The little creek turned twice in the course of its short run, concealing its source from anyone coming up the relatively larger stream's modest valley. In the rolling hills and plains of the territory, the settlement was hidden from view from all directions.

"Well, Alaric, Pete looks a little empty. Where is everyone? I expected to at least see a guard or two," Lothar asked, security still being at the forefront on his mind even in the seemingly endless wilderness.

"Ah, my friend, you doubt our competence? The guards are here; you just can't readily see them. We walked right past a couple of the bunkers, hidden in the grasses. Rest assured, if we'd been Fanatics we wouldn't have made it over the rise. But you'll get your chance to see all of that soon enough when you get to pull your guard duty. Everybody pulls their weight on the mundane tasks, too. Security is boring here, and we intend to keep it that way by being vigilant. In the meantime, almost everyone's waiting inside to greet you. We'd best not keep them waiting anymore." Then turning to the little Katherine, Alaric asked, "Shall we go meet your new friends?"

Katherine silently nodded her assent.

Lothar took his daughter's hand in his and led her to their new home. It was the first time in a long while that he allowed himself to relax. It was the first time in a long while that he felt safe. He was among friends once again.

But Lothar knew that the hunters were still out there. And the hunters would not stop looking for him. Nor would they stop hunting for little Clara. For he understood that it was not him that the hunters ultimately wanted. They wanted her.

3. Download

The mask hissed as he released the latch. He pulled the mask forward and off, his dark hair falling forward upon his brow. It took a split second for his mind to adjust from the 360-degree view of the mask to the narrow perspective of normal vision.

He placed his metal mask upon the stand. Turning, he walked around the large black chair and sat down. The chair gently reclined backward to the quiet whirl of electric motors. Two padded arms, one from each side, hummed as they swung upward on each side of his head. He closed his eyes as the warm pulse of the download began.

Michael Lightbringer, a Guardian of the West, relaxed during the routine conducted before and after each mission. The mission was downloaded from his brain to a central computer, an organic brain in the center of the floating castle, to be processed and analyzed before being reported to the Ancients. As he sat in the chair with the warm hum of the pads, more than just the mission was downloaded: his entire brain structure was scanned and stored. Michael understood that not only did this enable the Ancients to have a clearer picture of the mission, it also enabled the restoration of a Guardian should he fall in battle. But falling in battle was a rare occurrence for one such as him. It had not happened once in the last seven years. It was getting easier.

After a few seconds, a light turned blue, the arms retracted, and the chair up-righted itself. He stood and went to remove his suit of armor. His armor was like a second skin to him, but it was necessary to recharge and clean the suit on occasion. And standard operating procedure called for an inspection of the suit following each mission. The suit had never failed him before, and meticulous care was one of the reasons. If the slightest imperfection in a suit was identified, other identical suits awaited him to be used while the blemished suit was repaired.

In the room in which he stood there was a wall with twelve arched recesses slightly taller than a man. Into one of these recesses he stepped, placing his back against the wall. There was a latching sound and a small lurching upward as the maintenance bay gripped the suit on the back and at each foot. He placed his arms firmly in smaller latches on each side. Pressurized air hissed as the suit split open, liquid metal flowed to the sides, and Michael Lightbringer stepped out. The suit disappeared for inspection while another dropped into position, ready at a moment's notice.

"Are you coming to the dining hall?" his silver-haired mate asked. Her hair was not gray from stress, nor was it silver from age. Like him, she looked no older than twenty-five. Rather, it was metallic silver by design. Her hair shone with the glimmer of highly polished metal.

"Yes, it would be good to eat," he replied. It was time to settle in for another long wait. But he was patient. Missions did not come often, and the missions these days took little time.

Michael loved her more than anything else. Well, perhaps he loved her equally together with his job and serving the Ancients. But he didn't need to worry about separating his love, for he worked with her, and together they protected the Ancients. His love for her was the same as for his job and the Ancients. To him, all three were one thing. And she loved him the same. After all, they were designed for each other.

4. The Rebel

The boy slipped quietly into the room. Some 'old' guy he'd never seen before with thinning blond hair and a lame red beard was talking: "Without the Network's knowledge base and technology it will be very difficult for the Natural Human Alliance to maintain the capability to…"

The boy tuned him out. If he was talking about Fanatics, he might be worth sticking around for, but since it sounded like city politics, he wasn't interested. He thought he'd ask Conan anyway, just to make sure he didn't miss anything good.

"Hey Cone, does the new scape know anything about what the atics might be up to?"

"He hasn't said. He's just gotten started. Brian, you missed the entire welcoming dinner. You been running around outside as usual?"

"Of course," Brian nonchalantly replied.

"Well, don't let Meredith catch you. She was a little torqued that you weren't here to greet the new scapes."

"Thanks for the heads up, Cone. But don't worry, I'll be fine."

"I'm just trying to watch out for you little guys."

"Conan, I'm already eleven."

"That's right, your birthday was last week. My bad."

"And when I get old like you, I hope I'm not such a worrywart."

"Old? I'm only twenty-three!"

"Here comes Meredith, I gotta run," Brian said while coolly ducking behind Conan and then slipping into a connecting tunnel.

But he wasn't quite fast enough. Frieda had seen him, and after making eye contact with Meredith, Frieda pointed down the tunnel towards Brian in retreat.

"Brian, come back here right now!" Meredith barked. Nobody else in the room paid attention since it wasn't too uncommon of an occurrence.

Brian debated for an instant whether he shouldn't just continue down the tunnel and pretend he couldn't hear her, but then he thought better of it. Best to turn back around and deal with it now rather than the amplified wrath that would likely attend further delay.

"Where do you think you're going?"

"Well, out and about, you know," he replied. "Who wants to sit around here and hear them talk politics? It's got nothing to do with life here."

"Brian, it has everything to do with life here. But since I know you could not care less, you can go back outside."

"Seriously? You mean you aren't going to punish me for skipping the welcome dinner?" Immediately, Brian thought better of the question. He should have just let it go and gotten out of there while he could.

"Well, there is a catch," Meredith conceded.

"Oh, great." There was always a catch.

"But it's not that bad at all. Come with me." They walked across the room.

Odin was asking Lothar some questions and Brian caught a little more: "How many do you suppose were compromised?"

"At least seven," Lothar replied.

Meredith grabbed Brian by the shoulders and pointed him away from Odin and towards... a girl.

"Katherine, this is my little brother, Brian. Brian, say 'hello.'"

He complied, unenthusiastically. "Hello."

"Why don't you take Katherine out and show her around the settlement. And Brian, she may not feel like talking. She doesn't have to if she doesn't want to, understand?"

"Of course I understand, I'm not an idiot."

Meredith gave her younger brother the evil eye.

"Well, Katherine, let's go. Follow me."

Brian turned around and headed for the main door. Katherine hesitated. An encouraging head raise from Meredith was enough, however, and she trotted after him.

A little too late, Meredith called out in a hushed yell, trying not to disturb the others too much more: "And don't go out past the outer sentry!"

**

"See that ridge over there? That marks the river valley," Brian explained. "Chuck is just below that there – for now, anyway. We move Chuck around every once in a while, since it's harder to defend over there and we leave too much of a footprint or whatever cutting the wood. Everyone's too scared of the atics." Katherine wasn't following everything he rambled off, but she nodded anyway as if she did. Brian continued, "I guess we should get off the highpoint here. Odin would yell at us. He's got all these stupid rules. But you have to learn them if you want to stay out of trouble. Soon enough, though, you'll learn that Odin's rules don't mean much and figure out the real ones. Follow me."

Brian stood up and jogged down the gentle slope through the grasses. He turned back only for a moment to wave on the reluctant Katherine before continuing down between the hills. Katherine got up and ambled after. She wasn't quite sure about the people here, but her dad trusted them so they had to be good people. They just had to be.

5. Perfection

Gabriella Stormcaller tossed her silver hair behind her shoulders. "So, you think can run the scenario better than I can, do you?" she playfully called to Michael Lightbringer as the simulator in the belly of Fortress Magritte hummed to life.

Air jets sprang open from the floor as Gabriella jumped into the simulator. Powerful magnets and jets of air kept her afloat as she flew through a simulated city on the screens around, above, and below her. Lasers focused on her eyes to create the necessary multidimensional effects. Truds with various weapons popped up from behind buildings, and one by one Gabriella Stormcaller hit them with the precision of William Tell shooting the apple off his son's head. She just happened to aim a few inches lower than the imaginary apple.

Now she turned and dove on the invisible jets of air, aiming for a team of simulated trud-men setting up a canopy gun on street in the valley below. A virtual beam erupted from her outstretched hands and hit one of the men. A split second later and she had felled a second and third man. But the fourth trud now had the canopy gun set up, and he let forth a solid dome of fire. The simulated dome of energy slammed into Gabriella Stormcaller, the simulator screens went black, and the jets of air slowed. She reached her feet toward the floor as the magnets spun down and air jets cooled. Her feet gently kissed the floor.

Michael Lightbringer shook his head. "You should have hit the canopy gun first, and then worried about the men once they couldn't have harmed you, Gabriella," he chastised her.

"Ah, but you didn't watch the simulation closely enough," she replied. "Simulator, replay the last 10 seconds. See there, in the parallel street?"

"Yes, that's Dante Starmaker," he acknowledged.

"You see, Dante was below the dome of fire of the canopy gun. By taking out the other three, I left only one for him to worry about as he turned the corner. I may have gotten hit, but I gave Dante a chance to capture rather than destroy the canopy gun. With the gun intact, we could learn where it came from and ensure that no more were manufactured. The foot soldiers wouldn't have known; they'd make sure of that."

Michael Lightbringer smiled at her quick, if unconventional, reasoning. "But then you would have been unavailable for another mission for the three days you were in restoration."

"The intelligence about the manufacturing of the gun would have been worth it," she answered. And as proof, seemingly on cue, the simulator screen showed the analysis of her performance and her score: perfect.

She was just as he had always known her. Ever the same. Eternal. And he was always amazed at how she could see the solution to the most challenging scenarios the simulator would throw at her. Gabriella Stormcaller was not easy to trick.

6. Fanatics

Brian squinted into the binoculars. "Yep," he whispered. "Four atics down there."

Katherine felt her heart beat faster with fear and adrenaline. She instinctively grabbed the green pendant on her necklace with one hand and pulled the dog's collar down to the ground. "We should go."

"Just relax. They don't even know we're here. What are they going to do?"

"They could kill us," Katherine argued. That's what Fanatics did to people like her and Brian. She didn't think that was a risk worth taking. She got down even lower to the ground. Thunder, the dog, laid down, eyes looking up at Katherine.

"They're Fanatics, not murderers. You just have to understand their rules. And besides, like I said, they don't even know we are here."

"Brian, we need-"

"Shhhhh..." Brian hushed her. He did it primarily for the purpose of keeping Katherine from arguing rather than for security reasons. The atics were far enough away, the wind was to Brian's face, and they weren't yelling. There wasn't a chance in the world that the atics were going to hear them talking in low voices under those conditions. But he shushed her anyway. He just wanted her to shut up sometimes. When she first showed up, she didn't say a word and people were worried that she wouldn't talk. Now, several years later, sometimes she wouldn't shut up. Why couldn't there be a happy medium, Brian wondered.

Katherine was scared and wasn't about to make another peep. She tried to disappear into the grass, to will herself into invisibility. She imagined herself sinking into the earth, pressing herself lower, trying to hide from the dangerous eyes only several hills away. Thunder inched closer to her.

Brian studied them through the binoculars. These atics looked rather typical, if an atic could be considered normal. Normal in this case meant no clothes, a little dirty, unkempt hair, but human enough. He'd watched them before and thought he was beginning to understand them. Most people in the R.T. feared the Fanatics. Their marauding reputation, fearlessness, and animal-like behavior seemed to infect almost everyone with fear and disgust, Brian excepted. He knew from close observation that they didn't randomly kill each other. They only seemed to attack those who didn't follow their rules. Like stupid scapes from the cities. Stupid scapes offended nature and the atics, and therefore the scapes died. It wasn't that hard to figure out. Stupid scapes... Like Katherine was once, what seemed like a long time ago.

The atics rose, and Brian could see they carried wooden spears. The spears were blackened on the sharp end, as if they had been hardened in a fire. He was surprised that this group didn't seem to be carrying a blow gun or bows. This group's choice of weapons made them a safer group to observe since they couldn't attack from a distance. It might also be the group to one day approach for the same reasons. But he wasn't ready for that yet. He didn't understand them enough yet. Still, he was thinking about it.

The four atics ambled off along the riverfront and disappeared in the woodlands.

"Are they leaving?" Katherine asked.

"Yep," Brian responded.

"Good. We should get back to Pete," Katherine advised. She wanted nothing more than to put more distance between themselves and the Fanatics. She heard the stories and, unlike Brian, feared the atics and what they might do. A concrete home buried in the dirt with armed friends standing guard sounded really good at the moment.

"Nah, I was having fun watching them." Brian dismissed her worries. She didn't understand them like he did. Few people did. To understand them, one had to watch them. Most others ran or attacked when they saw atics. Most others died.

"They're dangerous," Katherine reminded him.

"Maybe to a scape like you."

"They'd kill you just as fast as they'd kill me. My dad says atics-"

"You'll have to learn pretty fast not to believe everything the old folks tell you."

"But-" she tried to continue.

"Don't be a stupid scape. Use your eyes. Observe the world! Observe them, the so-called Fanatics. Use your brain, think for yourself." Brian abruptly stood up, shouldered his backpack, and started walking back towards Pete.

Katherine didn't respond to Brian's rant immediately. They'd practically grown up together, and still he sometimes acted like she was a foreigner invading his space. A significant portion of her life had been spent in the R.T., and still Brian didn't treat her as one of them. She sometimes wondered why she hung out with him as much as she did instead of Lock, Heidi, or even Edda. They didn't roam as much, but was roaming worth it if you were always cut down? Lock and Heidi didn't insult her by calling her a scape, while Brian still did derisively. For him, it wasn't some chummy nickname like Edda used it. Even if it was perhaps technically true, it didn't feel good. Plus, Brian acted like a know-it-all. Sure, he knew more about the Refuge Territories. He was also a little older. But Katherine, scape or not, wasn't stupid. He kept talking down to her. Brian thought he understood the Territories better than anyone else. Maybe he did, at least his little corner of it, but that didn't make him better than everyone else. He didn't need to tell her she was stupid just because she hadn't had the opportunity to learn. He didn't need to act superior. He didn't need to be mean.

Katherine stood, shouldered her own pack, and looked down the hill towards Brian hiking away. Maybe he could work on being nicer, she thought. But was he going to change on his own? Brian? Ha! He'd need help. Maybe she was the one to help him work on that. Fat chance he was going to change, but maybe somebody ought to try.

She followed after.

They walked awhile before Brian spoke again. "Listen, the atics are different. That doesn't make them evil."

Hmph. Maybe Brian was feeling a little guilty about his outburst and wanted to justify himself. "Then how come they kill city escapes?" Katherine asked.

"Cause people aren't supposed to go into the Refuge Territories. It's illegal. Don't be stupid."

There was that word again that she hated. "You live here," she pointed out sharply.

"I was born here."

"Still technically illegal. And the atics are illegally living here, too."

"They aren't destroying the place with technology. They're just living naturally like the rest of the animals."

"Humans weren't meant to live like animals."

"Says who?" Brian asked.

7. Tag

Lightbringer stood on the edge of the floating castle. If the target was down there, he would find it. But there was only one way to be sure.

He leapt off the edge of Fortress Magritte. Stormcaller, Starmaker, and Suncatcher fell behind him, silver, red, and yellow falling stars trailing the blackness.

He was headed for the grassy plains, the lightly populated place the truds called the Refuge Territories, but which he knew as part of the Wild Lands. It was never hard to find what they were looking for there. With few humans and even fewer structures, everything stood out in sharp contrast on Michael's scanners.

He saw the settlement below. He checked the threat scan. It didn't look as if this settlement was armed with anything more than primitive ballistic slingers. Nothing to be worried about.

Even as the Guardians swooped low on their descent into the settlement, it seemed that no one saw them. This settlement took their safety from the hovering presence of Magritte for granted.

Michael's wings sprung from their pods, tore into the air, and rapidly decelerated his fall. His feet gently brushed the ground as he swooped forward before finally landing on the ledge of a wall. Michael crouched and studied the 360-degree view from his helmet and the swirling scanner analytics. The few people close by who saw him land on the wall stood frozen. His fellow Guardians landed on the outskirts of the settlement, preventing anyone from slipping out.

The scanners completed their work and confirmed what Magritte had estimated before the mission even began: there were four targets of interest. Three of them were in the schoolhouse building to his right, one was in a small house a little further into the settlement.

Michael leapt into the air towards the schoolhouse. He landed just short of the door and opened it. He walked swiftly down a short hallway before coming to a classroom door. He opened it and strode into the classroom.

Most of the children, large and small alike, froze, the most typical civilian response to a Guardian. A few children began to cry. The teacher began to plead but Michael ignored her. He put the scanners to work on the room. The three were here.

He moved closer to them. He held his open hand over each one of them in turn. The first two were rejected quickly. The third did not appear to be a match, but depending on the error parameters, she was worth noting.

Michael extended his finger and placed it on the girl's arm. She felt a sharp pain for a fraction of a second as a small amount of blood was extracted before the tracking fluid was inserted. Then the sharp pain subsided as quickly as it had arrived. Nothing but a slight red blemish remained, which would disappear by the end of the day, though the suspicions of her classmates and neighbors would last a lifetime.

The first part of the mission completed, Michael left the schoolhouse and looked for the fourth. The last target was here, somewhere. He would find her.

**

People were running around the settlement now, clearly agitated. Michael knew he had stirred them up, but it would not be for long. Soon, they would continue on with their primitive trud existence.

He approached the house. The scanner showed that the final target was inside. As Michael reached for the door, a man rounded the corner of the house, assault rifle in hand. The man's eyes grew wide at the sight of the black armored figure. The man lifted the assault rifle to his shoulder and let loose a torrent of fire at the invader.

The bullets plinked off Michael's armor of night. He slowly turned towards the man and calmly raised his gauntleted fist, pointing it directly at the man. The man dropped the gun and fled. "They aren't all completely stupid," Michael thought.

Michael again reached for the door, opened it, and entered. He found the girl, sleeping, in bed. The scanner indicated her body temperature was well above normal. Most likely it was due to some illness, because none of the other indicators were present. But just to be sure, he extended his finger to her arm. She only rolled over as he took a sample and tagged her in the same manner as he had with the girl at the schoolhouse. The girl continued sleeping.

Having gotten what he came for, Michael left the house. Three more men had now appeared with primitive weapons. Michael ignored them. They had done nothing illegal as far as he was concerned. They possessed no forbidden technology and didn't appear to have any knowledge of fortech, so there was no need to eliminate them. He called "Solid" into the comlink, and the four Guardians of the West flew once more to the hovering fortress above. A hail of lead tried to follow them towards the heavens and failed.

8. Understanding

The aroma of the eggs, hash browns, and onions smelled fantastic. Meredith stirred the skillet. "Are you learning a lot? Are you having fun this season?" Meredith asked.

"I guess so," Katherine answered as she scratched behind Thunder the Dog's ears and patiently waited for breakfast. "Most of the classes aren't too hard this year. Biology is still tough. I can't identify many plants around here. If it doesn't have a flower I think it's really hard. It still feels like I don't know anything."

Meredith smiled. "It will take a while for it to sink in." Truth be told, Meredith admitted to herself, lots of people who were born in the R.T. never mastered plant identification, especially as Rick taught it. She supposed it wasn't her place to tell Katherine what was, and what wasn't, an essential life skill.

It was hard for Meredith to believe Katherine was the same little girl who had shown up so many years ago. Katherine was practically a young woman now. She had shown up practically a mute, and now they talked practically every morning. Meredith almost felt like Katherine was more her little sister than Brian was her little brother. Katherine seemed to have recovered from the trauma that led them here, whatever it was. Meredith also noticed that Katherine was gradually becoming more assertive. Meredith even noticed that her sometimes almost intolerable 'little' brother Brian, who was now 'little' only in the sense of relative age, couldn't push Katherine around as easily anymore.

"I know. That's what my dad always tells me. But Brian knows so much more than I do, and he lets me know it."

Meredith turned down the stove and put a plate of breakfast food on the table for Katherine. Katherine set Thunder down on the floor. The dog cocked its head and stared up at Katherine as she reached for the plate of food. Meredith sat down across the table in the cramped underground room.

"Listen, I know more than anyone that my little brother can act like a know-it-all. Don't let it bug you. That's just the way he is."

Thunder barked and Meredith hushed him.

"But sometimes I think he's wrong, even if I don't know exactly why. And I can't get him to listen to me."

"He makes up his mind and it's hard to change. Katherine, it's called being stubborn. He has to learn some things for himself."

"But I'm worried that if he has to learn it for himself, he's going to get hurt." Katherine purposely let a bit of egg fall off her fork, and Thunder gobbled it up.

"Like from what?" Meredith asked, ignoring the 'accidental' food drop. Katherine was too good to that dog.

"Oh, I don't know. I guess like atics. He doesn't think they're all that bad."

Meredith leaned forward across the table, brow furrowed. "What do you mean? Is he talking like a Fanatic?" Her eyes narrowed and her ears listened intently. The dog whimpered, begging for another drop of food.

"No, nothing like that. He just thinks that if he learns their rules, he'll be safe. I try to tell him it's better to just keep your distance, but he won't listen. He watches them whenever he can."

"Is he telling Odin or Alaric about the atic sightings?"

"I don't know."

"Well, we need to find out."

9. Found Treasure

"Greendust allows it to be aerosolized, essentially. Without it, the compounds will not disperse properly," Damien explained.

Red picked up the argument, "Listen to me, Blue, that is how Baxter messed up the Cobra Operation. The whole cloud just sank to the bottom of the facility. Minimal effect. The bad guys were all still awake, ready to greet our assault team. Disaster."

"Red, I don't know how you uncovered this."

"As I was saying, Damien and I were looking in the tunnels for an appropriate operational site for the Big Project. And when we broke open one of the old bricked-up corridors, we found the stash, tucked away at the far end of a dead-end corridor. Well, actually, to be more precise, Damien found it. The Greendust must have been put there ages ago by an old NHA team, or perhaps it's even older, dating back to the Machine War or before. When the gens cleared out one of the old city units, nobody was left alive to operate it. Just a theory. In any case, everybody must have eventually forgotten about it."

"And you're certain it's Greendust?"

"Yes, Blue, I am certain. The good doctor confirmed it."

"What else was hidden down there, Red?"

"A few rocket packs, really-out-of-date rail guns, and a few other morsels of interest. The most relevant fact, though, is that the tunnel complex will in fact work for the Big Project and we're building it out now. But to answer what I think you were really asking: we found nothing else like the Greendust. It's a gift; I don't know why you think it's such a bad idea. The Greendust is useful. I'll bring up the topic with Chi if I have to."

"I'm concerned because it could be used in combination with Dreptex. It seems to me the Greendust would do the job as a combo agent. Might have even been designed for it," Blue said. "Isn't that right, Damien?"

Damien glanced at Red briefly. "Yeah, that's right, Blue. Greendust has multiple applications. If mixed with Dreptex, it would aerosolize it, for lack of a better lay-term." He answered with just the facts. This argument was above his pay grade, and though his life might depend on its outcome, he did what Red and Blue told him to do. He understood that when he signed up.

Red acknowledged the point on Dreptex. "Yes. It could be, Blue. But Dreptex has been completely suppressed, thankfully. It's all gone and nobody knows how to make it anymore. Nobody's going to kill everybody in a whole sector with a Dreptex and Greendust combination. We aren't talking about mixing it with Dreptex and killing off cities or everyone with a genetic marker. We're just talking about putting a bunch of the Core to sleep, and only temporarily at that. They all will wake up at the end of the day."

"But you admit it could be used to kill off a sector," she pressed.

"Theoretically. But, again, nobody knows how to make the stuff that actually does the killing, Blue. Dreptex is dead. It's lost to history. And even if they did figure out how to make it, they wouldn't be able find all the ingredients today. Too much forbidden tech involved. It's not just a poison. And if they had all of the ingredients, they don't have the processing machines. And if they have the processing machines, they don't have a delivery system. And if they have a delivery system, well, yeah, then we need to worry about them getting their hands on this dispersion agent, on the Greendust. But that's way too many 'ifs.' We can use this Greendust now, in a very limited way, and it will save NHA lives. We mix the Greendust with the sleeping agent and it will actively seep into every corner and put the whole Core facility to sleep. We can get in there to take what we need from the Core. Dreptex doesn't have anything to do with it. Dreptex is gone."

"Everyone thought all the Greendust was gone, too," Blue pointed out. "But here is a stash, put in place years ago but still hanging around. Nobody knows how to make Greendust anymore, either. But we have it. You haven't convinced me at all that it's safe, Red."

"Blue, if you insist we go after the True Core database, well, we need this. It's foolish not to use the Greendust. The Core compound is a hundred meters deep. There is no way we can get at the Core's database without it."

"Saying 'no way' is a high bar. You could do it," she replied.

"It would waste too many lives, both True Core and Natural Human Alliance. Damien here will be leading the operation. He's not crazy about a bloodbath and neither am I. Truds shouldn't be killing truds if we don't have to. Listen, I informed you because you're the intelligence boss around here and thought you should know, and I thought you'd see this Greendust is a godsend. The bottom line is this: I'm not destroying the Greendust stash and General Chi will back me up." Red had tried being nice. Sometimes he just had to tell Blue how it was.

"Okay, Red. Okay. We'll keep it for now. But I'm moving it to a vault." Blue knew when she was bettered but wasn't willing to concede total defeat. She'd read in the classified archives about what Dreptex could do if someone solved the dispersion problem, and she wanted to make that as difficult as possible.

"I have no problem with a vault. That's fine," Red said. He just needed to keep the Greendust compound around for now. Everything else could be straightened out later. This was more difficult than it was supposed to be. It was supposed to be straightforward: Find the stuff, realize how useful it could be, demonstrate its usefulness, and set aside the rest of the Greendust for a time when it was really needed. But Blue didn't always play along with Red's plans. Blue had her own ideas about how to fight and they didn't always align with Red's ideas. Sometimes, it even seemed Blue's plans were purposely opposed to Red's. But Red knew that might just be paranoia speaking. Still, one being paranoid didn't necessarily mean that one was wrong.

"In a few weeks, assuming I haven't changed my mind, someone can pick up just enough for the operation. The rest of it stays locked up," Blue said.

Red didn't need her permission, but arguing the issue was quite pointless. He'd gotten what he needed. It didn't really matter to Red whether Blue thought she was being gracious or using her authority.

She could think herself Queen as long as Red could still move forward, as far as he was concerned. In any case, Blue now knew about the Greendust and wasn't going to stop Red from using it and keeping the rest for later. That was enough. "I'll be sending Damien for it. Thank you."

Blue left the room.

"What's with her?" Damien asked.

"She doesn't like a lot of fortech. Even the non-modology stuff. I understand. I do." Greendust was in fact dangerous, and Red knew it. Perhaps it was even more dangerous than Blue thought.

"You may understand her opposition, but I don't understand it. We should use every tool at our disposal. Some of those tools are going to be dangerous. If it helps us win, I say we use it, no holds barred."

"That attitude, Damien, is why I selected you for this mission."

"I'm glad you did. I'm looking forward to finding out what the Core has been hiding down there."

Red nodded. But that wasn't exactly the mission Red had in mind.

10. Guests on High

Brian walked several paces ahead of Katherine through the wooded flood plain. "Seriously, I'm not letting you come with me if you are going to rat me out to my old hag of a sister. I can't believe you told Meredith that I've been tracking atics. We aren't children anymore and it's none of their business what we do."

"I just want to make sure you are safe. You don't need to be furious." She was having to jog every once in a while just to keep up. Little Thunder trotted after.

"I can take care of myself. I don't need you to keep me safe. I don't need you to try and change me," he said, accelerating his pace.

"Hey, wait up."

"Keep up or get lost." He went even faster, putting a little distance between them. Thunder stayed with Katherine.

**

Eventually he slowed, and she caught up to him but did not draw even. She remained a few paces behind. The two walked on in silence through the forest for a long time. The only sound Thunder occasionally pawing in the leaves.

Then Brian stopped dead in his tracks. Katherine froze a few feet behind him. Even the dog froze. She had learned a lot since she came to the Refuge Territories. And Brian only stopped dead in his tracks for a reason. Katherine focused on all her senses. She didn't see anything. She scanned the forest. There was nothing that she could see that was out of place. She strained to listen for anything unusual but heard only the birds. She attempted to see if she could smell something on the air. It had never worked before, but sniffed deeply, trying to smell whatever it was.

"Do you see it?" he asked quietly.

"See what?"

"Look up there through the branches."

Still, she saw nothing.

She walked a little closer to Brian and followed the point of his arm.

Then she saw it. "A floater!" she exclaimed.

She hadn't seen one since she arrived in the R.T. She couldn't even remember if she had ever seen one before, in the city, or if she had just heard stories about them. From class at Pete, she knew that what she saw in the sky was only one of several such ships floating above the earth. The large gray castles rarely moved with much, if any, speed. More often, the flying fortresses hovered lazily above a city for weeks before wandering farther across the countryside or before unleashing punishment for some technological offense.

No one could ever recall seeing a floating castle on the ground. Indeed, if it were to actually attempt to land, it appeared as if the fortress would fall over on its side on account of its pointy underside. From the ground, the underside appeared to be made of rough rock and had four peaks, like a mountain range turned upside down. About halfway up, the fortress appeared to have a horizon line where the rough rock changed to stone bricks worked smooth, laid in a fashion not unlike those of medieval Europe, long, long ago.

"What's it doing way out here?"

"I dunno," Brian nonchalantly answered.

"We should go tell Odin," Katherine urged. Thunder growled quietly.

"Just cool it. Let's watch it for a minute."

"But we should warn the others!"

"What are they going to be able to do about it?"

"We could get everyone to Mary where they'd be safe," Katherine rolled her eyes. "That's what the retreat is for, isn't it?" Katherine's heart raced. The dog leaned against her leg.

"If it's coming for us, there's no time to get to Mary." Brian's heart continued to calmly pump at seventy beats per minute. "Besides, what do the gens care about us? They couldn't care less that we're out here. Now quit talking and give me the binocs. I want to see if I can see a garg."

Katherine had to concede that he had a point. The gens didn't care who was out here, so long as they weren't building an army or playing with forbidden technology. If she were back in the city, it's not like the gens would just annihilate a random building for no reason. Come to think of it, she had never seen a gargoyle kill a civie. Not ever.

She relaxed a bit. Maybe, just maybe, she allowed that Brian might know what he was talking about. She scratched Thunder behind the ears and the dog visibly eased.

Brian focused the binoculars on the floater.

"What are you seeing?" Katherine asked.

"It looks just like a castle. Hey, let's move to the top of the bluff. Maybe we'll get a better view." Brian took off up the steep hill, away from the river, to the top of the bluff. The trees were thinner at the top and they could see for miles.

At the top, Brian squinted through the binoculars.

Katherine stumbled up the hill, completely out of breath, silently cursing the physical advantages of testosterone. At first Brian's physical advantages were just in years lived; now, several years later, it was clearly more. "Do you see anything?"

"No," Brian replied. "Just looks like a floater. Wait! I see a gargoyle! Two of 'em! They're plunging down over there... towards Miller's Place. Come on!" Brian yelled, as he took off running along the ridge towards yet a higher overlook.

At the crest, Brian cranked up the magnification. After trying for a moment to find the guardian in the binoculars, he lowered them. "The image is too shaky; I need something to stabilize it."

"Rest it in the crook on that tree," Katherine offered in between deep breaths.

"For once, a good idea." That was Brian's version of a compliment.

He did as she suggested and gazed through the binoculars.

"What's going on?" Katherine asked.

"It looks like they are doing something with the people in Miller's. I can't tell exactly. Kinda looks like some of the kids are being looked at. They're rubbing their arms... maybe like they got stung or something. Wait. I think... I think they're taking one. Look at that! They're flying back up and taking someone with them!"

"Let me look!" Katherine pleaded.

"Hold on a minute. Yep. Yep. They're flying back." Brian waited until the gargoyle almost reached the fortress before finally handing over the binoculars to Katherine. "Have a look."

Katherine struggled to focus the binoculars. With such powerful magnification, it was hard to hold the image of the floater in view even using the tree branch as support. But she couldn't see any gargoyles, only the fortress.

"I can't see anything."

"Check Miller's Place."

She turned her focus to the plains, but couldn't find the small hidden settlement. "I can't see it."

"Here give them back to me." Brian looked through the binoculars. "Everybody's already inside." He handed back the binoculars, keeping track of the angle at which he held them. "Try again. What do you see?"

"I see that patch of oaks."

"You need to go to the right more. About six of those patches wider."

"Oh. Okay. Yeah, I can just make out the dirt mounds."

"Yep, that's it, good ole Dumpyville. Miller's Place." Brian looked up at the floater again. "Hey, I think I see something up there again."

Katherine shifted her view and found the floater in the sky. "I think I see a garg! Up there on a ledge! He's... he's holding something. Someone!"

"He's jumped!" Brian grabbed the binoculars back. Thunder barked.

"Hey!" Katherine tried to argue before turning back to watch the black speck fall.

"They're taking her back!"

"What?"

"The girl the gargoyles took: they're bringing her back down."

11. Salvation in a Bottle

Damien studied the vial. Such a strange compound, such a small amount. The Greendust looked exactly like it sounded: it looked like metallic dust and it was green. Simple enough in appearance and name. But what made it special was what one could do with it. He had double-checked the classified archives, and it was just like Red had said. Nobody knew how to make it anymore. But those little vials that he had found in the tunnels were going to save lives, starting with this little vial and his little life.

The Core wasn't exactly an enemy. But they also weren't exactly on friendly terms with the Natural Human Alliance at present. The True Core was hoarding powerful information and not doing anything with it. Red and Damien were going to get at the information in that Core database and were actually going to exploit it. The NHA needed that information to fight the gens and the Core just sat on it. Well, the Organization had had enough of begging the True Core, and now they were going to take it.

And the almost magical Greendust was going to make it easy. Nothing dispersed faster and better. If everything went according to plan, he'd be tiptoeing through a sleeping fortress rather than tossing concussion grenades. Of course, if everything always went according to plan, the spies would have already gotten the True Core database a long time ago. So Damien set aside the vial to double-check that his rail gun was in perfect working order.

12. Knots

Alaric, Lothar, and Meredith listened carefully to Brian and Katherine as they told the story.

"So, how sure are you that they actually took someone up to the fortress?" Alaric asked.

"Positive. It was small with long hair," Brian said. "Those slobs in Miller's Place don't have any boys with long hair; they don't let them grow it long. Had to have been a girl or young woman."

Alaric and Lothar exchanged knowing looks.

"Okay. Thanks for telling us about this. Meredith, were you going to fix some food with the help of these two?"

"Yes, I think I was," Meredith replied. "Come with me, you two. What do you feel like eating?" Brian rolled his eyes. He knew when he was being ushered out even though he had just as much right to be involved in the conversation as anyone. They would never understand him.

**

Alaric and Lothar discussed the issue quietly, alone.

"If they are systematically checking known settlements, they could show up here soon," Alaric cautioned.

Lothar paced back and forth. "We're hidden from a lot of people here. But let's not fool ourselves: the gens aren't tricked by our set-up."

"We don't give them any reason to take any interest in us," Alaric noted. "Let's remember you've been here a long time and there's been almost no signs of anyone looking for you. I don't think it's related to you. If we panic and scatter, we'll only draw attention to ourselves. Some scanner floating up there will figure it out, it will see an anomaly, and it will investigate."

"But if they do come here, and they find her..."

"Let me think over this again. Maybe we could move a small group," Alaric conceded. Actually, Alaric realized it made a lot of sense. Small groups left Pete all of the time. Three or four people wouldn't draw any undue attention. There was no need for everyone to flee the settlement. If they were looking for her, they might not care about the others. It was only a couple that the gens would have any interest in looking for. His first instinct was to not do anything to call attention to the settlement, the first rule of survival. But upon further reflection, he began to see some possibilities.

"I'll take her-"

"Definitely not," Alaric said.

"She's my daughter, I'll-"

"That's exactly why you can't take her, Lothar. The chances that you are in one of their organic brains, one of those huge databases, are too great. It's almost a certainty. I mean, how could you not be? They find you and then they know they've found her. Hiding from other truds is one thing, hiding from gens is another."

"I don't like it," Lothar said flatly.

"Of course you don't like it. I don't like it. Nobody likes it. But it's the reality of the situation," Alaric stated. "We either just hunker down here or we send a small group with her to Mary or maybe even just on an excursion into the middle of nowhere. A few days should at least allow us to determine how extensive the gargoyle search pattern is. We can get on the secure comms and do some checking with our friends. I'm for sending her away, just for a short time. Just until we can get a better idea of what's going on."

"I'll want to discuss it with Odin."

"Are you crazy, Lothar? How on earth are you going to explain it to Odin?"

"Well, can you make it happen without Odin?" Lothar asked.

"Easily."

Lothar's stomach turned in knots. He wasn't sure which way to go. It was making him sick.

Alaric saw the pain on his friend's face. "Listen, I know you're worried. But it makes the most sense. I'll send her with Conan, Jimbo, and Dave Man. They're the best, and trusted."

"I know it's probably the right thing, but I'm going to go crazy holed up here in Pete while she's gone."

"Lothar, buddy, who said you're sticking around here? In a few hours, you'll be going in the opposite direction."

13. Red-Faced Robots

They were all asleep. Even the guards high up near the surface, where the air circulated and would be the freshest. There were fewer guards than Damien had expected, but every single body they came across was peacefully sleeping away. The gas had dispersed even into the far corner of the compound where Damien and his strike team made their entry, almost like the Greendust had a mind of its own and sought out the enemy in every crevice and hiding place. It was the easiest breach of a Core facility that Damien had ever experienced. And as much as Damien took a certain kind of pleasure in disintegrating things, he rather enjoyed not having to kill other natural humans, united in opposition to the gens if not in their methods and beliefs.

The breathing hoods that the strike team wore were very uncomfortable, but the problem with Greendust was that it could be a little too effective and take out the assault team if they weren't cautious. Without the masks, the assault team would be napping, too. So the team had to deal with a little discomfort and restricted vision.

Damien and his team made it deep in the Core's underground base before encountering their first hiccup. On level 9, they discovered that, unfortunately for the team, robots don't need to sleep.

The first robot quizzed them about who they were and what had happened. They talked to the bot just long enough for Specialist Wu to put a rail round perfectly through the robot's comm block. But it was a networked bot and after it went offline unexpectedly, the rest of the bots weren't interested in conversation anymore. But no worries: The bots weren't dedicated combat robos and Specialist Wu had a lot more rail gun rounds.

They were now deep in the base and here the Core defense systems were clearly not up to par. The True Core was rarely this sloppy in their work. Damien figured that the base designers thought that if anyone got this deep, it was all over anyway. The best defense was making sure that no one knew where you were and what you had. The NHA spies at least solved the first part of that defensive problem, even if they failed to get at the database itself. And Damien would soon have part two firmly in hand.

"There it is," Damien said through the hood.

"Doesn't look like much," Specialist Wu said in a muffled voice.

"Doesn't need to," Damien said, already working to get the most critically important data extracted. They didn't have time for it all, for the guards would not sleep forever and back-up could conceivably be on the way, but he knew how to look for the juicy stuff. And it looked like it was there.

It was a little painful for Damien to wait for what seemed like too long as the database tap scanned the Core system and began downloading data. Would the True Corers continue to sleep peacefully? Did the networked bots not only alert each other, but an outside team? Would better robots or battle drones emerge from the shafts, park themselves on the steps, and make it impossible to climb out? Did the Core have a quick reaction combat unit in the neighborhood? With each minute watching the slow scan and download, Damien seemed to imagine increasingly worse scenarios. The rest of the team, hidden behind their chem hoods, silently watched the corridor approaches, crouched in defensive positions, guns ready at the shoulder.

Finally, Damien was able to confirm that the most important information was downloading. After it completed and he double checked it, it wasn't worth the risk or the time to wait for more. It'd have been nice to duplicate the whole database and surely there were other hidden gems in there somewhere, but they had gotten what they came for and a little more. No need to press their luck. "Okay team, got it. Now for the tricky part."

"You mean going *down* the stairs was the easy part?" Specialist Wu joked, knowing that getting out was the real issue all along.

It was easier than expected for once. No battle drones crawled from the shafts. There was no quick reaction combat team. Had only the True Core humans in the base awoken, the team's escape would have been highly in doubt, having to fight their way all the way back up or negotiate terms. However, the Greendust did its job and nobody on the True Core side was awake but the robots. And these particular robots had especially bad brains when it came to keeping the enemy *in*. The team fought their way out with not a human life lost, neither from the Core nor from the Natural Human Alliance. And luckily, the robots didn't feel anything, not even embarrassment.

14. Shadow of the Past

Dave Man took point. Jimbo followed far behind. Conan, rail gun over his shoulder, walked with Katherine. Thunder the Dog trailed immediately behind Katherine.

"Where do you plan to go, Cone?" Katherine asked, having adopted long ago Brian's nickname for Conan. Cone wasn't so massive as when little Clara first met him. Of course she had grown up, but he had also gotten leaner and meaner looking. Conan said it had to do with training for ranging more rather than for power. If Brian had a rival for knowledge of the wilderness, it was Cone.

"I figure we'll follow the river north, then turn east into the hills. There are some woods there that should provide some good cover. Another thing in our favor is that there haven't been too many reports of Fanatics up that way. Even if we don't find any game, there are some berry bushes tucked in there that should be ripe. Good eat'n."

The group walked on through the rolling hills in silence. They talked among each other occasionally, though too much talking too often was certainly out of the question. Human voices carried a long way in the wilderness, and the hills might conceal bandits, or worse, atics. They were disciplined and knew this wasn't a game or a simple stroll. The dog could sense it, too.

It was a long way to hike. They alternately zoned out in the activity of hiking, got lost in their own thoughts, or kept wary eyes on the hills until boredom once again caused their minds to wander.

Katherine spent much of the time thinking of the time before. Of her mother. Of the city. How one day everything had suddenly changed. How she could no longer talk of her mother. How she had to change her name, how Clara had disappeared into Katherine, how her dad was slowly becoming a stranger named Lothar who had to disappear from the settlement for long periods of time. How she had to deny a past that was slowly slipping from her memory.

Katherine looked down to watch her step as she hopped over a small stream. When she looked up, she saw the black shape standing there, dark wings still spread wide.

Conan suddenly saw the gargoyle and raised his rail gun to his shoulder. Michael already had his fist pointed forward. A stun beam pulsed from his gauntleted hand, knocking Conan to the ground unconscious.

Katherine stood frozen staring at the huge gargoyle before her. Thunder barked aggressively.

Lightbringer looked back at the girl.

Time seemed to freeze.

A shadow passed overhead.

Michael felt a slight buzzing in his mind. Something about her... no, it couldn't be her. She wasn't the one they were looking for. He was certain.

He didn't even double-check the scanner. He leapt into the sky and was gone.

15. Odin Rules

There was a flurry of activity in Pete's community room upon their return and Conan's report.

"Did it touch you? Did you feel anything?" Alaric asked.

"No, it just looked at me for a second, and then flew away," Katherine explained.

"Would she even remember if it happened, Alaric?" Odin asked.

Alaric answered, "I would think there would be some discontinuity."

"But you can't know for sure, can you? None of us can."

"No, Odin, we can't know for sure. But there are probabilities-"

"We can't risk the whole community based on probabilities," Odin stated.

"But..." Alaric tried to explain that everything was based on probabilities. There were no certainties. One had to take calculated risks.

"No. This risk is too great. If you are wrong, it could mean everything. Lothar and Katherine must leave. I'm sorry, but this is more than coincidence. They have to move on."

16. No Closer to Home?

Once again, Katherine was hiking through the endless plains and rolling hills of grasses only broken by the occasional oasis of oaks. As a child she had walked across the plains, and now as a young woman she was doing it once again. She had been Clara, then she became Katherine. Was she about to become someone else? It hurt to be rejected and thrown out of the settlement. Her father tried to explain that wasn't what happened at all, but it sure felt like it to Katherine. Maybe she was a foreigner the whole time after all. Maybe Brian was right. Years had passed since they fled to the Refuge Territories, and they were no closer to home. Indeed, they were walking farther away.

Then she thought about Meredith. Lock and Heidi. Edda. Cone. Thunder. Even Brian. It was a home, wasn't it? Maybe the years she had spent in the R.T. under a new name were as close to something called a home as she would ever have. Or maybe there no longer was a home and never would be. Maybe home was a false concept, a mirage in the distance, a trick of the mind about the past, or an unrealistic dream of the future. The thoughts sat there for a moment, before she shook her head in rejection. She tried to banish the thoughts from her mind. She wouldn't accept that it could be gone, or that it could never be found. No. They would find it. They would find a new home. It could be done. They had loved her, she just had to go. That was the flawed world they lived in. They didn't love her less. It was just that she was… too dangerous.

It was a long way across the R.T. to the Towers, but maybe a new home was there. Or maybe home was farther still, beyond the Towers. She just had to keep walking. Eventually, she must find it.

"Don't you think we could go back to the city?" Katherine asked her father, knowing in her heart of hearts the impossibility of it. For now.

"I'm afraid too many people would recognize me there. You'd probably be all right because you've grown so much. But I'm afraid I won't ever be able to go back."

"Well, I'm not going back without you." She looked up to the blue sky. A black bird circled in the cloudless sky. There was no fortress in sight, no winged gargoyles, no machines.

"We never know what lies over the next hill, my daughter."

"Hey, Jimbo is waving us over," Katherine noted. She wished it were Cone, but Odin wouldn't let him come along. As they were leaving, Conan had to restrain Thunder. Katherine had never seen the dog bark so much as when they were walking away. It broke her heart. So, they were on the trail again, with just Jimbo and Dave Man to accompany them part of the way.

"Guess we'll be taking a break in that oasis."

"The shade will be nice. I could use a drink of water, too."

They walked over to the cluster of oaks. Dave Man met them there.

"We can go with you through tomorrow morning, then we need to head back to Pete," Jimbo offered.

"I understand," Lothar said. The black bird landed in an oak and crowed.

"We'd go with you farther," Dave Man explained, "but Odin is really concerned about the garg activity and gave us a deadline. He wants as many men there as possible."

"I understand," Lothar said again. Self-preservation. He didn't blame Odin. He might do the same thing in his position. He would have preferred for Odin to let Alaric accompany them. There was much that should have been discussed between Lothar and Alaric, but that couldn't be talked about among others. Only they knew what Katherine meant. What Clara meant. Only they knew why some wanted to steal her and why others wanted to kill her, why both gen and trud sought possession of her. Only they knew why her mother had been killed. Now it was just Alaric and Lothar left. And Katherine.

But the discussions with Alaric would have to wait. In a short time, Alaric would find an excuse and Odin would let him disappear for a while. Alaric would find his way to the Towers. Then they could come up with a better plan. A better hiding place. But for now, the Towers would have to do. Lothar knew a few people in the Towers. It wasn't ideal, but nothing was. They would make it. They would survive. Any way they could.

Dave Man unwrapped some jerky and offered it to the others. He sat down and took a big bite out of the salted and dried meat. Then he moaned.

Katherine looked up to see a large wooden spear protruding from Dave Man's chest.

The Fanatics let loose a bloodcurdling howl. The black bird screeched and took flight.

Lothar reached for his weapon, but an atic emerged from the brush behind him, clubbing him in the head with a heavy knotted oak baton. Lothar fell forward, unconscious. Just as quickly as he had appeared, the naked atic fled back into the brush.

Katherine screamed.

Jimbo held his rifle at the ready, turning left and right, but did not see any atics.

The Fanatics howled again.

Jimbo saw a shape run through the woods and fired a round in its direction. "I'm right here, monkeys! Come get me!" Jimbo fired another round into the brush.

Katherine went to her father's side. Blood streamed from the gash on his head. She shook him, but he did not respond.

Jimbo spoke, "Katherine, get Dave's gun. We have to go."

"I'm not leaving my dad."

"We can come back, right now we need to get someplace defensible."

"I said I'm not leaving him!"

"You can't help him if you're dead," Jimbo said, all the while scanning the woods.

Just then, an atic crashed through the thick brush towards Katherine, club in hand. Jimbo shot him in the face. The atic fell dead at Katherine's side.

"Let's go!" Jimbo yelled.

Katherine ran over, grabbed Dave's gun, and followed Jimbo as they ran through the woods towards the grassy hills.

MODIFIED HORIZON

Another atic jumped in front of them on the path, screaming at the top of her lungs. Jimbo shot her twice. She fell to her knees, still screaming as loud as she could as dark blood began to gush in spurts from the wounds.

The two kept running. As they passed a large oak, two atics leaped down from the branches. One broke his leg, but continued to howl and crawl after them. The other one was fast and before Jimbo could turn his rifle towards him, the atic had tackled Jimbo. The two fell to the ground, wrestling. The two rolled over into a ravine and out of Katherine's sight.

"Jimbo!" she yelled. She heard no response.

But another atic was closing in on her. She fired Dave's heavy gun once, but missed. And now the atic was upon her. The atic knocked the gun from her hand. Katherine felt his putrid breath as the atic yelled in her face. Then the atic punched her in the face and she fell to the ground. The atic raised his arms. Katherine closed her eyes as his arms came down for the final blow.

17. Congratulations

"Well, Red, congratulations are in order. You finally have the True Core's database."

"Part of it," Red corrected her.

"If it contains what we think it contains, it will be enough," Blue said.

"Yes, it makes the Big Project possible. It would have taken us years to figure all of it out. This database answers so many questions... We should have seized it years ago, if only we knew where to look. But we have it now. And not too soon either, if the rumors about the Event are true."

"All my sources point in that direction," Blue said. "The gens actually want to finally get rid of us. And they're going to do it, with this so-called Event, whatever it is. We know that in the minds of the gens, the Event means no more truds to worry about. The Big Project needs to go forward before the gens launch their Event. We'll knock them out before they have a chance to do the same to us. Intel isn't clear on how much time we have before the Event, but it seems to be big and complex enough that we are thankfully talking years, not weeks or months. Nevertheless, there is no time to waste."

"Agreed. Our own plan could take years until we are ready, but it only needs to take one day less than their plan. They are going to try the Event, but we will beat them to the punch. We're going to stop those who want to destroy us. I'm not planning on going anywhere."

Just then, the secure communicator on his belt buzzed. He looked at the coded message. "Blue, it is General Win," Red lied. It wasn't necessarily a wise thing to do with the local director of intelligence, but Red didn't have time for an elaborate story, and General Win was certainly a plausible alibi. "I need to leave immediately."

And as he left, he caught a glimpse of a shadow in the corridor ahead.

18. Hanging in the Balance

The steady rocking and swaying seemed almost gentle. The sun felt warm on her face and closed eyes. Then she became aware of the burning pain around her wrists. Her mind fired to consciousness and her eyes sprung open only to be blinded by the sky and the midday sun.

Katherine hung on a pole, her arms and legs tied to the branch by a rope. The crude and coarse strands dug into her wrists with each sway as the atics carried her across the plain. Her necklace had swung around to the back of her neck, and she could feel it swing to the cadence of footsteps.

She couldn't breathe through her nose. It was clogged, with blood. Her head throbbed. She tried to lift it to look around, but the effort caused the world to fade to black once more.

**

A cool breeze stirred, but her wrists still burned. She eased her eyes open. It was night. She was sideways on top of matted grass and dirt, still tied to the pole. Katherine lifted her head and looked around: no one. She couldn't see anything, not even the glow of a fire.

She listened carefully. Only the rustle of grass in the night air. Not even the sound of insects.

Katherine tried to move her hands before grunting at the pain. The crude ropes had worn her wrists raw. Her fingers were so swollen that she could barely move them. She tried to wiggle the rough rope loose before the pain forced her to stop.

She let her head fall to the matted grass again and exhaled deeply. The ropes were too strong. She was exhausted, in pain, confused, with no way out.

Katherine lay there in the night air. She looked up at the night sky. A few high clouds broke apart, revealing a view into the eternity of space. Against the dark canopy, space debris sparkled as it spun across the steady field of stars. Her breathing slowed and her mind cleared.

Maybe there appeared to be no way out, but she would not give up. Maybe the clouds of adversity would part and, if they did, she needed to be ready. She scooted closer to the pole and brought her wrists to her mouth. She struggled to get her swollen jaw open enough to get around one of the thick strands and began gnawing.

Her mouth was parched. The twine was dry and tough. She willed herself to keep moving her sore jaw. Each chew was a split second longer than the last. She began to fade into sleep.

She shook herself awake. She had to try to escape. She continued to gnaw the dry strands. She just... had to... keep chewing... and...

**

She awoke to the morning light. Her head hurt like it had never hurt before. Her mouth was cracked and dry. One strand of rope was a quarter of the way through. The thought was still in her mind: keep trying. She moved her wrists back toward her mouth to begin again before she looked up.

An atic sat cross-legged in the dirt, staring at her. She stopped gnawing and looked back at the gaunt face and empty eyes.

They studied each other without saying a word. The atic was a young man, perhaps about her age. He did not yet have the typical fanatic long beard. He probably had not chosen this life; he had probably never known a life other than as a Fanatic.

Then she heard people moving through the grass. She turned away from the seated atic to see two atics running with a pole, and suspended from the pole was her father!

"Dad!" she tried to yell, but produced only a hoarse exhalation.

But he merely hung limp from the branch. She wasn't sure if he was alive.

"Dad!" she tried to yell again, before the atics had carried him out of sight. It was only a split second. But it was enough for hope.

She turned back to the young man. "Listen," she rasped, thinking back to the logic of Brian. "We aren't here to interfere with anything you are doing. We're just passing through. Please, you need to let us go."

The young atic did not answer. He studied her without emotion, with the same empty eyes.

"Please," she pleaded. She knew it was probably pointless trying to reason with an atic, but the way the young man stared...

The atic's eyes suddenly came alive. He stood and turned his head to the right as if something from that direction caught his attention.

Katherine saw a red dot appear on the atic's forehead before it erupted in red mist. Katherine heard the crack of assault rifles and then explosions. She curled up as much as she could while still tied to the pole.

More assault rifles cracked overhead.

Then, silence.

The grass rustled in the breeze.

A short while later, Katherine heard voices: "Did you get them all?"

"Yeah."

"Chuck a few more frags just to be sure. I'm not climbing down in there with those crazies."

Katherine heard two more muffled explosions.

"One more, over where you shot the guy in the noggin."

"Wait!" Katherine yelled, "Wait, I'm alive!"

"Was that a voice?!" she heard one ask with concern, before the concussion blast knocked her unconscious.

19. Jack

She was strapped to a stretcher in the back of a ground transport. The ride was rough, typical of a transport vehicle so old and obsolete. Still, it was more modern than anything she'd been around in the years she had lived in the Territories. She slowly realized where she was as two men in the front of the transport were talking.

"How the heck did Red know we'd find scapes way out here? At this time? What are the chances? It was like a needle in a haystack and we found them on the first go. Way out in the middle of nowhere, we find the group of Fanatics with the scapes right where he said they would be. How does Red get that kind of detailed information? I mean, he must have Fanatics on the payroll or something, huh?" The man's companion chuckled at the ridiculous thought of a Fanatic on the take. What would an atic possibly do with cash?

"With Red, it's pointless to ask. He has his sources and methods that will forever remain a mystery to me and you. Just do the job and don't ask so many dang questions, cuz you ain't figuring it out."

"Good thing your aim sucks with nades or you would have killed the-"

"Hey, she's waking up," the tech noted while looking over the medical monitor.

"Well, we know she's not an atic. The question is, who is she?"

63

"You can ask her in a moment," the tech replied.

Katherine heard the voices and understood the language. She opened her eyes.

"Hello, everything is going to be okay," a young man said. "Who are you?"

"Ka..." she began, before regretting it. Even in the fog of the drugs, she remembered well the lessons her father had taught her. Saying "Katherine" could mean death. Could she trust these people? What did they know already? Were they friends, neutrals, or worse? Her name could be a death sentence, and she nearly slipped up.

"Ka?" the young man asked.

"Ka... Ca… Can you say that again?"

"I was just explaining that you're safe now. We rescued you. No need to worry about anything. You've got a concussion, taken a couple real serious hits to the head, so you might be a little confused. But give it time and the medicine is going to work. What's your name?"

"Maren," she answered knowing that, for now at least, Katherine had to be dead, just like little Clara before her.

"Just Maren?" he asked.

"Uh, Bern," faking a little more grogginess than she actually felt. "My name is Maren Bern," she lied. "Who are you?"

"We, my friend, are the Natural Human Alliance, and I'm Jack. Welcome back to civilization."

20. Bumpy Ride

She was riding in the back of the transport. The conversation with the young man, Jack, was quite enjoyable. He was explaining everything that had happened since she'd been gone, when suddenly, a wooden spear burst through his chest. Blood flowed out of his chest and Jack collapsed.

Then the man driving the transport turned around. She saw his full beard and he looked like he had never bathed in his life. Maren froze in horror as she realized the driver was an atic. He leaned towards her and exhaled his rancid breath onto her neck.

Suddenly, a black gargoyle ripped off the roof of the transport, his dark wings spread wide. He pointed his fist at the atic's head and it exploded in red mist. Next, he turned his fist towards Maren.

Maren let out a scream and started awake. Sweat beaded on her forehead.

Jack yawned and sat up. He put his arm around Maren, "Oh, no. Another nightmare?"

"Yes," she said. She felt at her neck. Her green pendant was still there. She rubbed it between her fingers, an old habit. It grounded her, it was real. "I... I dreamed I was back in the R.T., when you found me." She paused to catch her breath, "And the atics..." She couldn't begin to explain the horror she had felt seconds ago in her vivid nightmare.

"It's okay. Everything is okay. That was years ago," Jack consoled her as he brushed her red locks away from her forehead. "You're safe here, with me."

Maren looked around her familiar, comfortable room. Everything was there, just like normal, in its place or out of its place, as the case might be, as the result of daily living. The pleasant pictures hung on the wall. Comfortable clothes were strewn about the room. The soft white sheets wrapped around her. And Jack was next to her in bed.

It had just been a nightmare. A horrible nightmare, but not reality. She inhaled and exhaled deeply, trying to slow her racing heart. "I hadn't had a nightmare in a while. I thought it was getting better."

"With the mission tempo increasing, everyone is under stress," Jack offered. "Heck, you know I've barely been able to sleep. You can't expect to be immune to it. When the body is under stress, the mind feels it too and recalls when it felt similar, the traumatic events of the past."

Maren snuggled closer to Jack. No, she wasn't immune to it. So many people had been lost. So much depended on the few who were left. Though she was only a small part of it, she felt it. Maybe Jack had told her more than he should have, but if she could lose him at any time, she at least wanted to know why. And when Jack told her he could help stop the Event, that they were working to prevent the gens from destroying natural humans, she had to believe him. She had to trust that stopping it was worth his life. Indeed, she had to believe that stopping it was worth her own life. Yet now and then, she asked to be reassured anyway.

"Do you think it can work?"

Jack stroked her hair. "Maren, the Natural Human Alliance has been working on this one for a long time. The Event will be stopped. Humanity will not be wiped from the face of the earth. Our plan will work. It has to."

21. Robos

Michael and Gabriella flew through the city night, racing among the skyscrapers. The light reflected off the silver armor of Gabriella while the shadows were seemingly absorbed by the black armor of Michael. Seeking their quarry in the streets below, the pair swooped and dove through the canyons of glass and steel.

The pair was familiar with the city, and they knew most of its great urban canyons by heart. The city seemed more natural to them than the great expanses of the Wild Lands. Almost all of their missions were flown in the great cityscapes of the truds. Their quarry cowered beneath the supposed protection of the masses. By doing so, they not only attempted to hide their heat signatures and prevent the direct firing of energy weapons from the floating castle, but also sought to dissuade "attack" by surrounding themselves with "innocents." *"The fools,"* Michael thought. *"Primitives, not much advanced beyond animals,"* he thought back to the teachings of Rex Skyguard, as Michael Lightbringer swooped down on the racing vehicle.

As they closed in on the vehicle carrying the hostiles, Michael noticed something wasn't quite right. The people riding on the vehicle did not seem to be moving naturally. He increased the magnification and shifted the spectrum of his visor. He was right.

"Gabriella, they have robos. Looks like Icers. Call for the machines."

"Already done," she replied.

The few robotic fighters riding the racing vehicle were not a major threat in and of themselves. At a certain level of analysis, the robots were certainly more deadly than human fighters, since the robots had dramatically better targeting computers and the ability to continue fighting even when half of the robo's body had been blown away. They could also mask their heat better than a human. At a higher level of analysis, it was the creative humans that caused the real problems. But the combination of the two, robot and human: that was the nub of the problem. A creative human could deploy robots in unexpected ways and maximize their effectiveness.

Another aspect that made a robo dangerous in the hands of the right user was the fact that where there were a few robots, there were often many. Truds rarely let an Inorganic Combat Robot out in the open until a sizable army had been developed for fear that the manufacturing facility would be located, a strategy justified by historical experience. An Inorganic Combat Robot's heat signature, unlike a human's, could be easily changed to blend in with the environment. Thus, unlike a human army that could be easily detected from the fortress above, an inorganic army had been known to seemingly materialize out of nothingness. Ambush was to be expected.

But these were trud tactics of the past. It had been over five years since a hidden Inorganic Combat Robot manufacturing center had been destroyed. Michael and Gabriella betrayed no sense of worry. The gen's machines were superior in every possible way to an ICR, even a whole army of them. And the machines were on their way. Not that Michael and Gabriella couldn't handle the small group of Icers before them.

Michael folded his wings back and accelerated as he came into range of the robos as Gabriella swooped higher. They obviously didn't have a canopy gun, or he would have been hit in the solid dome of fire immediately after he had been seen. Instead, they attempted to lose him in the maze of city canyons, firing rail guns and energy blasts along the way.

He was in range with his own weapons now. He'd been hit twice so far (further evidence of an Icer's superior targeting -- no trud could shoot like that), but only with nearly spent energy blasts. A rail gun round had come dangerously close, but a defensive magnetic pulse from his armor had knocked the round off course, clearing his head by a good two inches. Or so the computer told him.

He let loose a controlled ray from his right fist, fusing an inorganic's rail gun to its own arm as a useless pile of slag. The robot rolled off the fleeing vehicle along with two others, as the rest sped ahead.

Lightbringer spread his wings wider and barrel-rolled as the two Icer robos on the ground fired a hail of energy blasts. The one with the slag arm stood his ground, ready to crush the approaching Guardian. But Michael continued his spin, and as the slag-armed inorganic leaped to crush him, Michael's wing sprang forward and cut him clean in two. In the same motion, his left fist zeroed on the pair with the energy guns. At this close range, both were reduced to slag in an instant. The top half of the slag-armed one crawled across the pavement after the deadly raptor, but Michael was already flying higher and accelerating once more after the vehicle.

Just then it happened, and the truds' robos sprung their trap. Michael's scanners came alive with movement from every conceivable hiding place in the steel alley's walls. He saw Gabriella high above for an instant before she was consumed by a hail of energy pulses.

He retracted his wings and dove for the deck. The computer had swiftly calculated the projected pattern of fire from the known locations and had determined he might have a chance on the street below. A blast slammed into the back of his leg, violently sending him into a backward spin. As he spun, he saw the deck approaching rapidly. His wings were nearly ripped off as he extended them once more, grabbing the air in a desperate effort to slow his descent. Lightbringer came to a violent halt as he hit the ground. He wrapped his wings around himself for added protection.

Concrete exploded around him as he rolled in an effort to dodge the incoming blasts. A blast pierced his right wing and the stomach area of his armor. Another blast hit his leg before he managed to roll under an overhanging building. He did not waste any time. He dragged himself to the corner and began to pick off the robots as they attempted to descend upon him.

Then there was a roar as an army of machines came upon them all. The gen machines vaporized entire buildings like a locust swarm devours a field. Gabriella had been taken out. The rest of the team was gone too. Michael wondered if they had done the right thing. This time he wasn't sure.

Then the world went black, and the simulator's lights came back on. The door silently slid open and Rex Skyguard entered the room. "Lightbringer, you'll have to review that simulation later. Right now, you have to prep for a real mission. Assemble your team for briefing in three."

22. Reaching Towards the Sky

The middle-aged engineer gazed up at the massive structure being built module by module. At fifty stories, it barely peaked above the surrounding monuments of metal and glass. "Reaching for the sky," he thought. "Will it ever get there?" Felix smirked. "Where does the sky begin?"

The structure would be rooted to the ground, like everything built by natural humans had to be, a law enforced from the heavens above. Half a lifetime ago, when he was only learning to build toward the sky, he had seen a machine designed to soar untethered among the clouds. A sled of sleek lines and beauty, like the young woman who crafted it. Then, long ago, he had seen the same machine melted and destroyed, and he had seen her die for it, for even the dream was forbidden.

He ran his hand across the top of his now bald head. He contemplated the exposed metal structure. Who will live their lives there? What will they be like? Will they be like him? Will they be like her? What kind of world will they live in? Will it be like this one? What will they gaze out upon from the fiftieth floor? Will taller towers eventually hide the structure before him in shadows, or will it be the tallest structure on the block for eternity, never to be surpassed? How many will reach higher? And one day, when the building comes down, what will cause it?

The bald engineer turned away from the structure. "Will it stand?" he asked silently, though no longer thinking about the steel structure growing behind him. He had studied his whole life to learn how things were put together, what made things stand up, what made things fall down.

Today he built, tomorrow he destroyed.

23. The Dragonfly

There was rarely a hurry before a mission. This was one of those exceptions. Lightbringer had assembled the four Guardians of the West that composed his team: himself, Gabriella Stormcaller, Dante Starmaker, and Martha Suncatcher. Rex Skyguard commenced the briefing immediately.

In many ways, Skyguard's briefings were redundant. Mission data was automatically downloaded to their winged armor, and in some cases, directly to their brains. But the briefings had an additional effect in that they focused the team on the primary goals and more importantly, reinforced the sense of purpose in each Guardian. For good reasons, they each still had a brain inside their skulls, not a mechanical computer.

Rex Skyguard, along with the great computer-brain (for in many ways, they were one), was the chief authority on Fortress Magritte. He had even seen a real Ancient once. Rex Skyguard was talking: "There is movement in the Forest Quarter of the city. The preliminary scan indicates illegal chemical transport: biofluid and hydroil. As you know, both are used for EMP-proof organic components in the manufacture of advanced robos, and of more concern, robechs. Fortress Magritte has analyzed the situation, and determined that the transfer operation is guarded by a half-dozen unmodified humans, armed with no more than rail guns. Once the dragonfly drone has tracked the shipment to the termination point, you will proceed to capture it for analysis if possible, destroy it if necessary, and search for evidence of a forbidden technology manufacturing facility."

Michael stared firmly at the tactical display as Rex continued the short briefing. Fortress Magritte's computer-brain had probably already detected evidence of the fortech factory days before. That was why he was getting more simulations involving robo tactics. Now they just needed to follow the trail. It would be easy.

As Rex Skyguard finished the short briefing, Michael's chair leaned back slightly to meet two arms with black pads that swung up on either side of his head. He closed his eyes and felt the warm pulse as the pads hummed quietly in his ears, gently recording his memories and patterns of thought. After a short while, he opened his eyes to the blue light signaling the scan was complete and rose to go to the suiting chamber.

Michael Lightbringer stepped into the recess in the wall. With a chink and a hiss, his armor latched around him. Then the liquid metal flowed over, covering his arms and the flexible parts of the power suit with armor the color of night.

Four Guardians stepped out from their crevices: black, silver, red, and gold knights ready to defend their lords. It was a hazy day as the four leapt from their gray fortress in the heavens. Even with their designer eyes, they could barely see the cityscape below directly. A shift in their visors' spectrum and the earth below became clearer. Magnified and computer enhanced, their eyes saw even the pavement markings on the concrete streets.

The dragonfly drone had tracked the biofluid and hydroil to the far eastern part of the Forest Quarter. The dragonfly had seen the humans take their cargo through a trapdoor hidden by a sculpture. There, camouflaged on a reed in an English garden, the drone waited, quietly pulsing its location to the mother-brain above. The computer then sent the information back to the smooth metallic bodies plummeting toward the city.

One by one, the metal-feathered wings caught the air and gently set the warriors in the midst of the nature garden. Trees, bushes, plants, and flowers appeared to spring naturally from the earth and every crevice, though in some way it was an illusion, as the garden was in fact heavily manicured. It was a tranquil setting. Even with his amplified hearing, Michael could only hear the gentle rustling of leaves in the breeze and the buzzing of insects. All else was quiet.

The ground was soft and covered in a lush carpet of green. He began to walk towards the pulsing dragonfly drone, leaving deep and dark footprints in the fragile green grass behind him.

It was an odd location for a lab. But then, that was generally the point when conducting illegal activity.

Michael stopped before the trap door. Something else was odd. He wasn't getting the usual biosign readings that he should be getting at this close range. Dante's huge shape appeared beside him, "No readings, huh?"

"Is the plan modified?" Suncatcher asked with concern. Hesitation at the onset of an operation was nearly unheard of. But so were close range scans that differed materially from Magritte's scans.

Michael Lightbringer aimed both fists at the composite trapdoor and let loose with a wide invisible beam. In a split second, the tunnel below was revealed. "No, no change of plan, not yet," Michael coolly responded, jumping through the opening. Guardians existed for their applied creativity and initiative, and now they would be tested once again.

It was a dark, damp, narrow tunnel. Water dripped from the ceiling to small puddles below. It didn't fit what the computer-brain had downloaded prior to the mission. Lightbringer expected large labs and rooms; maybe even a robo assembly line. But there were none. There was only a tunnel ahead. There was but one way forward. He stepped further into the darkness, giving each of his teammates a chance to jump down into the underground warren. He amplified the spectrum in the darkness, only to see that the tunnel turned ninety degrees at a distance of a few meters.

Dante had jumped down immediately behind him. As the massive Dante Starmaker strode forward, he had to bow his head to avoid hitting it on the rough concrete ceiling. Stormcaller and Suncatcher followed closely behind.

Lightbringer rounded the first corner, only to see another short hallway terminating in another ninety degree turn. Then he noticed his communications link with Fortress Magritte was down. He called to the back of the line, "Suncatcher, go back to the entrance and report back. They are jamming our communications down here, and the configuration of the tunnel is going to cause problems circumventing the jamming. And send back a few drones so we can establish a relay link and scout ahead. It's nothing like the computer predicated down here. We're going to press the initiative and go forward, see if we can't catch the shipment."

"On my way to report," she responded.

Michael, Dante, and Gabriella filed down the tight corridor. Rounding the next corner, a large, low-ceilinged stone room appeared before them. Stranger still, it was empty. "There is another hallway there," Lightbringer said, pointing across the damp emptiness of the vault. A chemical trace suggested the targets had gone in that direction.

Michael stepped forward into the room. As Dante followed, a heavy armored door suddenly slammed downward, nearly cutting Dante in half and leaving Gabriella trapped in the corridor behind them. Dante quickly tried to contact Gabriella, but the communications couldn't penetrate the thick door. Not only that, but he found he could no longer talk with Lightbringer through the comlink.

Michael's voice slit opened in his visor so he could talk directly with Dante. "They were expecting us."

"We could melt the door, give ourselves more options," Dante responded as he prepared to release a fisted beam. But before he let loose, an explosion in the contained stone vault seemed to hit them from all sides, knocking Starmaker and Lightbringer to the ground and unconscious darkness.

24. Circle of Light

Michael saw nothing but darkness. He wasn't quite sure where he was. "*My visor must be broken; I don't have any light amplification,*" he thought. Then the blackness slowly receded as blood returned to his natural eyes. And suddenly the uncertainty was gone and he remembered: the explosion.

Michael jumped to his feet and saw four figures dragging Dante's body towards a newly revealed opening in the vault. He was sure the opening hadn't been there before. "Fallen!" he called, fruitlessly trying to send the signal for an injured or killed guardian. Communications were still down. He wasted no time. Michael raised his arm and fired at one of the figures dragging Dante's body, dropping the man to the floor, before another attacker fired a projectile back, penetrating the armor of Michael's right thigh.

Michael grimaced and charged forward, reducing two more attackers to pools of goo on the floor. At first, if he could see the enemy, they died. Until they massed. Several more figures appeared at the new opening and began firing rail guns and energy blasts as they charged forward. As Michael reached Dante, a slicing motion of his dark metallic feathers eliminated the last figure in his immediate vicinity. But more and more attackers were emerging from unknown passages, and they would be upon him in an instant. His armor was nearly at the breaking point as energy blast after energy blast pounded him.

Seeing the attackers approaching fast, Michael threw himself upon the sprawled Starmaker and extended his wings around them both, creating a small cocoon. There were too many. He waited for the charging figures to get closer. In fact, Lightbringer wanted the attackers to come closer. Into the kill zone.

Michael's armor began to glow with a faint blue light, and as the attackers neared, he activated the nova device. Blinding blue light erupted from Lightbringer as everything in a ten-meter radius was vaporized, creating a sphere of nothingness.

Michael and Dante fell to the bottom of the newly created ten-meter-deep pit and hit with a thud. Michael unwrapped his wings and looked up. Light flooded down like a spotlight. Directly above him was a large, perfectly circular hole in the ceiling. The tunnel was shallow enough that the nova device had vaporized all of the material up to the surface of the garden, revealing a circle of sky above and an escape route from the trap.

Lightbringer grabbed Dante under his arms and launched himself upward towards the light. No energy blasts followed him from below as he burst to the surface, extended his wings, and flew higher, leaving the garden behind. Ahead of him he saw Gabriella and Martha circling higher. Before he even had a chance to contact Fortress Magritte, a massive barrage of energy bolts thundered from its underside. The bolts sizzled over Lightbringer's shoulder, and he heard the muffled impact thuds in the garden below. By the time he reached the ledge of the fortress with Dante's lifeless body, the quiet English garden and the warren below were nothing but a smoldering memory.

25. Pulverized

It was black. Jack couldn't breathe. Pulverized granite and concrete filled his nostrils and coated his mouth. Jack coughed and hacked out the chalk-like substance, then vomited onto the rubble. His left arm screamed at him. The bright blue flash had scalded the exposed limb. Then the energy bolts had hit. The rail gun he once held was gone. Already, he could feel his arm oozing blood and liquid through the thin layer of powder that covered it and the rest of his body. He felt the weight of debris on his lower body.

He tried to call out to anyone else alive, but the only thing to emerge was a dust-clogged raspy exhale. Jack closed his eyes in the darkness and felt his breast pocket: it was still there. He took out the illuminator and flicked it on. A haze of pulverized rock hung in the air.

Jack lifted the debris off his legs, gritting his teeth at the pain emanating from his oozing arm. He gingerly lifted one leg, testing it, then the other. Each leg seemed to be okay.

As Jack struggled to his feet, he saw someone's dust-coasted leg sticking out from a pile of corridor panels. Jack stumbled over the rubble and started pulling panels off of the figure. By the time he got to the tactical vest, he knew it was Damien. A few more panels were removed to reveal Damien's unconscious face. Jack turned Damien's face sideways and dug out some of the grit from his mouth. As he did so, Damien gagged and came to consciousness.

Damien's eyes grew wide at the ghostly white figure looking down on him through the dusty haze.

"It's me: Jack." The rasp barely sounded like Jack, but Damien nodded anyway.

"Can you clear the rest here? I need to check for others." Damien nodded that he could.

Jack scrambled over the rubble. The corridor that led to the vault had completely collapsed. Even if anyone was alive on the other side, they were beyond Jack's help – if there was in fact another side: it might all be solid debris now.

Jack slid back to where he started and scanned the room for anyone else, randomly picking up panels, shining the illuminator, and coughing out a few "Anyone here?" inquiries. There was no one else. No bodies, no voices, no signs.

Damien found his voice. "Okay, kid, I don't know what in the world happened here, but it's time to leave before more of it happens."

"Agreed." Jack extended his good arm to Damien and helped him to his feet.

"I don't have a light. I'll follow you." Damien stepped forward with an obviously severe limp.

"Can you keep up?" Jack rasped.

"I'm not as young as you, kid, but I can still out march you. Let's get moving." He limped forward.

Jack nodded. "We'll have to go down. The only way out now is to go deeper."

26. The Green Light

Dante sat with his eyes closed in the large, black chair. Rex's briefing seemed straightforward enough. Biofluid was probably under that garden. Biofluid was dangerous in the wrong hands, it could mean EMP-proof robos or worse, and Dante was confident they would intercept it before any harm could come from it. The only challenge would be finding clues that might lead Magritte to the manufacturing facility. His eyes remained closed as he felt the warm pulse of the pad humming quietly near his ears, gently recording his memories and patterns of thought. After a short while, he opened his eyes and saw that the indicator light, rather than the normal cool blue, was a bright green. "Apparently," Dante thought to himself, "the mission was more challenging than I first surmised."

27. Time

He ran his hand across the top of his smooth bald head. He didn't have much time. The Event was nearing. The first plan should have worked. It had to work, otherwise none of the other pieces worked. They all had to be convinced. Everyone.

It was inexplicable that it had failed. So much planning, so many mistakes. Now, he would have to start over. And without his best people.

Felix entered the elevator and began his smooth descent to the street below. During the entire afternoon of meetings in which the construction of a new building had been discussed, Felix was his usual quiet self. At work, he was soft spoken. His managers and colleagues rarely even noticed him except when his professional engineering competence, gained over twenty nine years, was required. Despite his expertise, he had never risen to a high level of management.

It wasn't that he had never been offered the chance to climb the corporate ladder, but rather that he had turned down the offers. His managers were never quite surprised when he turned them down. To the managers, Felix didn't seem to have a strong leadership drive, and he rarely if ever worked long hours. Sometimes he would disappear in the middle of the day for a couple of hours, but his work always got done.

But his managers' view that Felix didn't have much ambition didn't bother Felix at all. He preferred relative anonymity in professional and social settings; it made climbing the ladder of his second job so much easier. Not to mention the fact that anonymity happened to make staying alive easier too.

The descending elevator came to a halt. The door slid open and Engineer Felix T. Katz stepped onto the street. The bright, golden light of the evening sun shone along the long axis of the skyscraper canyon. And a little black speck hung in the sky.

Felix casually walked through the spotless city streets. Occasionally, he stopped to look at the goods displayed in the windows for the holiday season. He studied each item as if the fate of the world depended on his choice of this one or that. His mind, however, was elsewhere.

He turned from a window displaying the finest time-pieces available. The old-fashioned watches, used almost purely for ornamental purposes, had refocused his mind on the matter at hand: Time. It was running out. And he needed to be prepared.

Rounding the corner of the city block, he entered a smaller cross street where the canyon was in deep shadow. He turned his head upward, as if checking the weather, to see what the clouds might bring today. Seeing nothing, he stepped sideways into a recessed doorway. Felix did not ring or announce his presence, but opened the door quickly, and boldly walked in. Engineer Katz was left on the street outside, and into the room stepped Colonel Red, Director of Special Operations, 3rd High Command, Natural Human Alliance.

28. Flora

The middle-aged woman walked through the small garden. Whereas thunderbolts had rained from the sky and destroyed a larger garden, this one remained, as did others. Small, overlooked, hidden. Life continued here unabated, and from pockets such as this, even the charred moonscape of the English garden would quickly recover to teem once more with all manner of plants.

Her small garden waited for its chance to flower. In some areas, shoots pressed up through the mulch. In others, flower buds waited patiently to burst into their full glory.

The woman leaned over the flower bed and pulled up one of the closed flowers by the roots. An intense shake loosened the dirt from the roots. She tore off the rest of the roots and took the stem in hand. It was amazing that such a narrow tube could support so many leaves and a large flower head. Such a little stem. If you cut the stem, the beauty of the flower would be yours. You could take it inside, put it in a vase, and enjoy the flower for a long time, even though it was cut off from its roots, from the very thing that nurtured the flower for so long, from before it had even had a flower. And later, from those roots, from the bulb hiding in the dark earth, the flower would emerge again. If, however, you pulled the flower up by the roots, it would never grow again. It would be gone forever. Some other plant would instead take its place. The ground would not remain vacant for long. Nature abhors a vacuum, and spaces are filled, either by the most fit, or the most desired.

She took the bud in her hand and squeezed it between her fingertips. The bud burst open to reveal the almost completely formed red petals, woven tightly together. They were glorious wings tucked in the womb, waiting to stretch out towards the heavens. But this flower would never bloom. The glorious wings would never open up to claim the sun and seduce the bees with their brilliant scent, their radiant crimson, their nectar of life. No, this flower would never blossom. The woman had cut its life short. Now, it was merely bits of red smeared across her fingers. Pretty red. Aromatic red. But not yet the flower it strove to be.

Flora looked down at the rest of the flowers that had not yet emerged. It was not yet their time. But their time would come soon enough. Very soon.

29. What's New?

Martha, Michael, and Gabriella were finishing up a post-simulator evaluation and exited to a long hallway that encircled Skyguard's Tower. Along one side, windows looked out upon billowing white clouds and a rich blue sky. As they walked along the corridor, a door opened to reveal a tall, assured looking Dante Starmaker.

Martha walked over to Dante and embraced him.

"What is new?" Dante asked the question that had become a Guardian ritual after restoration, though the question's original humor had long been lost to history. For Dante Starmaker, it was as if only a minute ago he was sitting in the black chair feeling the warm pulses of the brain scan, preparing for the raid on the small garden in the Forest Quarter. In actuality, the raid had taken place over three days ago. During that time, Fortress Magritte had been carefully growing a new body and imprinting it with Dante's stored memory and thinking patterns. Theoretically, there was no reason to assume that it wasn't possible to regenerate a guardian instantaneously. However, at that time even gen technology had its limits, and the three day restoration period was necessary to train the neural pathways in sequence. Now, three days later, Dante Starmaker felt great after awaking to the green light in the black chair.

And it was always good to have the full team back together.

"The surface has been quiet again," Martha responded. "It was bold of the truds to attempt the destruction of an entire guardian team, but I do not know what they hoped to accomplish. Skyguard says the post-mission analysis does not indicate that there was anything of value in the tunnel system."

"What mistakes did I make?" Dante asked, having no memory of the time between his last brain scan before the mission and his regeneration. The green light that appeared after a scan was his only clue that three days had elapsed rather than three minutes. Dante knew that a blue light indicated a complete, successful scan, while green indicated a full restoration. Since he had seen green, it was vital to learn what happened from the others and from Rex.

"There was not much you could have done differently," Martha said.

"Essentially, it was an elaborate trap," Gabriella added. "We surmise that the biofluid and hyrdroil were simply expensive lures. Thankfully, they did not seem to have a follow-up plan. Their only accomplishment was tipping their hand regarding some novel jamming devices they developed. If the truds had been smart, they would have saved the jamming devices for a situation when those technologies would have mattered."

Martha agreed, "That is one thing that is always certain: truds will make big mistakes. Rex has already upgraded the wings to prevent these new types of jammers."

"The rest of the team returned from the mission unscathed?" Dante questioned, in only a slightly astonished tone, his pride slightly wounded. The massive and powerful Dante had fallen before, but rarely had he done so alone.

Michael walked closer to his teammate and slapped him on the back. "I took twelve energy and kinetic hits, but took no damage that a regen bath could not heal in an hour. However, my wings were quite damaged," he said, referring to his power armor, "if that makes you feel any better." He didn't bother explaining that his suit had since been repaired. That was a given.

"How did we eliminate the aggressors?" Dante wondered, the question pointedly starting with "how," not "did." It was historical fact that the enemy was always ultimately destroyed. It had always been that way, and Dante had no reason to believe it would change.

Martha answered, "Lightbringer nova'd the aggressors in the immediate vicinity. Magritte then disintegrated the caverns as a precautionary measure when we had moved clear."

"I am sure Magritte will have new simulations for us given the novel tactics," Dante said, as he turned towards the simulation room which the others had left only a few minutes before.

The others followed not far behind. They lived for it.

30. Gathering in Shadow

Two was normal. Meetings of three or four High Officers were rare, while the meeting underway with five high command officers present was nearly unprecedented in the city's recent history. Such meetings were generally considered too risky. A single Gargoyle attack, a single Floater barrage, or even a little dragonfly drone could put an end to a generation of military planning for the natural human resistance. Nevertheless, sometimes things needed to be whispered among one another face to face.

Colonel Red was the last to arrive.

"Welcome, Red," General Win greeted Felix.

Compartmentalization was essential in the Natural Human Alliance, or the Organization, as the trud military element was sometimes called. The normal organs of trud government were quite open and visible to the general public. The military, however, was an underground organization in spite of its nearly universal public support. The gens were too effective at destroying any visible military elements. Experience had also taught that treason was an ever-present risk and an all-too-common occurrence. The gens could be very effective in recruiting turncoats.

Colonel Red quickly glanced around the room. There were five other individuals present. Felix clearly recognized four of them. There was Colonel Blue, the Director of Intelligence with whom Felix had a long history. They'd come up through the ranks together, for better or worse. Next was General Win, who as 3rd High Command City Commander was pretty much as high of an official as any of the others were ever likely to meet. Red also recognized General Chi, who frequently seemed to appear when new technologies were involved, though it was never entirely clear where his responsibilities began or ended. He'd been around for what seemed like forever in trud terms, and though rickety, still had the sharpest mind of the bunch. Then there was the gentleman with the burn scars on his lower jaw, whom Felix had met twice before, but who had never been named in his presence. Nevertheless, Felix knew exactly who he was. The scarred one wasn't a high command officer, wasn't even technically Natural Human Alliance, but he might as well have been when it came to the current project. In the shadows in the corner, a fifth person was present. Colonel Red did not bother asking who it was.

"I take complete responsibility for the garden mission failure," Colonel Red began. "The first error was failure to promptly activate the blast door, allowing two gargoyles to enter the kill room instead of one. Second, the team did not confirm the kill of the black garg. Third, the assault team did not react quickly enough due to-"

"We are well aware of the reasons for your failure," the scarred one interrupted. "It is far from necessary to spend our precious moments cataloging your many errors."

"Sir, I intended to-" Felix tried to continue, but General Win cut him off.

"Enough. Colonel Red, a tribunal has found that you were not responsible. The actions can be directly attributed to the planning elements for which Trenton had command authority. He has been reassigned. Your operational concept was not the problem, the execution was. You have been summoned here because you have been given complete command authority for our next operation. You'll plan it again, and this time you'll carry it out, too."

In his mind, Felix smiled grimly. He knew what this meant. He also knew the price that had been paid to give him one more go. He had one more chance, and with complete authority, this chance was worth more than all the others. He would not waste it.

General Win continued, "We all agreed that an exception to compartmentalization in this situation is now necessary. We trust you completely and thus you will be responsible for mission execution. You understand what we are trying to accomplish and you know the operational area. If the intel on the Event is accurate, that the date is drawing near, we do not have the luxury of time to reposition or bring in new personnel. We all know the operational mistakes that were made, and they will not happen again. We are here to move forward, not dwell on the past. Colonel Blue, go ahead."

"The new operation must take place before the end of the operational season," Blue began in her mildly accented voice. "Our source has indicated that plans are unfolding for the Event, and we must act soon-"

"Your source?" the scarred one interjected with derision. "Look at the resources we have wasted over the years on your source's ill-conceived plan. For how many years has this 'Event' been looming and yet you have done nothing? It's seems your so-called Big Project is a convenient myth, one that just happens to mean more resources for the Organization, and less for the people."

Blue, the Director of Intelligence, responded, "The planning for the Event has been corroborated by many sources. There is no doubt that a plan is afoot for the gens to be rid of us forever. And our key source has always been reliable."

"We don't have as much confidence in this so-called key source that you seem to have. As a matter of fact, it would be fair to say we don't trust the source at all. It seems your source may be acting at cross-purposes to our own. We see nothing but set-backs and delays. Just where exactly has the source's advice gotten us in the last twenty years?" the scarred one asked.

"Why, to this point of course," the one in shadow unexpectedly responded. "During these many years, has the source ever given you false information? Has not everything been just as the source said it would? Have you not had successes that would have been impossible without the source's input? Have your failures not been a result of your own actions, not the source's? And as for the Event, you need not take the key source's word for it. The evidence is abundant, from multiple sources, from multiple places, using multiple technologies. All the signs point to the same thing, and at an accelerated rate. The data is consistent with a nearing Event. We are now at a critical juncture. Everything has been building to the Event, and it is close at hand. This is why you must act now. Our timeline is tight. For reasons I cannot reveal, the window of opportunity will not be open forever. We have spent much time planting and tending the field. It is now time to collect the harvest."

General Win spoke sternly before the others had a chance to respond. General Win looked directly at the scarred one with hard eyes: "The Council had assumed that your concerns had been settled and that the Network would be assisting us. Are they in error?"

The scarred one inhaled slowly before responding slowly and deliberately. "Of course the Council is not in error. We have had discussions of our own. We have decided to supply the assistance as promised. The Network has shown extreme patience with the Organization, and we have abided by the Council's reasoning up to this point. But do not expect us to wait forever. If it fails this time, we will proceed with our own plans – with or without the Council's approval."

Blue attempted to make the case for waiting. "You must be patient. You must not strike before we've-"

"We've had enough of patience, but that is beside the point. The Network will assist with this final effort, and that is what we have come here to discuss." The scarred one continued, "The plans we have seen up to this point are doomed to fail. Fortress Magritte will simply annihilate the operational site and all will be lost. This operation cannot succeed as currently planned, and that is why we question the wisdom of your esteemed source."

The one in the shadows spoke a second time, "Your concerns would be justified, but for the fact that you have only seen the plans in part. The Floating Fortress will not fire a single shot during the operation."

General Chi expressed doubt, "How can you guarantee that Magritte won't respond when we have taken out part of a genbot squad? That is quite an extraordinary claim."

"I can guarantee it because the source has promised to see to it personally. This time, the source will help you directly. Instead of passing along the weakness the source discovered about the fortress, the source will personally use the weakness. The source is taking an extraordinary risk because the gens could track the source's exploit methods, and it is that which backs up my extraordinary claim. The Floating Fortress will not be able to launch a barrage, nor will it be able to release machines or more genbots. But only for a period of minutes, if that. And it will only work with one of the floaters, not them all. Still, that should be enough for this operation. This exploit will only be possible once. Once these loopholes are used, as with the jamming technique used in the garden operation, the gens' agents close them. The same will happen after silencing their weapons for a brief moment. The weapon systems will soon come back online and the loophole will be gone. The opportunity will never present itself again. There is no telling if the source will ever discover another weakness in their defenses to exploit. You must make it happen this time. There can be no errors."

"Don't worry. We will be ready. It will happen as planned."

"It has to. The Event is at hand."

31. Gray Refuge

"Have you told them about me yet?" he asked, stroking her blonde hair.

"Do you want me to keep our relationship a secret?" she asked in reply, looking up at his gray eyes and the lock of gray hair that hung over his forehead.

"No, not at all, Eve. Don't get me wrong. I've talked to all my friends about you. I've told them how wonderful you are, how happy you make me, how there's no one else like you in the whole world. I was just curious whether you talk about me with your friends. You don't seem to mention them much."

"You're my hidden fortress. I don't want to tell them about you. When I'm with you, I can forget the rest of the world," Eve said. "I feel safe with you. I feel a bit like if I told them about you, somehow just in their knowing they would intrude on us and our world, and I don't want them to. Do you know what I mean?"

"I thought that's how you felt, but I wasn't sure. I just wanted to make sure you didn't think there was something wrong with me, you know?"

"No, never!" she exclaimed, lifting her head up and looking at him. "Don't ever think that! You've been my refuge in this crazy world. I feel like you rescued me from the depths. But if you really wanted me to, I'd tell the whole world about you."

"No, Eve, I don't want that. I think it's rather romantic, your secret. I'll protect our hideaway from the rest of the world if you do. From this day hence, our world, the only world that matters, exits only between us, my love."

"You are my escape." Now, she stroked his prematurely gray hair and the long gray lock that hung down over his forehead. "I don't know how much longer I can stay there, living that life."

"Do you want to leave?"

"Yes, eventually. I'm tired of being around all of the dying. One day, I want to leave it all behind. I want to be among the living."

"Well, then, Eve: Eventually, we'll have to make that happen."

32. One More Chance

Jack was not his first choice for this operation. But he knew Lt. Jacques "Jack" Carlitos could be trusted, that his loyalty was absolute. And all of Colonel Red's first choices were dead.

There was no time to train anyone else, and time was of the essence. Jack knew many of the essential elements of the plan and was smart enough to figure out most of the rest. If he lost Jack, it would further complicate the follow-on operation, the part for which Carlitos was supposed to be a part of all along, but such risks were a necessity. Just as High Command had been forced to make Red responsible for planning and execution of the next mission, Red was now forced to ask Jack to take on two missions. Compromises had to be made when faced with limited resources and limited time.

"Lt. Carlitos, do you feel well enough to handle that portion of the operation?"

"Absolutely, Colonel. There is only mild pain now, and it will in no way interfere." He had been in an underground corridor when Magritte had bombarded the chambers beneath the Forest Quarter garden. Lt. Carlitos was lucky to survive with only a few mild energy burns to his arm. He was even luckier to have made it out of the area without being detected. He had been one of only three survivors of that doomed tactical team, thanks to Trenton's failures.

"Good." Colonel Red continued the briefing to his lieutenants. "I am sure I need not remind you of the importance of this operation. We know from multiple sources that the gens have a plan to eliminate us once and for all as a thorn in their side, called 'the Event.' It is said that the gens have given up on dominating us as self-perceived superiors and instead plan to be rid of us forever. We have a source who says the Event is near, and we must be successful in our follow-up operation. Well, we plan to show them once again that natural humans have some fight left in us. The best news is that this time we will receive some direct assistance from a valuable source. This source has found several technical weaknesses in their defenses, and we will exploit those weaknesses. I cannot offer any further details for operational security reasons. All that I can say is that this is a once in a generation opportunity, so we must succeed. With perfection. I am sure you all understand what is at stake here."

He looked at the men and women who would play a part in history. "We will not meet again as a group. You have all received your assignments. Each has a part to play, and each part is vital. I am depending on you. The Organization is depending on you. Humanity is depending on you. Good luck."

33. Down the Hatch

The two sat on the high rise balcony, looking out across the city. Fortress Magritte hung in the distance.

"This is the last time up here for us, perhaps for a long time, buddy," Jack said.

"I know, kid." Damien took a swig of his beer. "To tell you the truth, when I'm away from here, I don't miss it. I could take it or leave it, this life. Up here, I mean."

"Really?"

"Listen, as long as we're working to bring those guys down," Damien nodded towards Fortress Magritte, hanging in the sky, "I'm willing to stay down there in the tunnels forever."

"You realize that almost happened to us on the last mission." Jack stirred his beverage. Jack, for one, had no desire to be buried forever.

"Hmph. We made it out. They haven't killed me yet, and they've been trying quite a few more years than you've been around." Damien took another drink, making good progress on his journey toward 'grizzled' status.

Jack silently thought of all of those who couldn't say the same thing.

"How's the arm?" Damien asked.

"Superficial energy burn. Hurts like crazy, but will get better with a little time. The leg?"

"Already like it never happened." Which wasn't entirely true. But Damien wasn't one to complain. He changed the subject again. "Is our little toy ready?"

"Yes. Just waiting for the order."

"I'm coming along," Damien said.

"Really?"

"I wouldn't miss it."

"I can do this part alone." It was a one man job, and Jack was that man.

"I know. But I'm not passing on the opportunity to get back at the gargs."

"Well, okay then. I guess it will make my girlfriend feel better that the indestructible Damien will be riding along."

"Ah yes, the other project," Damien snickered.

"Don't talk about it like that."

"That's what it is, isn't it, Jack?"

"Yes, but-"

"But nothing. You're doing what has to be done. No holds barred. Do what it takes."

"But it's not going too well. I can't figure it out, Damien. She hasn't told me anything."

"What about the old archive?"

"The files aren't telling me anything either. There are all of these hints, but nothing that points to a reason."

"What makes her so important?"

"I wish I knew, Damien. But I don't have a clue. Red seems to have some ideas, since he's given me such specific orders. But he won't tell me why. I've asked, but he won't tell me anything other than to keep looking. It's almost as if he isn't sure and needs me to independently confirm something about her. Still, when he doesn't give me very many hints, it's hard to figure out what's important. I don't have any idea if I'm even going in the right direction."

"You should talk Red into giving her a scan." Damien pounded back the rest of his beer.

"Listen, Damien. We shouldn't even be talking about that here."

"I wasn't going to say anything specific."

"I know. I know." Jack threw the rest of his drink down his throat. "Well, that will do it for this R&R."

"Down the rabbit hole we go again."

34. Plans

The Doctor slid the paper file across the glass table to Red. "Well, that's the summary of the team, Red. Overall, the mental profiles are looking good. A few natural stressors, of course. How could there not be?" The Doctor snorted. "In total though, there is nothing to worry about. They are all clear. Everyone is on board. No threats identified."

"Excellent. Thanks. Good to have it all checked out before we move forward." Red took the folder and put it in his bag without opening it. He'd read it after the Doctor left, then destroy it. In the meantime, he didn't want it out in the open. One never knew who might show up and when, or when one might have to leave quite suddenly. "I appreciate you looking over everyone one last time."

The Doctor studied Red. "Well, there is one person we haven't discussed."

"Who's that? Blue? She doesn't fall into my chain of command."

"No, not Blue. You."

"Um, I didn't know there was a reason for me to have yet another test. I do them all the time though, so shoot away if you need to."

"You always pass the tests, Felix. That wasn't was I was getting at."

"Then what exactly *are* you getting at, Doc?"

"I know you, Felix. You have something planned."

"Of course I have something planned, Doctor. That's my job."

"You know that's not what I am talking about, Felix. I'm not talking about the Big Project or whatever it's called these days. You have a different plan."

"I do?" Red asked.

"Yes, you do," the Doctor said.

"I don't know where you get these ideas," Felix said.

"That is not a denial," Doctor Psycho observed.

"How can I deny something when I don't even know what you are talking about?"

"I am talking about the girl."

Red sat there in silence before answering. "Doctor, let me be clear: she is a separate issue entirely."

"Entirely?"

"Yes. Entirely."

35. Interception

Skyguard was curt and to the point: "Magritte's density scanners have registered new shipments requiring immediate action. The density scans leave only one possible conclusion: the truds are once again gathering materials for fission weapons. Intercept the shipment and retrieve the fissionable material, intact if possible, so it can be analyzed. Details have been downloaded to your combat wings. Launch immediately. That is all."

The black pads swung up quickly, and after a brief moment, the chairs' lights turned blue. The four Guardians rose from the black padded chairs and moved swiftly towards their power armor.

Michael stepped into the recessed archway, and after the familiar latching sounds and the flow of liquid metal, he emerged ready for battle. He secured his helmet, blinked once as his brain switched to interpreting images from the 360-degree vision his mask provided, and walked briskly down the corridor from the suiting chamber to a ledge overlooking the world below. Information on projected defenses, estimated number of truds, predicted travel routes, and surrounding land features streamed across his visor in rapid succession.

It was night. Michael stood on the dark ledge, looking once more upon the city. The city's many lights formed a pattern of red, amber, orange, yellow, and blue that was at once familiar, yet different. Even though the city was ever changing, he felt there were few parts he did not know.

To Lightbringer's right stood his mate, Stormcaller, and to his left stood Starmaker and Suncatcher. They paused for a moment, waiting to dive upon their enemies after a final data download from Magritte. Uncharacteristically, Michael turned his mind's eye to gaze upon the silver figure at his side. Gabriella continued staring ahead, intent on the data stream flowing across her visor. Even in her armor, she was magnificent. A red crosshair suddenly flashed across Michael's visor screen as Magritte sent the final targeting information, indicating the dive point on the surface far below. Michael noted the spot, and with a leap, began his descent to the world below.

The crosshairs indicated a residential neighborhood subtly lit by the orange glow of street lamps. Lightbringer amplified the surface streets. At the center of the target, a hoverbike was moving to the south, with a single rider wearing a large backpack. Very little fission material was necessary to make a weapon, and Lightbringer could not be sure whether the contraband was on the person riding the bike, on the bike, or in the bike itself. The low power density scanners were only accurate to a few feet when the target was moving, and the signal from a more powerful scan would tip off the truds. So, he had to satisfy himself with a little ambiguity. Michael also noticed a hovervan trailing 50 meters behind the bike, at precisely the same speed, and which Magritte had just indicated contained four heat signatures and the chemical traces of advanced energy weapons.

"Gabriella will target the hoverbike, I will target the rider, Dante will target the trailers, and Martha will fly high cover," Michael ordered.

Martha extended her golden wings first, and began a slower spiral to the surface. Dante veered left and accelerated towards the hovervan, while Michael and Gabriella fell side by side, intent on the lone rider speeding through the dark night.

As Lightbringer and Stormcaller fell silently through the blackness, the rider suddenly looked directly up at the pair. "How did he know we were here?" Michael thought briefly, before modifying the angle of his fall to track the now accelerating hoverbike.

The van did not accelerate to follow the bike. Nor was there any fire from the surrounding buildings. Instead, the rider seemed to be all alone as he went faster and faster.

Michael came within weapons range and prepared to disable the hoverbike. His wings sprang open to glide him in at a more horizontal angle, slowing his speed so that he did not overtake the fleeing trud. He raised his fist and fired at the hovenbike's engine, but the blast was absorbed at the last instant by a pulse shield.

"Did you see that?" Michael asked Gabriella, unaware that the truds had the capability of mounting such a device on a small vehicle.

"We want the material intact. We shouldn't use a solid-state projectile or amp up the ray if we want it in one piece," Gabriella responded. "We'll neutralize him at close range with the wings."

The rider turned and fired an energy blast at Gabriella, the weak bolt hitting her armor harmlessly in the chest.

Meanwhile, Dante fell upon the trailing van, blasted a hole in its roof, and prepared to annihilate the unsuspecting inhabitants. But as he landed on the now slowing vehicle, it became apparent that it was unoccupied. All that sat in the back of the vehicle were four heat generators and some chemically laced rags. Dante crackled across the comlink, "This is another weird one, team. The van's empty."

"What?" Martha asked.

"The van is empty – it's a decoy. Watch out for that bike, Michael." Dante warned.

"We're almost on him," Michael replied. "He doesn't have anywhere to run. And judging from the blasts he's firing at us, he's very much real, unlike your van occupants." But as they were closing the gap, the rider stood up on the hoverbike seat and leapt into the air. At the apex of his leap, his backpack erupted into blue flame, and he jetted upward into the night sky.

"I'll get the bike," Gabriella called as she flew after the now riderless vehicle. The hoverbike could be programmed to travel independently with the material. Perhaps the rider was taking off to distract them, hoping that the contraband would escape unnoticed. There was no guarantee the rider was even a biologic.

"Rex," Martha called up to Magritte, "Where do the density scanners indicate the material is: with the bike or with the rider?" There was no response.

Michael zeroed in on the jetpacker. Even with his wings folded back and accelerating at near maximum speed, Lightbringer could not close the gap. But Michael knew he had an advantage the jetpacker didn't: time. The rider's fuel would run out much quicker than Michael's.

The jetpacker turned toward the large lake next to the city and dove towards its black surface. Lightbringer followed behind. "Martha, do you have an intercept angle?" he asked, hoping to cut the pursuit short across the water. Martha did not respond. "Suncatcher?" Michael asked again. Still, the comlink was silent. "Dante?" Nothing. Apparently, the truds had more than a few novel jamming devices. But never mind, he was gaining on the jetpacker now.

The two raced only feet above the dark waters. Then, the jetpacker began a steep ascent. The blue flames from his pack suddenly diminished as a heavy mist began to be emitted from the engine. Michael could smell the heavy fumes of the flammable gas and thought the rider's jetpack must have malfunctioned.

But this time, Michael was wrong. The heavy mist was intentional; it was filling the air for the purpose of being ignited and creating a massive pressure wave. He saw a brief flash before the wave from the fuel-air pressure bomb knocked him unconscious. Lightbringer's black body fell backward from the night sky. With a splash, he hit the water and was swallowed by the dark waves.

Martha circled alone high in the sky, calling to her companions above and below. But there was no reply.

Golden light grew on the horizon. One could not yet see the sun, but the dawn and the new day that it would bring was on its way.

36. The Grab

Perspiration beaded on his brow. A line of sweat ran down his cheek and paused in the stubble of his jawbone before dropping through the stale air and onto the deck. Condensation collected in tiny puddles beneath the small port windows. Jack checked the temperature gauge and saw that it was actually cool in the compartment. Nonetheless, he sweated.

He took another deep breath, and exhaled through tight lips. It was taking longer than expected.

"Where is it?" Jack asked.

"It will show up. Be patient," Damien advised, trying to convince himself as much as the Lieutenant.

Jack wiped the stinging sweat from his eyes and looked at the console once more, striving to see what he was waiting for. And finally, it was there.

Lt. Carlitos moved the submersible into position.

Damien extended the robotic arm, reaching for the black object falling through the murky darkness. The mechanical arm scraped the forearm of the sinking armored body before it settled on the sandy bottom. Damien gripped the black one's forearm tighter and retracted the submersible's robotic arm, bringing the dark armored form closer to the sub's skin. The catch was then deposited into a small bay for the underwater journey.

"All set?" Jack asked.

106

"Affirmative. We have one gargoyle safely contained," Damien smiled. They had actually done it. "Please proceed, Lieutenant."

The genbot had fallen a little further toward the south end of the lake than had been planned, but not so far as to jeopardize the mission. Considering all the variables, it was a small miracle it worked at all. Having the cargo safely stored away, Lt. Carlitos released the decoy debris as planned and then sped away to the north under the dark waves.

37. A New Day

"What was living in the Refuge like?" She stared out across the dark water, killing time.

"The Territories? I don't know, Eve," Maren replied, her mind not really on the conversation at hand. "It seemed pretty normal at the time." She struggled to see if there was anything out there in the near darkness.

"Didn't you wonder what you were missing, what was possible?" Eve asked, absentmindedly plinking the aluminum rod supporting the overhead tarp that extended out over the water from the van parked at the shoreline.

"Do you mean did I feel 'primitive'?" Maren responded with a hint of annoyance. "No, not really. It was just all I knew, and besides, it wasn't all that primitive anyway. It seemed like a pretty good life." Her eyes stayed on the black lake ahead of her.

Eve still couldn't comprehend why anyone would choose to live like they did in the olden days. "I think it might be interesting to see the Refuge Territories, but I certainly wouldn't want to live there. Like, what would you do all day? I would get so bor... Wait a minute. Is that it?" Eve pointed out into the water and suddenly became more businesslike. Before waiting for a response, she turned away from her red-haired companion and walked to the front of the hovervan.

Maren strained her deep blue eyes in the twilight of the morning. At first she wasn't sure, but with a second look she saw it, too. How'd she miss what Eve saw? There was indeed a faint green dye in the water. She double-checked that her pendant was tucked inside her rash guard top, then leaned over to pick up the end and several loops of a cable woven from spiderlyn. Maren waded out into the shallows. Soon, she was treading water. Out a little farther, the green dye gently stirred from a subtle current flowing underneath.

Maren lowered her goggles, flicked them on, took a deep breath, and dove under the surface. The water was murky, made more so by the green signal dye. Yet she knew it was there. The goggles eventually highlighted it. She kicked harder and the black shape came into view. Grabbing ahold of the heavy armored figure that was resting on the sandy bottom to keep herself and the light cable submerged, she worked the spiderlyn sling under its arms and secured it tight. When her red hair breached the surface, she signaled the shore with a short salute.

Eve started the winch, and the body was slowly reeled up to the shoreline and into the back of the waiting hovervan. By the time it breached the surface, it was under the tarp, and then it was only a few more seconds before the body was inside and the doors where shut tight.

As they started up the van, the morning rays shown through the wooded shoreline. A bird sang in a tree. "Take a good look at the sunlight. It'll be the last time we see it for a while. The downside to our little success here is that we'll be locked down for weeks now."

"Yep," Eve said. Maren's statement was true, Eve thought, as long as "we" did not include Eve.

They drove away into the light of morning. The new day had fully begun.

38. Held Down

Clouds and water swirled around him. He needed to protect them. At first he tried to control where he was going, but he soon realized he was caught in the tumult, being carried away with no control of his own. He wanted to fly. A large hand kept him under. Trying to fight his way out, he tried to fire an energy wave from his fist at the large hand, but his gauntlet was missing. His fingers were cold. Then, for a moment, he felt the warmth. She was there, reaching for him. But her hair was not the color of silver, but of flame. Then she fell away into the swirling cloud below as the water covered him above. He tried to fight against the current with his wings, to make it back home. There was nothing there. They must have been ripped off in the fall. Even if he had his wings, there was no going back. For he looked in the sky, and the fortress was gone; to where, he didn't know. He needed to protect them, but they weren't there. Then he was sitting in the dirt, all alone, away from the city. The large hand was gone and the sun was shining brightly. But he was still cold. He thought of her again. Looking across the plain, he did not see her. Mist began to cover the ground, yet the sun was still shining brightly. Too bright; it hurt his eyes. He tried to lower the visor of his mask, but it would not go down. The light grew stronger…

"It's coming around."

"Wait until the beta scans show full consciousness. We only get one shot at this."

"Be ready with the rail gun. If it comes after us, it's going to be tough to stop it."

"Calm down and pay attention. It's not going to have a chance to do anything. It'll be fried in a moment. Franklin, make sure you have the stasis shot ready."

"B-scan at 90%. Priming the charge."

"Here we go, people…"

"B-scan 100%, go."

"Engaging pulse."

Michael's body wretched, his spine arching backward as all the muscles in his body seemed to contract at once. The black pads on either side of his head did not emit the warm humming pulse of Magritte's scanners. Instead, the padded scanners burned and pounded into his skull. And instead of the few seconds in the chair on Magritte, this seemed to last forever. He writhed in agonizing pain.

Then it was over, and the light fell again to darkness.

"Did we get it?"

"We got it. Oh yeah, we got it."

"Wait a minute… It's still alive. It actually survived the procedure! It wasn't supposed to do that, was it?"

"Confirm, we have the scan? It's perfect?"

"Yes, sir. Scan and backup data chip both read 100% clean."

"Then give me the stasis shot."

"But that will definitely kill it, Lieutenant," Franklin objected.

"The stasis isn't necessary, he is still alive!"

"Maren, we're sticking with the procedure. Franklin, give me the shot. I'm going to freeze its-" Jack said, his face set in a determined mask.

"But you can't just kill him, Jack!" Maren said, grabbing Jack's arm and preventing him from reaching the stasis shot. Jack recoiled at her hand. His burns from the ambush under the English garden had not yet completely healed. Maren let go immediately.

Jack stepped back and spoke to the room. "The plan was to freeze his neural network which means we kill it. We do it now and get it over with. What are you looking at me like that for? It's a genbot! Its sole purpose in life is to kill us. It is a machine, a robot, designed by the gens, designed for one purpose: Hunting and killing us: *me* and *you*!"

"We don't need to freeze the structures and pathways if-" Maren tried to continue.

"The plan was to kill it and study it and then-" Jack interrupted.

Then from the back of the room came an unexpected voice, but one they all recognized instantly. With the first words, the rest of the room went silent. "We didn't think he could survive the scan, and it was questionable whether he would even survive the pressure bomb. Well, he didn't die. That changes the plan," Colonel Red calmly stated. "If he dies later, we can just as easily freeze the neurons then," he said almost as an afterthought.

"You've got to be kidding me!" Jack argued, amazed that he was even having this conversation about a deadly machine built to kill him and everyone else. "Do you know what kind of risk we are taking? I mean, what are we going to do with it?! Its heat signature alone is enough for them to find us! What does the Doctor think about this? If the neural pathways change-"

"We might be able to learn something from questioning the genbot, learning not just what it knows but how it thinks," Colonel Red reasoned. "We don't know yet what purpose he might serve, but-"

"The only way the Organization stays alive is through discipline, and we can't go changing the plan," Jack responded with fire in his eyes, as if his life depended on it. Jack believed it did. "It could get out and kill all of us even without its armor!"

"He isn't going to be killing anyone in his current state. But you're right about one thing: discipline keeps the organization going. And so I'm making it an order," the Colonel commanded, but in the same level tone he had used all along. Jack was loyal, passionate, and persistent. That's why Red picked him. Jack wouldn't like it, but he'd do it. One way or another.

Jack murmured, "This is going to get us killed."

"I said it's an order. We are presented with a new opportunity and I intend to seize it. If the genbot is hurt... no... if the genbot doesn't recover – fully, mind you Lieutenant – before we transfer him to Colonel Blue, I will hold you personally responsible, Lt. Carlitos. To the fullest extent of military law. Full recovery. On you. Is that clear?" Red was annoyed that he had to explain himself. The stress was getting to everyone. Jack didn't normally argue about an order or a change in plan. Red knew immediately that his threat was more than necessary, but it got the job done quickly.

"Yes, Sir!" Jack responded crisply. He had forgotten himself. Even if it got him killed, which he thought it quite possibly could, he would follow the order. That's what good lieutenants did.

"See that it's done." Colonel Red turned and walked briskly out the door as the genbot drifted once more out of consciousness. Red had work to do.

39. The Odds

"My good Doctor Psycho, it actually worked," Red said.

"Hmph," the Doctor smirked. "Of course it worked." He told them it would work. Why should anyone be surprised when it did?

"I wasn't so confident," Red admitted.

There was never a doubt in the Doctor's mind. He had worked on it for years. He had seen it tested. He had used it in other applications. They were just patterns and biology. The information was encoded, and he had the keys. Of course it worked. "The rest will work, too."

"I hope so."

"We take each step as carefully designed." Doctor Psycho and Colonel Red had worked it all out. With General Chi, Colonel Blue, and the others, it all came together, just as planned. Perhaps it was even the most difficult part of the plan. There was only a little more to go. Then, they could stop the Event. They could stop the gens from destroying the truds. Natural humans were still smart enough to fight back. And Doctor Psycho led this part of the charge. "It's just a matter now of assembling the blocks, like one of your buildings. We put in place one piece at a time."

"Agreed..." Red dragged out the word.

"But?" The Doctor knew there was more.

"But there is always the unanticipated. Our little enterprise isn't physics and engineering. There is chance."

"Always. Which is why we planned for the unanticipated." Doctor Psycho smiled. "Relax, we've done everything humanly possible to make sure this works."

"I know. I'm just worried that everything humanly possible isn't enough."

40. Awakening

Once again the light grew brighter, and the world slowly began to seep back into Michael's mind. Something was preventing him from lifting his arms. He tried to sit up, but failed. He tried to open his eyes, but the light was still too bright. And to make it worse, his head hurt. The pounding in his skull made him remember: the painful scan, the voices and before that... the explosion. Now the world raced back into his head. He remembered chasing the jetpacker and the split second hint of the smell of a petrol-like substance.

He again tried to get up, to give a report to Rex, but he couldn't. Finally, he managed to open one eye against the white light to see the blurry room around him.

Spiderlyn straps crossed his body and ended in bolts fastened to the floor. The impossibly strong cord made of synthetic spider silk also secured his wrists and ankles to the cold concrete floor. In the stark room, there was only one item intended for his comfort: a small mat underneath the trunk of his body.

"Well," he thought to himself, "I am obviously not on Fortress Magritte." The thought was cold, not said with humor or emotion. It was merely a statement of observation and therefore fact. He expected a barrage from Magritte at any moment. Or perhaps Gabriella, Dante, and Martha might burst through the wall or ceiling.

MODIFIED HORIZON

He waited there.

The room was quiet. Michael slowly opened both eyes and stared skyward at the white ceiling and florescent lights. He turned his head, partly to see the rest of the room and partly to turn away from the lights, and the pounding pain between his ears began again.

He was alone. Despite the strange pulsing pain that came with each pump of his heart, Michael Lightbringer tried to observe the conditions around him. Regardless of his current circumstances, he would likely soon need to give a report to Rex. Each detail needed to be recorded accurately. The room was stark and nearly bare, but even in its bareness, it offered clues. There were no windows. Most likely, he was in the center of a large building, perhaps buried deep beneath the earth, or in the belly of a vehicle carrying him somewhere. If it was a vehicle, it would have to be a large ship or submersible, because there were no land vehicles of which he knew that were large enough to contain the room in which he now found himself. The possibility that he was in an airship did not even occur to him, for the gens jealously guarded the sky. Only trud buildings strove for the sky. Anything detached from the firmness of the earth was not allowed to exist for long.

Michael's eyes were focusing better now, and he took note of the metal bars and energy shield transecting the large room. On the other side of the energy shield and bars were several desks, unoccupied, and a bank of recording equipment obviously focused on him.

Michael recognized the purpose: the room had some similarities to the holding pen on Fortress Magritte, though the last time they had held a prisoner in it for any significant length of time was decades ago. Prisoners typically held little value. If information could not be extracted from them through the scanner, chemical tracing, or bribery, further detention usually proved fruitless. So, any detainee's stay on Magritte was usually quite short, often only minutes. Still, Lightbringer was certain of the similarities of the two rooms. And the pattern recognition led to an inevitable conclusion.

The thought had never occurred to him that the truds might actually attempt to capture him. For what purpose could holding him possibly serve? He could understand the truds trying to kill him, for he was often preventing them from creating technologies and manufacturing weapons that were deemed a threat. Indeed, the situation often dictated that he go so far as to kill them. They had been trying to kill the gens, the Ancients, for generations. It was only natural for them to try to kill him, the gens' Guardian. But to hold him as a prisoner? He held no special information, nor a special place in the eyes of the Ancients, and his mere presence was a danger to them.

None of his training had prepared him for this situation. Nor had he been designed to deal with it. Yet a major feature of Guardians was their adaptability, which Michael understood. He was in uncertain circumstances, but he would nevertheless seek to advance the primary mission: Protect the Ancients.

Realizing that if he was deep underground or underwater and if this group of truds were technologically advanced enough, as the energy field indicated, Michael considered that rescue or destruction of the building/bunker/ship might not be imminent. This meant he must consider escape. He was not considering escape out of fear of death or fear of anything else. As a matter of fact, had he been able to reveal his location to a floating fortress but for a moment, he would have done so and called down a barrage upon himself. After all, he would be restored in a short period of time while his enemy would not. In his situation, flight was not fear, but power. If he could get back to Magritte, Skyguard would be able to read his thoughts, analyze everything he'd seen, discover what the truds were trying to accomplish, and destroy not only this base of operations, but others as well. Escape then.

Straining his head against the throbbing pain, he looked down to examine the spiderlyn straps that secured him to the floor. What he noticed first was not the spiderlyn, but the large gash in his right arm. Michael had no memory of the submersible's mechanical arm cutting through the malfunctioning liquid metal and into his arm when it retrieved him from beneath the dark waves of the lake. Though Michael was aware of the gash now, it did not particularly hurt. While pain produces useful information, it also can inhibit functionality. Thus, the pain sensory abilities of Guardians had been significantly reduced, and that pain they did feel was typically more of an awareness of something wrong rather than agony. An exception had been the agony of the crude scanner-like device he was subjected to upon his arrival, and the strange continuance of the throbbing pain in his head. Studying the gash more carefully, it was clear that it had already been treated with crude stitches, though he did not know who had done it. He did not understand why the savages were helping him and actually healing his wounds. Like the purpose for holding him prisoner, it was a mystery.

Not able to recall where the gash was received, Michael returned to his original purpose. He noted the two straps crisscrossing his body and the smaller ones securing his wrists. The spiderlyn securing his ankles was out of his line of vision. He flexed his muscles against the straps. The spiderlyn was high quality, construction grade. Likewise the bolts on the floor. He was strong, but brute force would not likely extract him from his current circumstances. Besides, the energy field presented a second impossible barrier. Even if he might extract himself from the spiderlyn, he would not be able to find a way to neutralize the energy shield before the truds would be alerted. As for the poor-quality steel bars: They were thick enough to stop a trud, but they did not concern a Guardian such as himself. He could tell just by looking at the bars that it was subgrade metal, and old. His body and, more importantly, mind were more than capable of defeating that crude technology. However, he decided it would be best to conserve his energy rather than fight against straps that could likely not be broken. His captors may have crudely stitched up his arm, but he had no idea if they would provide him with energy or how long it might be before the best opportunity for escape might present itself.

So he would wait. Patiently. Calmly. Coldly. Until there was an opening.

41. Mortar and Pestle

Flora took the assorted plants from the strainer, and placed them in the bowl. She picked up the pestle and began to smash the plants into a paste. It would take a long time. The fibers needed to be broken down. Then the paste would go into the flask, and the chemistry could commence.

Flowers and plants. Full of strange compounds with miraculous properties. Medicine, healing, salves, elixirs, life from some. Poison, decay, rashes, acids, death from others.

In fact, one could bring forth both good and evil from some of the same unemotional, unthinking, unfeeling botanical wonders. The plants and flowers were just naturally there, waiting to be used for a higher purpose. It was not for the plant or flower to decide.

And many of those flowers could be bought from a local market. Most people just appreciated the superficial beauty of the flowers, but there was an internal beauty that was so much more magnificent, so much more powerful.

Flora knew how to draw the beauty out. And a few others would share in that beauty. For a brief moment of their lives, at the end.

42. In Red We Trust

"Listen, I'm sorry I yelled at you." Jack was trying, and failing, to apologize properly to Maren. "It's just that I don't think we should be risking the whole operation by keeping the genbot alive. I've seen last minute changes to operational plans get people killed before, like with Trenton. I still think it's a mistake to nurse that killing machine back to health. A genbot is like a homing beacon. It attracts trouble. It's just a matter of time before some havoc emerges from above looking for it. Somehow the gens always find one of them when a genbot goes missing. And that doesn't even factor in the danger of it going berserk and killing people down here. Those things are stronger than the strongest man and faster than the fastest. We should be putting the body back in the lake."

"He's in a cage, Jack."

"There's a whole army of his friends up there that would try to free the genbot from it if they knew where it was."

"But they aren't going to find out where it is."

"It's the possibility that-"

"What can you do about, Jack? Red gave the orders. And I know you: you are going to following the orders. You're worrying too much about things you can't control and won't change. We have to trust a little bit that High Command knows what they are doing."

Jack stood there and let Maren's comments sink in for a little while before responding. "I know. You are right. Orders are orders.

121

And maybe there is some wisdom in it. Maybe the Colonel knows something I don't that makes it all worth the risk. Anyway, I'm sorry about yelling." He moved closer to Maren and put his arms around her waist.

Ultimately, Jack knew he trusted Red, despite his current frustration. The Colonel had almost always done the right thing. And Red knew things. Colonel Red always knew more than the others, often even more than Colonel Blue, and Blue was the director of intelligence for the whole city. And if he needed proof for how much Red always knew, he had it in his arms. They'd found her out there in the midst of the Refuge Territories, that vast wilderness, right where he said they'd be. She'd been in his arms pretty much ever since. Over the years, it grew into something like a real relationship. Jack trusted Red that Maren was important, though despite Jack's best efforts, he didn't know why. Jack had to accept he couldn't see the whole picture and would probably never have most of the answers. Still, it was within his power to decide, based on the evidence, who he trusted. There was no question that he trusted Colonel Red.

When it came to Maren, however, Jack wasn't sure he could ever trust her completely. He didn't have an answer for why that was the case, either.

43. Puzzles

The pieces didn't fit together. Felix sat at his computer, supposedly drafting structural components of a new gleaming tower of glass and metal. It was to be 75 stories tall, one of dozens of medium-sized towers his firm was in the process of designing in the city of mirrored pillars. With the combination of intelligence and years of experience, Engineer Katz could do his day job while simultaneously working out the problems of Colonel Red. Instead of drafting, he was thinking. And the pieces didn't fit. It didn't make sense.

All of the data said it couldn't survive the scan. Now what was he going to do with it? He had saved its life because Felix was the type of man who preserved options when he could.

Yet this option came with risk. But maybe the risk was worth the opportunity. The idea grew in his mind. Something in his mind hummed ever so slightly. Slowly, gradually, as he manipulated the structural components on the screen, the pieces began to fit together. Soon, the proper course of action naturally dropped into place.

But he had to put that out of his mind for a bit, to be returned to later. Now, it was time to focus on the primary concern: the Event.

44. Machine Watching

The door opened and two women tentatively walked into the room.

"I'm telling you, it was moving around."

"I believe you. I just think we should see him for ourselves. You've been staring at the monitor for hours, and I know what that can do to one's eyes," the red-haired female said somewhat skeptically.

The genbot blinked its now opened eyes.

"You see, it *is* awake. I knew it wasn't dead!" the blonde one exclaimed.

"Of course he wasn't dead, Eve. It was just a question of whether or not he would gain consciousness." *Then the blonde one is named Eve.*

"Then why have you been so nervous, Private Bern?" *The red one is Bern. She was there before, during the pain-*

"The lieutenant gave the strictest instructions that he needed to make a full recovery. I was nervous because whether he woke up or not was really out of my control," Private Bern replied.

"If you can't control it, Maren, you shouldn't worry about it," Eve counseled as she moved closer to the bars and the energy barrier to get a better look. They were words of advice she herself had often ignored. Eve often said things as much as to convince herself of the truth of her statement as to converse with her friend.

124

"Easier said than done, Eve," Maren said, thinking back to her own conversation with Jack and the nightmares that visited in the darkness.

"Should we try to talk to it?"

Maren arched her eyebrows at her friend and made a half frown, held it for a moment, and then turned her palms upward in an expression of "Why not?" Private Maren Bern motioned towards the genbot. "If you want the first shot, Corporal, be my guest."

"Your guest? It's the prerogative of rank," she winked.

Eve looked at the killing machine. It wasn't even looking at her, though she had seen the gen's warrior blink half a dozen times. She desperately wanted its attention. "Hello? Genbot, can you hear me?" Eve rattled her sidearm against the steel bars just outside of the energy shield. "Genbot, are you in there?" She paused for a brief second before turning to Maren. "I've asked it a bunch of stuff and I don't think it is listening to any of it."

"First of all, I was right here listening, and I'm not sure I'd respond to you either. Second, why don't you try asking him something he would care to answer? Besides, you asked him only, like, two questions."

Eve turned quickly back to the body formerly enclosed in gargoyle-like armor and asked in a seductive voice, "Mr. Gargoyle, do you want to be let out of the cage?"

"Quit kidding around," Maren said as she grabbed Eve's arm. "Let me give it a try." Now Maren moved closer to the cage and asked in a caring tone, "Are you hungry?" The genbot did not seem to register the question. Eve smirked. It sounded a bit like Maren was trying to talk to a little kid. Maren tried again. "Excuse me, would you like something to eat?"

Nothing.

"Do you have a name?" she persisted.

"Come on, Maren, it's a machine." Eve didn't think a machine would call itself anything.

"Without his armor, he is just blood and flesh and bone," Maren replied. She'd seen him bleed. He had been unconscious and in captivity for three days. He had to be hungry, so asking him if he wanted something to eat seemed perfectly logical to Maren. Maren remembered being a prisoner once. She had wanted her captors to show some sign of humanity, some glimpse of understanding. She had been thirsty and hungry.

RAN VANT

Eve waved her hand dismissively. "Sure, it has blood and stuff... it's a biological machine, like a fancy robech, but still a machine nonetheless," Corporal Eve Mortier insisted.

"Whatever it is, they still have to call him something," Maren insisted. She turned again to the genbot, trying one more time, "Excuse me, what are you called?"

"Maybe it doesn't even speak our language," Eve pondered, more to the air than to anyone in particular. "Who knows how they communicate up there on the floater?"

"Eve, that is a good insight; it's possible he's not understanding," Maren acknowledged. "I guess I just assumed they spoke the same language as us. But even if he spoke a different language, you'd expect him to at least acknowledge our presence."

Maren turned away from the bars and began walking back towards the door. "Well, now that he's awake, it will make cleaning the wound more interesting."

"I'm willing to bet Franklin will be jumpy," Eve predicted. "I'll try to make sure he doesn't shoot you when you're in there."

"You'll try? Why, thanks, I guess."

"You know what I meant."

Maren pressed the release on the room's door. "We should probably get out of here. Since he's awake, they'll probably want somebody else to do the interrogations, in spite of our expert performance."

"I hope we still get to visit it."

"Why?"

Eve looked back at the cage and then turned back to Maren and said in a hushed tone, "I think he is kind of good looking."

"Eve, I thought you thought he was just a ruthless machine?"

"Well, let's just say that's one good looking machine then."

"Just remember, everything is being recorded," Maren pointed out, and in a joking tone she continued, "After the lieutenant reviews the recording, I'm not sure he'll let you near him anymore."

"Hey, I'm not the one dating an officer."

Maren looked at Eve with her head crooked sideways, eyebrows lifted, and big eyes, as if to say, "Stop talking about that," but thanks to the recording devices, which were indeed likely to be reviewed by the lieutenant, she said nothing.

"Let's get out of here," Eve said, with a big grin.

45. Play Along

A new twist, a new opportunity. He had a course of action now.

But there was already much to manage. And Red knew which was the most important: The Event.

Everything, every action, all must converge on it.

The most important early objective had been accomplished. Now, time would take care of much of the rest. But others were already impatient, and their impatience could ruin everything forever.

It was now time to ensure that the others played along. And he knew who was going to help him do it. Indeed, he had known for a long time.

46. Thoughts

The women were gone. He was sure now they were the same ones he glimpsed in the midst of the painful scanner. There were others there, too. But these two visited again. And again. They spoke to him, they asked questions. Michael had said nothing. They were truds. And Guardians of the West did not answer to truds. Guardians of the West answered to the Ancients through Rex and the other Fortress Overlords. Truds were like cattle to be managed at the Ancients' directions. Dangerous cattle at times, to be sure, but clearly beneath those who watched from the sky.

And this made things all the more strange for Michael. Lightbringer did not know why, but he had felt an urge to answer the redheaded trud woman, the one he had learned was named Maren Bern. He had nearly said that he did not require food as often as the weak truds did. He had nearly told her that he was called Michael Lightbringer, Guardian of the West. He had nearly said that he understood everything they said and more.

But he had not said anything.

Michael merely lay there, waiting. The answers would be forthcoming soon enough.

47. Some Assembly Required

Damien Musashi carefully assembled the rail gun. The energy core had needed a thorough cleaning. Now, with the fuel scrubbed, he was carefully realigning the rails and magnetic runners. Even as a child, Damien had a knack for technologies and weapons. Years of experience had honed the innate talent. Not just anyone could align the magnetic runners properly. It took patience, attention to detail, and knowledge. Now middle aged, he'd had years to practice and had made the most of them.

Damien finished the assembly and grabbed a plastic projectile at the center of which was a very small speck of ferrous material. The plastic projectile allowed Damien to test the alignment with a high drag, low velocity, low mass object. He placed the weapon in the firing test vice and stepped back to initiate the weapon charging. Safety first. A moment later, he pressed the button to remotely pull the trigger. The plastic slug flew out of the rail gun and hit the centering mark.

"Perfect, dead center. And on the first attempt. Impressive." Red observed.

"Colonel Red, I didn't realize you were here."

"I just arrived." Red stepped further into the room. "Do you mind?" he asked, pointing towards the calibrated rail gun.

"Of course not," Damien answered, appreciating the Colonel's asking permission where everyone knew none was required or even expected. They were different ranks, but Damien always felt as if the Colonel treated him as a peer.

Felix began to casually release the rail gun from the alignment apparatus. "Damien, you seem to have a talent for aligning rails and runners. You're patient and meticulous. I haven't seen many center it on the first try. It was your first try, correct? I didn't miss thirty minutes of swearing, did I?"

Damien chuckled. "No, sir, you did not. It was my first go. If you take your time and are careful, it usually works." Damien was being modest. While it sounded simple, the assembly was quite difficult and it almost universally required extensive fine-tuning to center the slug shot. "Most people just rush it. And another factor is that most people neglect to put the same effort into maintaining the realignment equipment. You have to put in the prep work."

"The first hour sharpening the axe, eh?"

"Heck, it also doesn't hurt to have been doing it for years now. I've been at this game a long time."

"So true. So true. But you aren't the only one who's been at this a long time. Believe it or not, I had hair when I started this game, as you say. I've seen a lot of operatives, Damien, and you are one of the most capable and persistent. Few people have patience and are willing to set the groundwork in place."

Felix finished releasing the weapon from the alignment harness and slowly looked down its sights. "The thing is, I need someone with patience. Someone who understands certain technology, and someone loyal to the cause of natural humans. Forget all the squabbles between the Natural Human Alliance, the True Core, the Pure, and all the others." Felix mock fired the weapon, then slowly lowered it back to the table. "Those differences are nothing compared with preserving natural humans, with saving them from a world where they are always in danger of destruction."

Damien nodded.

Felix patted the rail gun. "If we are going to stop the Event, we are going to need the technology of all of them."

Damien pointed to the equipment in the room. "This stuff is good. Rail guns, skip drives, the works. But I'm worried it's not enough," Damien confessed. "I know I don't know all of the plans, it would be foolish to tell me or anyone who doesn't have a need-to-know, but to me it doesn't quite add up to victory. The gens have some mean stuff: armies of machines, guardians, the floaters, and who-knows-what in reserve. In my years of fighting them, if there is one thing I've learned is that they should not be underestimated. I'm not sure if you are asking, sir, but I think we're going to need something more to take them all out. I sure hope you have something up your sleeve."

"A couple somethings, actually. But one which you may prove especially helpful with."

"Should I even ask?"

"We're going to be hitting them harder than ever before, with things not seen before. Your analysis is correct: with only what you've seen, we could not defeat them. However, we can defeat them with new tools. But in order to do that, we've had to make arrangements with some whom we'd generally rather avoid."

"Like the Core?"

"Much worse, in my humble opinion."

"Who?"

"The Network."

Damien scoffed. "We can't trust the Network. Everyone knows that," Damien said, pointing out the obvious. "They seem practically half gen to me."

"I understand, and on certain days I would be inclined to agree with you. As I've said, I generally prefer to avoid the Network and the Network is certainly not a fan of me. But we have to play all our cards to make this operation work. And the Network can be played."

Colonel Red continued. "They have developed a... a... a *capability* that is powerful. Very powerful. But dangerous if used incorrectly, and I fear they plan to use it incorrectly."

"So you want me to steal it?"

"Not this time, Damien. But it could be valuable to our own efforts if the Network could be persuaded to see the benefits of cooperation. Indeed, it could be key. But if they use their technology on their own, according to their own plans... disaster will result. Of that, be assured."

"And you want me to do what exactly?"

"They've agreed to help us. You're going to see that they do."

48. Clues and Concealment

The Refuge Territories had long posed a special problem for Jack. The people who lived there did so illegally. There were thus no official records on those people for Lt. Carlitos to use. The NHA didn't even have a good idea of the number of settlements out there in the wilderness set aside for nature, let alone the number of people hiding out in the wilds. It was not the place where members of mainstream society went. It wasn't worth the risk for most.

The fact that Maren grew up in the R.T., but by her own account wasn't born there, meant that she or somebody close to her probably had something to hide or was a nut job. She certainly didn't walk there as a kid by herself. Somebody went with her. She, of course, claimed she didn't know. She claimed she didn't know much before Jack found her tied to a pole on a hill covered in tall grass. The question was: who was that person that brought her to the R.T. so long ago?

The archives didn't explicitly answer the question, either. But sometimes there were holes in the archives. And the lack of information was in itself information that could be used. Yet there were other sources of information. Many of the illegals were literate and did the same as people in the cities: they felt the need to write down every detail about their lives, and those around them, in diaries. Hunting down NHA traitors in the R.T., which was unfortunately sometimes necessary, also occasionally would turn up a rare stash of documents that shed light on the local power structures.

So Jack had clues, but nothing that pointed to why Red should care at all about Maren. This wasn't new. He'd been working the problem literally for years. Despite his best efforts to pry it out of her one way or another, Jack hadn't gotten anywhere in a long time. She either didn't know why Red thought she was important or she was very good at concealing it. The former possibility was a concern, but it was the later possibility that really worried him.

49. The Network

The burn scars on his lower jaw turned his lips down at the corners. Damien thought the scars gave the man a perpetual scowl. "We, of course, have much to show you," the man said.

"And I look forward to seeing it, Niles," General Chi said.

"Why does Red insist on calling us that? We can only assume it is because he thinks of us as we were before. But we are no longer that which Red remembers."

"I'm sorry?" General Chi didn't know why Niles was offended or what the scarred one was talking about. That was the scarred body's name after all: Niles.

"We are so much more than just the man Niles," the scarred one answered.

General Chi, for all he knew of the world, would never understand the Network. "Naturally," General Chi said, using the most inappropriate and at the same time appropriate word for the circumstances.

The one word response seemed to please the scarred one and he went on: "Please, follow us and we will continue with the inspection."

The scarred one turned and walked down the corridor. Damien used the opportunity to turn around in the middle of the room, allowing the cameras hidden in the buttons on his cuffs and the front of his shirt to get a panoramic view of the facility. It wasn't every day that the NHA got people inside a Network base of operations, let alone a manufacturing facility. The Organization could learn a thing or two from the Network. A few quick steps and he caught up again with Niles and General Chi.

They entered another room with racks and racks of equipment piled to the ceiling. A woman brought in two packs hanging from straps on each arm, and set them on a table in the center of the room. Damien recognized her from Colonel Red's briefing as the woman called Zhe.

Zhe spoke: "These packs contain modern skip drives. Better than the rockets or old skips and certainly better than those sputter packs the True Core is churning out. We've done the math: put these in a jetpack and you will out-climb a Guardian, like a sputter pack but with more control, better reliability, and more endurance. And they are easy to use. An idiot could launch himself and, more importantly, land himself without getting hurt. No operational training necessary. We have them all ready now. Please, inspect those you wish. Unfortunately, it is of course impossible to fly them at this location."

"Of course." The floater still hovered above them, and they never forgot it, least of all General Chi.

"Shall we look at the rest? You may come back and look at these more closely if you wish, but we have much to see and only limited time."

"Lead the way," General Chi responded.

Damien did another covert camera spin in the skip drive room and followed Zhe, Niles, and Chi down a very long but wide corridor, through two sets of blast doors, and into a cavernous room that looked as if it had been carved directly from the bedrock.

Zhe spoke again. "And this is the real reason why you are here."

"This is why the Natural Human Alliance deigns to deal with the Network," Niles said.

"This is how we shall destroy the gens," Zhe said.

General Chi looked at the weapons. They had not been lying. The weapons were here. The weapons were ready. No matter how crazy he thought the Network was, they sure could churn out the hardware.

Damien was the one to actually say it: "Nova bombs."

"Radius of total disintegration?" Chi asked.

Zhe spoke, "Enough. 10 to 20 meters. If placed in the right place, deep inside near the float generator, one of the devices could take out a fortress."

Niles continued, "Alternatively, multiple novas could be used in sequence to tunnel into the fortress. Either way, it will crash to the ground. We've trained enough people to properly use them, without those people understanding exactly what we have developed or what they will be used against."

Zhe went on, "The novas would also be devastating to a machine army if deployed properly. We can make them larger, but then their mobility suffers further."

"They could do a lot of damage to the city, too," General Chi said.

"Which is why we are going to be very careful with them, General."

"And the delivery vehicles?" The bombs in this primitive form were too heavy to be carried.

"Combat sleds," Niles said. "It will be like the days of the fighter pilot."

Damien smiled at the thought of racing through the sky in a combat sled, delivering a nova bombardment to the homes of those who had ruled the skies for so long.

"I need to see the sleds," Chi said.

"This way."

At the end of the corridor, Zhe peeled off from the group, and disappeared into the labyrinth of the complex.

General Chi and Niles did not chitchat on the way. Both were stone cold. Both knew this was an alliance of necessity, not love. And both knew they would not get any information from the other except that which they wanted to reveal.

Finally, they reached it. The door opened, and for the first time in his life, Damien saw something made by the hands of truds that could truly reach the heavens. "Amazing."

"Do you like what we have created?" Niles asked.

"It's about time we took to the skies to fight them," Damien said.

General Chi was not so easily impressed. "There are only five."

"We will have all of the combat sleds in place when the time comes, but they aren't ready now," the scarred one said. "We will have everything ready to deliver the weapons in due time."

"Niles, you promised that you would have all the technology-"

"And we will, General Chi," he hissed. Chi had called him Niles again. This is why the NHA is weak, he thought. Their leaders cannot remember even the simplest facts. He was no longer just Niles.

"Then where are the sleds?" Chi asked.

"All of the combat sleds will be in place in time. And everything is just as we have said. Damien will be able to verify it, with his own eyes as well as with all those cameras he is wearing."

Damien grew white. How did Niles know? Damien instinctively thought to deny it, but Niles spoke again first.

"Isn't that why Red sent you? To ensure that everything is in place and on time?"

"Yes." Damien said matter-of-factly. There was no point in lying.

General Chi was not so quick to give up. "Niles, what are you saying? If this man was spying, I had no-"

"Don't worry, gentlemen," Niles cut him off, pleased in a way to see Chi squirm but eager to quickly establish the Network's superiority. "You cannot keep secrets from the Network. Colonel Red has always been suspicious of the Network, but you can assure him that his goals are the same as ours: revenge against the gens and ensuring that they are wiped from the face of the earth. If Red wants to verify that we keep our word, we have no problem with that. We invited you here, after all. But rather than sneak a look here and there, Damien may as well settle in and make himself comfortable. There is no reason he can't see what we have made here. We will show him it all."

"Everything?" Damien asked.

"Everything," Niles said. And for the first time, Damien thought the scowl on Niles' face turned to smile.

50. Triple Redundancy

Michael heard the door open. He thought about continuing to stare upward so as not to reveal any capability or thought of escape. The truds seemed to think he was not fully functional. Continuing to support such fictions might create an opportunity where his enemy was overly relaxed. In the end, however, he decided to turn his head to see if he couldn't gain more information about his location through a brief glance into whatever lay beyond the doorway. Any bit of information might be the key for understanding how to escape.

Two men walked into the room carrying rail guns, but he did not concentrate on the men with weapons, for they were nothing he hadn't seen before. Instead, he looked past them, straining to see any important details in the corridor beyond. It appeared to be a white corridor, similar in construction to his cell, but obviously a passageway rather than an adjoining room. As the door shut, Michael knew he had gained little of practical value.

A second time the door opened, and this time the two females who had visited before entered. He saw another person dressed in coveralls and carrying dirty excavating equipment walking down the corridor. Lightbringer surmised he was likely in an underground bunker or building core, not on a ship. It would be highly unlikely to have those kinds of drilling rigs on a ship, especially given that the equipment's dirty condition indicated recent use. As the door shut a second time, he continued staring in its general direction at the four truds now staring back at him.

"Hey, it's been turning its head," Eve whispered to Maren, in what Maren viewed as one of Eve's typical statements of the obvious.

One of the men holding a rail gun spoke up. "Genbot, we are going to clean your wound again so it doesn't become infected. It may hurt, but it is actually for your own good. Do you understand?"

They did not understand that Michael's body already made its own version of the antibiotics. Of course, Michael did not have any need to understand this minor part of his biology either. Michael did not make a sound in response to the query, but continued starting at the door. Gildur shrugged his shoulders.

"See, I'm not sure it even understands us. How do we even know it speaks our language?" Eve said in an attempt to make the sergeant understand her hard won wisdom.

"It understands, Corporal," the sergeant stubbornly asserted, though in fact he had no clue if it spoke the common tongue or not. Sergeant Stern turned towards Maren. "Private, go ahead. The spiderlyn has a safety factor of over 10 for this application, so don't worry," implying that there was no way the tied-down genbot could hurt her when she entered his confinement area.

"I'm not the one who feels the need to carry a rail gun," she playfully teased the strait-faced, by-the-book sergeant.

"Triple redundancy, Private. It's the regs. We won't need 'em," he said as he patted the rail gun and flicked off the safety. That was his idea of a joke, but nobody else seemed to notice. After he realized that no one else got it, he flicked the safety back on immediately. The regs said a weapon was not supposed to be live, that is, with the safety off, unless there was A) clearly identified and B) potentially imminent danger where C) the weapon could serve to D) destroy, E) damage, F) immobilize, or G) distract the enemy or, in rare cases, H) signal an ally. Of course, that would be just the abbreviated Reg 1984(a) Summary Paragraph 3.

Maren rubbed her emerald pendant between her fingers for good luck, then took the key and opened the mechanical lock on the metal bars. She stepped forward into the narrow gap between the bars and the energy field and pulled the barred gate shut behind her. Tossing the key to Eve, she called, "Lock me in with handsome, Corporal."

"You're all alone with the big boy, now."

"Thanks. I'm ready to step across the shield now."

"Okay, Private. Shield down in 3… 2… 1… down," Maren stepped across the threshold, "Shield up in 2… 1… up."

"Everything okay, Maren?" Franklin asked with his voice having that slightly metallic sound that occurs when two people are on opposite sides of an energy field.

"Just fine, Franklin."

Private Bern stepped slowly toward the bound genbot. "Hello. I'm Maren," she said as she set down her small duffel bag and knelt beside him. She took the cleaning tool out of her bag. "This will probably hurt, but it removes the dead tissue, kills the bacteria, and adds some cells that aid in healing." At least she expected the cells to help. She didn't actually know enough about the tool or his genetic structure to know if it would really be effective. As for the pain, she knew from experience that it could be excruciating. Regardless, the deep gash in his arm needed to be cleaned, according to the doctor. Putting the nozzle over the wound, she pressed the button and the tool began its work, spaying the wound with solution and immediately vacuuming it up again. She worked it across the wound twice. She expected the genbot to wince and perhaps utter a curse word like most patients did, and as she had, but this one did not even grimace.

Michael did not feel anything other than a slight rubbing sensation on his arm. If this process was expected to hurt a trud, he felt pity for them. They were such weak, primitive creatures.

"That's all of the cleaning," Maren explained to the unanimated genbot. "Now I'll just give you a nutrient injection, and let you get back to your busy day." She took the injector, placed it against his arm, and pulled the trigger. "That's it." She placed the injector back in the bag, closed it up, and stood. "That was easy enough. I'm done with Mr. Talkative. Now let me out of here."

51. Fading Beauty

Flora took the flowers from the vase, shook the water off of the stems into the bathroom sink, and then dumped them in the trash container under the counter top. The flowers had been beautiful, but all beauty fades. And once a flower's beauty has faded, what is a flower good for?

She used to hate having to throw away the flowers, many years ago. Over time, however, she gradually grew accustomed to it. And while she certainly wouldn't say that she enjoyed throwing out the flowers or that she wanted to see them go, she accepted it as a fact of life. Maybe there was even still a tinge of remorse at throwing away the once-glorious petals, but she wasn't even sure of that. Things served their purpose and then were used up. Nothing lasts. That was just life.

She closed the cupboard under the sink that concealed the trashcan, shutting the faded flowers off from the light forever. She leaned against the sink and stared into the mirror.

Her face had a round blandness that was a clear signal to all of her obviously pure trud lineage. The natural imperfections indicated the existence of unmodified genes, and her dated clothing indicated the existence of unmodified fashion sense. But where some might see a disadvantage, she found an advantage. Hers was the advantage found in the anonymity of her face and the ability to blend into crowds. She always hated attention. Maybe she hated attention out of jealousy of the more beautiful and not wanting anything associated with their lifestyles because it could not be hers. Maybe she hated attention because she thought that there was an air of arrogance to it, an implication that those seeking attention were somehow better or more special or more important than somebody else. In her mind, nobody was too important. But when someone acted as if they were too important, there were ways to restore equality.

She turned from the bathroom mirror. There might be time to be reflective later. And if it came to pass that there was no time, what did it really matter?

52. Survival

"Has he done anything yet?" Maren asked as she walked up to Eve, who was slouching at the desk, her chin resting in both palms.

"It hasn't so much as lifted its pinky," she droned in a monotone voice.

"Has he said anything?"

"Um, Maren, I think it's safe to say I would have told you if it could talk. Talking qualifies as 'doing something,'" She had lifted her head just long enough to make finger quotes in the air around 'doing something' before plopping her head back into its cradle. At first, watching the genbot was exciting. Not just exciting; thrilling. The danger, its admittedly handsome features, the fact that one had never been caught like this before, wondering what it might do. That had lasted about fifteen minutes. Now, Eve was the most incredibly bored person in the world. NHA life was generally boredom punctuated by death and sorrow. Her current task now fell firmly into the general boredom category. She didn't really want to be wasting her life staring at a vegetable. She wanted to get out of the tunnels, back to life, back to her hidden refuge with the man she loved on the surface, away from the boredom with spikes of terror, away from the hint of death around every corner and in every cage. Her refuge was her secret and what got her through the monotony of staring at the almost lifeless genbot. "You know, I think maybe the scan scrambled its brains after all."

143

Maren pulled up a chair next to her friend. "All the readings indicated normal gen brain patterns, as far as we know what normal for a gen is, but I guess it's possible he's scrambled up there since he wasn't even supposed to survive." Maren leaned back on the back two legs of her chair and stared across the empty white space to the bars and the gargoyle blankly staring back. "Has he been looking this direction the entire time?"

"It's eerie. It's just been staring this direction. Hardly ever even blinks. I tried counting the blinks for a while, but, you know... I think I liked it better when it didn't even look toward us. The fact that it has blinked a couple of times means I'm pretty sure it isn't dead. But he might as well be, as far as I can tell."

"Hmm... it looks like it's going to be another boring wait."

"I'll say. I don't know why we have to watch it. The sensors can do a good enough job."

"Well, I agree. I certainly don't think he's going anywhere. But orders are orders. Doctor P wants him watched all the time now after he started showing signs of moving and looking around. And in a couple hours, the genbot's scheduled for another cleaning and nutrient treatment."

"Ugh, can you imagine, days of nothing but nutrient? I had to take that stuff for three days once. They wouldn't let me eat anything else. Clogged me up for a week." Eve was glad to at least have Maren to banter with again.

"I wonder what he eats up there on the floater?"

"For all I know, all they eat is nutrient. Maybe they have a greenhouse or something up there. It certainly doesn't look like anything green would grow up that high. It wouldn't surprise me if they stole some food from us every once in a while."

"They probably manufacture something to eat up there. They'd have to, it's so isolated and you don't see anyone coming and going regularly."

"Well, what did you eat in your isolation out there in the boondocks growing up?" Eve asked, almost always finding a way to steer the conversation towards the strange and remote Refuge Territories. It was a way to vicariously image freedom. Limited freedom, to be sure, but a kind of freedom nevertheless, away from everything in the tunnels.

"What's with your obsession about me and the Refuge Territories?"

"First of all, it is *not* an obsession. Second of all, you have to admit it's interesting."

"Seems pretty normal to me," Maren replied truthfully. "We ate, we laughed, we cried, we played, we worked. Normal stuff. It was life pretty much like anywhere else." Maren didn't quite understand what Eve found so fascinating.

Eve wouldn't have any of that. She knew Maren had a million good stories from living outside the cities. And Eve prided herself at being pretty good about prying those stories out of Maren. Well, except for some things. "Come on, give me a break. You know it's a least a little bit exotic. Most people never even get to see the Refuge, let alone get to grow up there."

"I know. I guess I'm tired of people asking me about it. Jack is always asking me, you are always asking me, anyone who happens to find out I grew up there quizzes me," Maren took a deep breath and pivoted the chair back to all four legs. She folded her arms on the table and set her head down on them sideways. Looking up at Eve, she continued, "It's like growing up in the Territories makes me different, like somehow less than a fully modern human being."

"Well, most of the people from the Territories are a little bit messed up in the head."

"Eve, you've said yourself that I am the only one you've met from the Territories."

Eve lifted her head from its cushion of palms again and turned to look at Maren. "I know. Like I said: Most of them are a little messed up in the head," she joked, twirling her right index finger in a circle around her temple. "Now quit stalling. Seriously, I want to know what you ate. You couldn't have eaten nutrient all the time, that's for sure."

"Well, we grew some of our food, traded for other stuff, went searching for berries and certain types of roots, and we did a fair amount of hunting."

"Hunting?!"

"Sure, the Territories are full of animals."

"That's the whole point of the Refuge Territories! I can't believe you killed animals!"

"If you ever had the chance to live there, you'd see that that's how lots of animals eat. Everything is so ordered here in the city that you forget how violent the wilderness is, and how normal that actually is. People here imagine everything in nature is as they wish it should be, as somehow perfect. But I know a lot of the animals are cruel, and vicious, and violent, because I've seen it. People here think of animals as pets, all cuddly and cute-"

"Okay, okay, okay... Enough with the sermon, already. I know animals eat other animals, but we aren't animals!"

53. Blue Books

Colonel Blue set the package down on Jack's desk.

Lt. Jack Carlitos carefully opened the box and took out a stack of notebooks.

"You can't say anything to Red," Blue said.

"I remember what we agreed." Jack knew that Red wouldn't care anyway if he got help from Blue on the project. Blue was cleared to see everything and knew all the NHA's secrets. After Jack had run into one of many dead ends, he had told Blue to keep an eye out for items that might help. She had taken an interest in the mystery. Blue agreed to help if Jack didn't tell Red. Everybody knew there was more than a little rivalry between Blue and Red. And she probably just wanted to avoid the bickering that sometimes went along with working with Red. Red and Blue sometimes saw things differently, that was all. Jack would take help where he could get it. Personal rivalries and frictions shouldn't get in the way of a professional.

The lieutenant spread out the notebooks. "Where were these found?"

"In a burnt out lab two sectors over," Blue said.

"How many others did you tell about this?"

"Give me a little credit, Jack."

"Had to ask."

"No you didn't." Colonel Blue exhaled. Sometimes young officers could grate.

Jack flipped through the crinkled pages of the first one. "Looks like research notes."

"Probably. They're old."

"How old?"

"Maybe 25 years. At least 20." Blue said.

"If these are over 20 years old, then she's too young for there to be a connection, unless she was a genius toddler filling notebooks with scientific theories."

"I'm not so sure."

"You think she's older than she is saying she is?" Jack doubted it. She didn't act older. She seemed like practically a kid when they met.

"No, I don't think she's lying about her age."

"Then what could these old research notes have to do with her?"

"The man who wrote those notebooks fled to the R.T."

"And?"

"And when he did so, he had a young daughter. With bright red hair."

54. What Then?

"Hello, Gentlemen." Maren called to the sergeants, Gildur and Rosie, as they entered the room. Franklin tagged along behind.

"Hello, Corporal, Private," Gildur greeted the women.

"Do you really think you still need the rail guns?" Maren teased.

"The regs call for triple-" he began to recite like a programmed machine, seemingly oblivious to her kidding tone of voice.

"Yeah, yeah. Triple redundancy. Sorry I asked." Some people have no sense of humor.

Maren picked up her bag, went through the gate and stood before the invisible shield. "Let's go."

"Shield down in 3... 2... 1... down," Maren stepped across the threshold, "Shield up in 2... 1... up."

"What do you think, Private? Is this going to be the last treatment?" Sgt. Rosie Krantz asked.

"Are we playing at questions?"

"No, it's a real question."

"I'm not the Doctor, but it sure looks like he is healing up fast," Maren commented as she knelt to apply the treatment. "The Doctor says we probably will be done with the cleaning treatments after this one, but he'll look him over one more time at least. My guess is Doctor P will say it will be up to his own body after this. After we're done with the treatments, the Doctor says we'll need to start exercising him to prevent muscle atrophy."

"I'm not even convinced his brain works, let alone worrying about his muscles," Franklin thought aloud. "Why on earth do we need to have him walking around, anyway? I much prefer him tied to the ground. We should let his muscles atrophy to nothingness. It'd be safer for us, don't you think?"

"Look at him. He almost looks normal," Maren observed. "It's hard to imagine it's one of the genbots that's taken so many lives."

"Without its armor, it doesn't look like a killer," Eve piped in. "He almost looks normal. What do you think, Maren? How tough does he look close up? Does it look like a killer?"

"I don't know. I don't think so. But how does one know what a killer looks like?"

"It's a killing machine, make no mistake about that," Gildur said. "Just because its circumstances have changed, it doesn't change the fact of its origin and purpose. It's designed to kill. You guys all seem to have forgotten that fact, but I haven't. That's why I'm keeping the R-290 right here. In fact…" Gildur the Sergeant continued to drone on.

Maren tuned the sergeant out. Sergeant Gildur Stern didn't talk all that much, but when he did, he tended to quickly wander off on some technical tangent. Now the Sergeant was going into the specs on one of his side arms. Maren muttered under breath to the still genbot, "You certainly don't look like one of the Ancients' killers. And you certainly don't look like a machine." She paused for a moment, staring into his black eyes. "You don't look like a killing machine, but I know you aren't a human."

"What am I then?" Michael asked.

"Oooawwk," Maren screamed, as she jumped back from the tied down body.

Sergeant Gildur Stern raised his rail gun to his shoulder, Michael in his sights, "What is it?! What happened? Did it try to attack you?"

Maren stammered, trying to find her voice, "He… he talked!"

"What?! What did it say? Could you understand it?" The cacophony of questions erupted simultaneously from the assembled group, before settling into a silence as they waited for Maren to answer.

"He asked what he was," she said, still staring into his eyes. Michael continued to stare back.

Again the chorus erupted with questions, "Do you think he has amnesia? What do you mean he asked what he was?" Then Sergeant Stern's voice rose above the others and took charge.

"Maren, do we need to let you out?"

"Yes… No. Wait a minute." Maren saw Michael blink, and just maybe his eyebrows moved. They stared at each other. She tried to see what was inside those orbs of blackness. "Everybody just be quiet. Let me try and talk to him some more." Maren took a deep breath. Engage him. He wanted to know what he was. "Um, I'm Maren. Who are you?"

Michael stared into the blue eyes of the red haired woman, a mere trud, and after a long pause, replied, "I am Michael Lightbringer, Guardian of the West. For what purpose are you holding me?" Having asked a question, he expected an answer from the primitive. But this time, Michael was not encased in his black armor demanding answers from cowering truds. However, he was not yet accustomed to such circumstances.

"Um, we are… well, I don't know exactly why we are holding you," she answered.

"Don't answer it!" the Sergeant commanded, as if the lowly private would have told the genbot all of the Natural Human Alliance's secrets. But what Maren had said was in fact partially true. She had a general idea of a few portions of the plan, but didn't know really why Michael was being kept captive, or rather, why he was being kept alive.

"Don't you think we should call in the lieutenant?" Eve asked, the obvious not having occurred yet to any of the others. Those were the orders after all.

"Go ahead. In the meantime, leave the questioning to me," Sergeant Gildur Stern commanded.

"Franklin, go get the lieutenant," Eve commanded, since she didn't want to miss any of it. Franklin outranked Eve, but he wasn't the type of guy to disobey any order, no matter who it came from.

Now, the sergeant had his chance to show what he was capable of. He always thought he should be in intelligence rather than security, and now he'd have his first shot at wringing information out of the gargoyle. He knew other soldiers in the Natural Human Alliance who would kill for the opportunity. And he knew others who had died for the opportunity. He had dreamed about this chance ever since the operation was conceived. The sergeant puffed up his chest and moved closer to the bars. Raising his weapon back to his shoulder, began, "Gargoyle-," before stopping abruptly. He turned toward Eve and whispered, "What was its name?"

"Michael, I think. Michael Lightbringer," she responded.

"Lightbringer-," Gildur began again before stopping just as abruptly. Now that he actually had a genbot gargoyle before him, he didn't know what to say!

55. Priorities

Outside of the make-shift security chamber, down the hall, in a room full of ancient looking document boxes, Lt. Carlitos shifted through the old notebooks. A slightly winded Franklin peeked his head into the room. Lt. Jacques 'Jack' Carlitos kept working. There was no time for distractions.

Franklin didn't say a word. He just looked at Jack, hoping the direct approach wasn't required. The lieutenant was digging through one of the boxes, as he had been for a long as Franklin had known him, searching for some piece of information. Franklin didn't know what Jack was looking for or why he was looking for it. Personally, Franklin didn't know why the lieutenant didn't have all the paperwork scanned and then let the computers analyze it to look for whatever he was looking for. It would be infinitely more efficient. Franklin had thought about suggesting it, but the lieutenant wasn't one who generally accepted suggestions, especially suggestions from Franklin. Besides that, Franklin knew he wasn't even supposed to notice that Jack had been spending as much time in the room as he had been. He'd just get in trouble for asking why, let alone suggesting something. Nobody was allowed to ask why, but it was still obvious that the lieutenant seemed to be spending more and more time in there, presumably for some good reason. Franklin stomped down his curiosity and braced himself for the expected onslaught questioning why the lieutenant was being disturbed.

The lieutenant was ignoring him, so Franklin tentatively approached him, as Jack was engrossed in an old notebook binder. Technically, nobody besides the lieutenant was even supposed to have access to the room or ever enter it. And "nobody" definitely meant Franklin. Franklin could only imagine what Sergeant Stern was saying to the genbot now, and he knew he needed to tell the lieutenant what was going on with the gargoyle talking and all, but he wasn't quite sure how to interrupt him. Thankfully, as he neared the desk, he didn't have to.

Jack looked up to see Franklin over his desk. He quickly stuffed the binder and other papers back into the box out of view, while simultaneously berating Franklin. "I thought I made it clear that no one is supposed to-"

Quite uncharacteristically, out of nowhere really, Franklin interrupted, "Lieutenant, sir, he's started talking."

"What?" The question was equal parts not registering Franklin's comment and being utterly astonished that Franklin had interrupted him mid-sentence.

"He's started talking," Franklin managed to utter quietly.

"Who?"

"The genbot, sir."

"It's been talking! Why didn't somebody come in here and get me?!"

"Well, sir-"

"Never mind that! Hurry up and tell me: what's it said?" Jack quizzed Franklin as he stuffed the rest of the papers on the desk into a box.

"So far, just his name."

Jack walked swiftly to the door, Franklin in tow. "It has a name? Well, what is it?"

"Michael Lightbringer, sir."

"Yes, of course. And what else did it say?" he asked as swiped his palm over the scanlock, securing the room with the old paper records.

"Sir, as I said, just his name. That's all," Franklin answered, trailing behind Jack as the lieutenant swiftly strode toward the chamber housing the genbot.

"That's all?" Jack asked, turning his head for a moment to look at the diminutive Franklin, while still striding briskly onward, lengthening the gap between them.

Franklin gave a curt confirming nod. "That's all. They decided to call you before they asked him any questions." Franklin had to run every few steps now just to keep up.

"Hmph. I guess they aren't all idiots," he mumbled, not really under his breath, as he approached the holding chamber. Lt. Jacques Carlitos stopped before the door for a second, before again motioning his hand over a scanlock. "Let's go…" And with that, he was through the door.

56. Answers

"Genbot, my name is Lt. Jacques Carlitos. I am going to ask you questions, and I expect answers." Jack confidently strode back and forth behind the iron bars. He went into what Maren called 'Lieutenant Mode' where he acted like he had all the answers and was in complete control. Maren recognized it for the fiction it was. Jack put on the show occasionally at work, especially (really only) in front of subordinates. Maren thought it was ridiculous on several levels, but she knew better than to call him out on it.

Jack stopped pacing and asked in a slow inquiring tone, as if he were asking a question he already knew the answer to: "Let's talk about the Event, shall we?" Michael stared in silence at the wall beyond. "Do you understand what I am saying?" Jack asked, his tone indicating annoyance and increased questioning.

There was silence.

Then Jack hissed between clenched teeth, "You will answer my questions, or we will be making your stay with us very uncomfortable. Is that clear?"

Silence from the Genbot. Maren cringed.

Jack turned towards the usual assembled audience of Gildur, Rosie, Franklin, Eve, and Maren, "All right, is this some kind of joke?"

"No, sir," they all replied, in one form or another.

156

"Come on, it's not saying anything," Jack said with a dismissive wave of his arm. He smiled and his shoulders drooped just a little. They were just messing with him. "Its brain was fried in the operation, just like we thought would happen." He chuckled a little. "It's just a vegetable now, right? You guys are pulling my chain, aren't you?"

"No, sir. This is no joke. I swear, he talked to me," Maren said.

"You can check the recordings," Franklin offered.

The lieutenant stiffened. "If this is a prank, soldiers, I'm going to-"

"Sir, she is right, sir," Sergeant Stern spoke up. "We all heard him. He definitely talked."

The lieutenant studied them for a few seconds longer and then turned serious again. "Well, then. Let's try again." Turning once more towards the metal bars, once again turning on 'Lieutenant Mode,' he continued his pacing back and forth, hands clasped behind his back, chin held high. He began again: "Genbot, what do you know about the Event?"

Silence greeted him.

"How are the gens going to try to get rid of us? What are they planning?" he tried again.

Silence.

Jack stopped his pacing and turned suddenly towards the others. "I'm going in there. Open it," Jack commanded. The gate was opened, the shield was lowered and he stepped across it. Lt. Carlitos stood above the gargoyle, spiderlyn cord still securely tying the biological machine to the concrete floor. He knelt and tried to place himself in the line of the genbot's blank stare.

"The Event, do you understand? Maybe you call it something else. It's the gens' plan to kill off all the humans on earth."

Silence.

"What do you know about the Event?" Now his temper flared again. "Answer me!" He slammed his hand against the cold concrete floor, but it only echoed in the quiet. Actually, it hurt Jack's hand more than a little.

"Talk!" he yelled. He was roughly following the script Doctor Psycho had outlined, but embellishing it a bit much. He calmed down a little, and gaining his composure again, he leaned in closer to Michael. "Listen here, Genbot, you *are* going to answer my questions, one way or the other."

The cameras and monitoring equipment stared.

After a few more questions, all unacknowledged and unanswered, Jack pulled a ballistic sidearm from his holster. The Doctor's formula didn't seem to be working, so Jack decided to break off from the Doctor's recommended course of action and tried a different approach. "Do you see this? Do you know what it is? It's an old fashioned ballistic slinger: the kind used way before your gen masters were even born. But it still works. It rips apart your insides. In the gut, it's a bit more painful than an energy blast."

Maren wanted to hide. Beyond Jack being ridiculous in his performance act and her being embarrassed about even being associated with him at this moment, she knew Jack was actually capable of it. She knew Jack thought of Michael as an evil robot that needed to be dismantled in order to avert the disaster of the Event. Jack would kill it, Jack would torture it, Jack would threaten it if it meant discovering the smallest clue about the Event. Maren understood that. She understood why they did it. But still, to Maren this talk seemed... inhumane.

He moved the steel barrel across Michael's cheek. "But before we even get to that, I'm sure I can find an arc-welder down here someplace. You ever seen what that does to flesh?" Jack looked down at Michael's exposed arm where Maren had not too long ago cleaned the deep wound. Then Jack's eyes moved to his own energy burned arm. He tossed the ballistic slinger from his right hand into his left and jabbed his right index finger into the still-tender-looking gash on the genbot's arm. "And from what I've seen the sub's retractor did to your arm, I think you're still very much made of flesh, no matter what's up inside that thick skull of yours." Michael did not even adjust the focal point of his blank stare. "Listen, you stupid machine, I'm an officer and I'm the one who is controlling whether you live or die," he lied. "Say something!"

**

Michael listened calmly but did not feel compelled to answer. He knew the hierarchy of the world. Michael was submissive to, and answered questions from, Rex Skyguard and Magritte. He extended the courtesy of answering his fellow Guardians, as they did to him. Michael did not, however, answer to the machines on Magritte. And he certainly didn't answer to primitives. But here was a trud ranting and raving about answering his questions. And now he was making threats, too.

Perhaps such techniques worked on other primitives, but this lieutenant was foolish to equate a Guardian of the West with a primitive and to think Michael would answer out of fear. Michael would answer questions that he felt that he should answer to further his mission as he now understood it: find a way to report the facility in which he was imprisoned to Magritte along with any other intelligence he was able to divine.

But threats? What did threats matter to a Guardian of the West? The idea of him being forced by truds to answer a question was absurd. It was as absurd as the idea of Michael demanding an answer from an Ancient. Michael would answer as he willed. And this primitive, this lieutenant, would get none.

57. Through the Tunnels

Eve had finally rotated off duty, and she wasted no time before starting to work her way through the underground network of service tunnels, conduit routes, piping tracks, and abandoned transport corridors: the living, dying, and dead guts of the city.

Un-sensored in many areas to avoid any potential gen wiretapping, the tunnels and hidden pathways had served the Organization well over the years. Additionally, the subterranean system served other underground elements, common and not-so-common criminals not the least among them. But Eve was not a criminal. She merely needed a break from time to time. In this case, Eve was using the tunnels to escape. Temporarily, of course. In her mind, it was more a well-earned (if unauthorized) R&R than anything criminal. She'd be back in time for her next scheduled shift, just as always.

She emerged at one of her usual locations, a storm drain in a hidden corner of a city park in a rather wealthy neighborhood. It was actually a fairly small opening, and she had to push her bag out first before squeezing herself through the drain and into the shaded cover of a well maintained shrub. Eve brushed herself off, before exchanging the coveralls she was wearing for the civilian skirt and top she had brought along in the bag. Her hair was never to her satisfaction after working her way through the tight, sometimes humid corridors below the earth. Despite her best efforts, a smudge or two of some foul smelling substance always made it onto her check or hands, too. Yet, these things cleaned up easily enough.

Eve walked the block to the apartment. She didn't bother ringing. Instead, she took out the key he had given her and let herself in.

Two candles were lit. The table was set. The aroma of classic Mediterranean food filled the air. And he was sitting there, at the table, reading a slim book.

She observed him for a few seconds, before he quietly closed the book and looked up, smiling. "…'Her waters renewed me, like the Springs of Eden'… I read of beauty, but days of reading the most beautiful poetry are nothing compared with a split second glance of you."

Eve blushed, and then dropped her bag and moved quickly to him as he rose from his chair to embrace her.

"I couldn't stand it for another hour. I needed to escape. I needed to get back to you."

"Welcome back to the hidden fortress, where nothing can hurt you."

58. For Every Season

She walked through the flowering city park. The blossoms were open. It was their time. It was their brief moment in the sun, their short season to radiate their glory to the world.

Each flower had grown, had waited, existed for this time.

Flora, too, had waited. She had made the preparations. She had taken her time. She knew the moment would arrive eventually. There was a cycle to everything. Everything had its proper time. And now she was ready.

Someone's time was up. Again it was the season; it was time for someone to die.

59. Action and Reaction

Doctor Psycho looked both ways down the tunnel before stepping back into the room and shutting the door. "Private Bern, I know this sounds extraordinary, because, in fact, it is. But we need you to undertake a rather special assignment. We want you to continue using your training to ensure that the genbot heals appropriately."

"I've had the basic NHA medical care class. It can't be that hard to find someone else to do it. Over half the people here could do it. What's so extraordinary about that?"

"Well, Maren, that takes a little explaining. I want you to not only to continue using your NHA training. I also want you to continue to pretend to be healing him after it's technically no longer necessary, which may actually be about now."

"Doctor, now it is starting to sound strange. Why on earth am I to pretend to-"

"Wait, that's not all," the Doctor smiled. "You may find this strange, but I also need you to tell him stories."

"Stories?"

"Yes, stories."

"What kind of stories?"

"Anything you can think of. Anything that might solicit a response. Tell him about the Refuge Territories. Tell him about life on the surface. Tell him about what you did last night. Stories. Simple stories."

"Doctor, now I think you're the one who perhaps has experienced the brain damage."

Doctor Psycho laughed. "I admit, it sounds crazy, but it is absolutely critical. I need neural processing data. I need to better understand how it thinks, and you're going to help me. He may not answer Jack's questions, but he appears willing to engage you. There is more than one way to crack an egg."

60. A Mustache and a Drink

Flora ran her fingers over the brass flower pin attached to the strap of her apron and casually eyed the mustached man from behind the counter. His mustache was perfectly groomed, as usual. He looked at the menu with precision even though he always ordered the same thing. She waited for him to make his order. She was patient.

There was really no reason the job couldn't be automated, but there was something about the corner beverage café that made customers in the rich neighborhoods crave a smiling face behind the counter, even if the other faces in the café were more often in a state of serious contemplation or studious concentration. Because the delivery mechanism for some of the more mild modification technologies had been via beverage shops, for a long time some truds remained skeptical of beverage cafés and those who frequented them. But some habits were hard to break, and the beverage shops had lasted longer than anyone could have predicted. Of course, the cafes were highly regulated and even the mildest modification technologies had been banned since the Conflict. Still, a stimulant or two could yet be found at the corner shop.

Truth be told, she would count herself as one of the few truds who still looked askance at beverage café patrons. And if she wasn't thrilled about working at a job that once delivered mild modology in a cup, she at least found the job convenient for delivering another substance. Besides, even if she hated the job, she'd only been at it three weeks. And if her service to the next customer went well, she would only stick around for a few more weeks after today. Just long enough to avoid suspicion.

The mustached man stepped up to the counter. It was his daily habit to visit the shop and enjoy a beverage. He found it helped him wake up before facing a long day at his job. It was also, on occasion, a useful spot for quietly passing along information. He ordered his usual drink, and the middle aged woman proceeded to mix it. She was new to the job and really not that good at it, he thought. She never got the cream on top quite right. And compared to the types who normally worked at this location, she wasn't very attractive and certainly didn't make up for it in trendiness. Frankly, he didn't know why they had hired her at all. He demanded perfection, and she and her service certainly weren't it.

She finished mixing the perfectly-groomed mustached man's beverage, dashed in a little something extra, and added the cream on top.

He took the beverage, shook his head slightly at the imperfect cream placement and how it hung sloppily on the rim of the cup, and took a long draught as he turned towards the seating area. Flora didn't bother even looking in his direction for the rest of the time he was in the café or when, twenty minutes later, he got up and left.

61. Unrestrained

"Don't worry, Private. We're right outside the door if you need us," Gildur said, patting his rail gun.

"Just hit the panic button on your wrist band if you need us, Maren," Franklin confirmed, essentially repeating what the others had said.

Maren looked at the two and was not especially inspired with confidence. She looked towards Eve. Eve raised her eyebrows, smiled without parting her lips, cocked her head, and gave a quick shrug of her shoulders in an expression of "Well, you've got to die sometime" and hit the button, opening the door to the room.

"Thanks, Eve," Maren grumbled.

The doorway hissed, closing behind her. There he was: Still on the hard floor, still strapped down by the spiderlyn. For a few more minutes.

After taking in the scene, the voice in her head began again.

I don't even know what they want me to find out about him. How on earth did I get this assignment? Then out loud she made an attempt at conversation, "I must apologize about the lieutenant. My boyfriend, the lieutenant, he hasn't always been that way."

At least I don't remember him that way. The attack on the caverns changed him, when most his team was killed. Well, maybe he started changing before then, but it's certainly gotten worse as a result.

"When we first met, this was years ago, when I wasn't even a part of this whole thing, he wasn't quite so bitter." She needed to distance herself from the threats Jack had made against the Doctor's plan. She needed to try to build rapport. "But you don't want to hear about any of that, do you? You probably don't even know what a boyfriend is. And if you do, don't go gabbing about it with everyone, OK? It's supposed to be a secret… but everyone knows already, so why shouldn't you, too?" *Tell him personal stories, the Doctor said. No repercussions. It's important that they are personal stories. Her stomach turned: this seems dumb and dangerous.* "I'm not exactly thrilled about this, but…" *Yikes, confessions with a genbot. What am I doing? 'No repercussions,' yeah right. Jack's going to flip if the Doctor doesn't hold to the promise that he's the only one who will see the raw data and video feeds.*

She moved the magnetic key over the bolts, and the spiderlyn that crisscrossed across Michael's chest was released.

"The instructions say I'm not supposed to remove the ankle restraints today, and I'm not going to." She swiped the magnetic key again over the binding on his wrists and stepped back quickly as the small diode light on the restraints began to flash red, first slowly, then faster. "But you do get the arms freed." It was another two seconds or so before the delayed-release clicked on the lock and his arms, both gashed and ungashed, were relieved of their metal bands. Michael applied tension once more to the spiderlyn and found it released easily. Maren was already back behind the energy shield, but still on the genbot's side of the metal bars, and thus held her left wrist with its panic button bracelet, just in case. She was observing him, waiting to see his reaction.

Now that his arms and upper body were free, he was tempted to immediately throw his whole weight against the ankle restraints. With the proper leverage and momentum, the bolts might pull free from the concrete floor, depending on the precise construction techniques. But there was still the matter of the energy shield. Once past the shield, the metal bars should not prove problematic: he could see the hints of decay on them from moist air and age. But he was getting ahead of himself. They were waiting to see his reaction and would be most alert to his actions now. Later, however…

"So, I guess you might be wondering what's going on. Well, we don't want your muscles to atrophy, and the Doctor says you'd probably get some nasty sores if we kept you tied down like that forever. If you don't use your muscles, flex them and move around, they'll waste away and eventually you won't even be able to walk," she explained, not knowing that Lightbringer was engineered to have a constant level of muscle mass. He could lay there for a decade and, assuming proper nutrition, still rise up with the same strength as if he had been training every day for two years.

Why should it matter to you if I should walk? Michael thought, not realizing himself that atrophy was no issue for him. He didn't really even know what muscle atrophy was. It wasn't relevant to his existence.

Maren continued talking. "The Doctor says that it's a priority that you become able to walk again, so the restraints have to go."

Ah, Michael thought. In some matter of time the other restraints will indeed be removed. Lightbringer didn't understand why the truds should care if he walked again, but her superior officers must have their reasons. He reflexively pulled against the ankle restraints, flexing his muscles at the thought of movement.

Maren noticed. It was the first real sign of physical vigor that she'd seen. "Try to move around a bit, but don't go yanking on the ankle restraints or lunging at me or anything. Anything erratic and you get the cords again for a long time."

She guessed it was good that he was coming around, but it didn't make her any more thrilled about the risk associated with being near him. She'd nursed his wounds as she was required to and as she'd been trained. But she wasn't sure about keeping him company beyond that, let alone telling him stories. He looked so human, yet she reminded herself what he really was.

"Well," she said, "that's about it for now. Just take it easy and... you know... don't go anywhere." As Maren passed through the metal bars and then out to the hallway, she exhaled deeply. *Argh,* she thought. *I didn't get him to say a word. On the other hand, I survived...*

Michael noted that the trud with the red hair, Maren, seemed to need to verbalize everything to him. He would find a way to use it to his advantage. The truds had plans for him, but Michael was working on plans of his own.

62. Avoiding the Claudius Effect

He strolled down the street. He could already picture it. The museum lights, the beautiful and elegant black dresses... at least one of which would be holding perfection. It was going to be a grand evening. Anyone who was anyone in the city would be there. And that, of course, included him. He was not one to miss one of the major social events of the summer. A haircut was in order. It had been a week and he could not stand having one hair out of place. The thought made him lift his hand to stroke his mustache. Tonight he would be at his peak. He would be magnificent.

She watched the mustached man through the tiny scope and slowly squeezed the trigger. An invisible wave flew forth and hit the mustached man in the back, though he didn't feel a thing and kept on walking along at a leisurely pace. The wave activated the chemicals that he had ingested with his morning beverage earlier and were now concentrated in his kidneys. She was always cautious about making sure she hit the right target. A two-phase approach was often the best. Not only did a two-phase approach make it harder to identify the source of the poison, but the requirement of an activator signal to make the poison effective also helped to avoid the "Claudius Effect," that is, killing off someone (or yourself) rather than the person for whom the poison has intended.

MODIFIED HORIZON

The poison having been triggered from a safe, anonymous distance, she placed the small activator unit in her pocket and turned back toward her apartment. Come morning, he wouldn't ever have to worry about his mustache or cream placement on his beverage again. Before heading home, however, she thought she might pick up some flowers. Flora would enjoy their aroma, no matter how briefly they lasted.

63. All the Way

Damien lay prone in the cockpit of the combat sled, cycling through the displays. The sleds had to work perfectly the first time. And so the pilots had to be ready the first time, too. Once he saw one, Damien knew he had to fly one.

This sled checked out fine. It was a beautiful creation. A fast, powerful weapon. One day, this very sled would fly to the heavens with nova bombs. With a little luck, it would make it all the way there and a fortress would come crashing to the earth.

One combat sled, however, would not be enough. To be honest, Damien wasn't sure hundreds would be enough. If the fortress was active, if the machine armies were released, if the fortress weapons saw them, it would all be over in an instant.

And what would the loss of a few fortresses really do to the gens? How powerful were they really? Were the fortresses the pinnacle of the gens' military capabilities? Or were the fortresses just the outer ring, with even deadlier weapons waiting out of sight? What did the gens hold in reserve?

Damien crawled out of the sled and stood.

Niles sat reclined in a chair.

"This one tests okay," Damien said.

Niles did not say anything. His eyes were open but they darted back and forth, as if he was watching something, but not something in the room.

"I'll check another one," Damien said, more to himself than to Niles.

But Niles' eyes suddenly focused on Damien. "Yes," the scarred one said. "Yes, we understand."

"Huh?" Damien said.

"We don't know how powerful they truly are. But we know how to kill them."

Damien was confused. Had Damien actually been talking to himself out loud when he was in the sled such that Niles overheard him? He didn't think so...

Niles went on. "What do you think of the combat sleds? Of our plan?"

Damien answered with a question of his own. "Do you think this is going to work?" Damien regretted it immediately; it wasn't his place to question it.

The scarred one arched his left eyebrow and studied Damien. The expression was calibrated to make Damien think he was surprised at the comment.

"I know better, we shouldn't be taking about operational details," Damien responded, backpedaling away from the implication that he had doubt. It was a mistake to express a lack of confidence in the NHA to those whom you didn't trust completely. Damien had been around a long time and knew that what he had said would not be viewed with charity by all.

"No, please, share your concerns. There is probably no more secure place on earth than our current location," the scarred one encouraged him. He was right, in a way.

"Well..." Damien hesitated. It could be dangerous. Niles was part of the Network. If Niles wanted to destroy him, Niles probably could. Yet risks had to be taken. And Damien felt that if he didn't take the risk now, he might never have the chance again. None of them would. So he spoke honestly. "It just seems like there are too many things that could go wrong. Look how many things haven't gone as planned up to this point. I fear we'll only be making a dent."

"Ah, but the Natural Human Alliance has its sources."

"Personally, I don't know why they put such faith in them. Who knows their true motives?" Damien said, as he stared out across the facility at the combat sleds in various states of construction.

"Who, indeed. Who, indeed. But what do you suggest we do?"

"I know of the power some are rumored to possess," Damien said, now turning and deliberately looking into the eyes of the scarred one. If he was going to take the risk, if he was putting his life on the line, if he was going to trust Niles, Damien was going to go all the way. "I know of these powers. What I don't know is why the Organization is so hesitant to use it."

"That, Damien, is an excellent question."

64. No More Death

Eve cried uncontrollably.

"What's the matter, my darling?"

Eve continued to sob.

"It's okay." He held her closer. "It's okay. I'm here."

She gradually gained control of herself. The sobs slowed to a few tears and sniffles.

He stroked her shoulder and waited in silence. Sometimes it was better not to talk. Sometimes a person just needed another person to be there. Not to judge, not to rationalize, not to try and make it go away. Just to be there.

They laid there in silence.

"They all died," Eve said.

"Who did, Eve?"

"Almost all of them. Almost all of my friends. I had a sudden feeling that it was happening all over again, just like before."

He knew what it was like to lose loved ones. He knew the pain. Once. "I'm so sorry."

"I'm sorry. Sometimes it just hits me. I can't explain why. They died... it happened a while ago. A mission went horribly wrong." Eve needed to talk about it now. She needed someone outside of the Natural Human Alliance to understand her. She needed to talk with someone who didn't view the death of friends as just a normal price to be paid in a seemingly never ending war. She needed a safe place

175

of understanding and acceptance far away from all of the pain and fear and violence. She could only pretend for so long before she needed to retreat, to regroup for another round of the struggle. But she was beginning to wonder if the struggle was worth it. She was tired of it. She told herself she just needed a break. That's why she snuck out. That's why she found him. That's why she told him.

"I don't want to be part of the dying anymore. I don't want any more death. Promise me that you won't die. Promise me you'll never leave me."

"No one else is going to die. I'm not going to die, Eve. I'll never leave you. Don't cry."

65. Learning

It was the third day since Michael first talked, and Maren was at it again. Eve got a scheduled break, but on Doctor Psycho's orders, Maren was back at it. The pressure for results combined with incredible boredom of the actual experience was beginning to take its toll on her.

Make friends with him, the Doctor says. It's like trying to make friends with a brick wall! What am I doing here? This has got to be one of the worst assignments.

Maren was frustrated at the lack of response from the genbot. She knew he could talk. And the Doctor had assured her that if she just keep on talking, honestly sharing whatever she could, that eventually she would find a trigger and he would talk again. She wasn't convinced. As a matter of fact, she was beginning to get a bit angry. It was getting ridiculous, her talking to the vegetable all day, telling him everything, having everything *recorded* by the Doctor, and probably reviewable by Jack despite the Doctor's assurances to the contrary, and still nothing to show for it. It felt as if she was half the experiment and she was getting tired of it. She was also getting tired of him, the genbot. The thought even entered her mind that he could use a good kick.

Instead, she took in a deep breath and prepared herself. *Honest talk is what the Doctor told me to do, so here it goes, like it or not...*

177

"At first it seemed like a huge opportunity, when we found out you'd lived through the procedure. I'd thought I'd learn all about you, about life up in the floater. Maybe even hear what an old gen fart is like, one of the guys who has been around since the start. They've got to have some good stories, having been alive for so long. It would be pretty cool to hear about them, about the olden days, about what they are like now.

"Instead, you just sit there. You talk to me once just to get us all excited, just once TO ME so that I get this lousy assignment, and now you sit there and clam up. And because you talk TO ME once, and not to the lieutenant when he shows up, everyone thinks you'll talk with me again. Oh, this is pointless." Maren stood up, and began pacing around. She tugged at her necklace with the green pendant. *Great, brilliant plan. Tell him all about your boredom and impossible task and maybe he'll talk. I'm not sure that's what the Doctor had in mind when he wanted me to be honest to build rapport.*

Maren remembered back to her talk with the good Doctor Psycho. She remember his calm, smooth, reassuring voice. "Just talking with it might stimulate a response," the Doctor had said. "You should continue to talk out loud to it even if it does not appear to respond. The scanners seem to indicate recognition in the verbal center when someone in the vicinity of the genbot is talking, and they spike when you talk to it. All indications are that he is conscious and understanding everything. He is just choosing not to respond. Our work with captured Fanatics suggests that if you talk to them long enough, eventually they will talk back, the ones who have verbal language, anyway. And then you start to build a relationship, and from there, extract information. My guess is it should be the same with the genbot."

Maren remembered her response to Doctor Psycho after he had gone on about the genbot's capabilities, "If you know so much about it, why don't you go live with him and do the talking?"

"Frankly, I'd relish the opportunity," the Doctor had responded. "However, the fact that he talked with you once, and only you, suggests he may feel more comfortable talking with you. Regardless of whether I want to, and believe me, despite the connection you may have established, I want to give it a try… Regardless, the powers that be have said you're the one who is going to do it." He hadn't mentioned that he was one of those powers.

The Doctor had concluded, "It may seem tedious, but you must try to continuously talk with him. The stimulation of the verbal center is vitally important. I need data for the mission."

Talk to him. Tell him stories, the Doctor had said, Maren thought the words to herself. *Easier said than done. You try talking out loud to nobody for a couple days.* She took another deep breath and calmed down a bit. *Think…* "Well, what could I tell you about? Hmm. Are you curious about the R.T.?" She'd been avoiding the topic, even though the Doctor had suggested it. But after a few days, she was running out of other things to say. Life in the R.T., the Refuge Territories, wasn't her favorite thing to talk about, mainly because for some reason everyone was always questioning her about it and she rebelled at the inquisition. She didn't like being singled out as different. But she felt she had definitely run out of anything else to talk about. And once she got going, she figured she could probably talk about the Refuge Territories forever. "Everybody else is curious about the R.T., so you might be, too. They're always asking me about it. And I guess it's something I know about.

"It's been more than a few years since I left. On the one hand, it seems like I was just there yesterday. On the other hand, it seems like that was another lifetime. My life was so different. *I* was so different.

"We went to the Territories when I was young, just a child, but I remember the day exactly. It's not something you easily forget, when your whole life changes in what seems like an instant. I remember walking through the grasses for the first time that afternoon. It was incredible. I could just barely see the head and shoulders of my dad walking through the tall grass ahead of me. The stems came right up to the height of my eyes. In much of the Refuge Territories, the grasses are long and golden and sway in the wind. Here, in the city, when you can even find grass, it's short and cut and green. Most of the time, they don't even want you to walk on it. In the R.T., you can see to the horizon where the grass meets the sky. The nights are darker and the days are brighter. In the city, these deep canyons of metal and glass make it… it seems that someplace is always suffocating in a shadow here. And the lights always seem to me to be artificial. But it's cleaner here too. You never see dirt in the city. It so spotless and clean in the city."

Michael was pleased to hear the new information, though certainly not because he was learning about the great grassy plains, of which he had patrolled often. Instead, he valued her story because of the last part: He now knew with certainty that he was within the city, thanks to her comparison with the R.T. Magritte was probably no farther than a few miles away, maybe only a few thousand feet straight up. The more she talked, even about seemingly innocuous things, the more Michael was bound to learn, and the closer he was to the clues that would lead to his escape.

Maren continued, "It's so spotless. Everything is polished, so much so that I don't think people on the surface even know what rust is. I mean, in the R.T., half the stuff we'd make would rust out eventually. We didn't have the capability of making the higher end rust-proof metals. That's one thing about the city. Life is certainly easier here. It's safer, too. No wild animals or wild people who have sworn off technology, no floods or fires on the plain. Doctors, nurses, knowledge, plentiful food. There's law and life is ordered. I try to keep a realistic perspective. Jack tells me I romanticize the R.T., and he's probably right. Both places have their good sides and their bad sides. It's just hard to adjust when you've known one way of life for so long. I guess I don't need to tell you that. That's probably why you are just sitting there. I know this place must be different for you."

Maren stared at Michael, who stared blankly back. He was just lying down there, not even moving his arms after his restraints had been removed. She was trying to talk with him, she knew he could talk and that he understood her, he knew she knew he understood her, and still he played mute! She was angry again.

"Listen, you can just sit there forever and waste away. I certainly feel like I'm wasting away when you just sit there like a stone. So you can just sit there, or you can take advantage of the situation, talk with me, ask some questions, and actually learn something about us. I thought you were human-like, but maybe I was wrong. Maybe you are just a machine that kills and doesn't know how to learn. Or maybe you just aren't interested in learning more about the people that you and your gen overlords kill."

"I already know much about those," Michael responded in a calm, cool tone. "I kill those who would try to kill me and who seek to wipe the Ancients from the face of the earth." He would lose his only source of intelligence if she stopped talking. He could help prevent that.

Maren was astonished. She stood there with her mouth agape. *He was talking again! What could possibility have made him decide to respond to*

180

that? She struggled to find a response that wouldn't shut him down again. Talking to herself for days was beginning to drive her crazy. So she didn't want to antagonize him by responding that it was the so-called Ancients, the old gens, who had on several occasions nearly wiped out humanity while pursuing their goals of making themselves gods.

After a few moments of stunned silence, she responded, a bit haltingly and at the same time a bit rushed, trying not to let the momentum slip, "Is there anything you would like to know about us? What questions do you want to ask?"

"You say I may ask you questions?" Michael asked. Though it sounded like an honest question because of the calmness and lack of facial expression in the asking, Michael was slightly amused that a trud, a small one at that, was granting a Guardian permission to do anything. Yet he still asked the question. He found something compelling about the woman.

"I do." She decided that if her superiors wanted him to talk, she might as well try to get him to talk about things he wanted to talk about. She would work in the intelligence questions later, if they even mattered. Doctor Psycho seemed more interested in having the genbot talk, no matter what the topic. She would get him to talk.

Realizing that she was completely serious, Michael played along. He might indeed learn something just as she suggested. "Where are we?"

Maren smiled at his obvious angle, or rather, his lack of any angle at all. There were obviously some things her superiors would not be pleased to learn she had divulged. "Well, you can ask me questions, but I'm certainly not going to answer some of them. And where we are is definitely one of them. But, hey, we've started a conversation," she tried to sound relaxed, though her heart felt like it was beating a bass drum in her chest. "Please, try again. Ask away."

"What are you doing with me?"

Haven't you asked that one before? she thought. She didn't want to say that one was out of bounds, yet she couldn't really answer it. She stammered out a response, trying to keep the conversation alive. "Well, I guess you could say we're learning from you."

"What are you learning?"

"How you talk… how you interact with us… other things. What it means to be you, I guess."

"Why?"

181

"Michael, there are some things that don't have answers." In her mind she was panicking. She needed to keep him talking, but he kept on asking rather direct questions that she didn't know how to answer. She had to obey her orders to get him, and keep him, talking, but she also had to obey orders not to give the enemy intelligence.

It was obvious to Michael that the trud female either didn't know anything or wouldn't divulge it. As in warfare, when you can't get a direct answer, try flanking. "I can see the horizon from Magritte."

"What?" Once again Michael had caught Maren off guard. *You'd think I'd learn,* she thought to herself.

Michael continued. "On Magritte, I've also seen where the oceans of grass meet the sky."

All right, this is progress. "What's Magritte?"

"The Fortress, where I live."

"Oh, the floater? I would guess you could see a long way from up there. You can see a long way from the tops of the city towers, if you're important enough to be able to get up there. But I guess you could see quite a bit more from your castle in the sky."

"Do you often go to the tops of the towers here?"

"No, mostly I stay down here. When I'm off, I…" Maren continued. *Down here*, the words repeated in Michael's mind. *Down here… under the city.* As she talked, Michael continued learning. And planning. Bit by bit, he was getting what he needed for escape.

66. Intelligence

Blue shut the office door behind her. The room was cramped. Jack leaned back and crossed his arms, waiting for Blue to ask the question he knew she'd come to ask. "Did you learn anything from those files, the notebooks I delivered? Could you find anything that helps?" Blue inquired.

"Sure, I feel completely ready to start building nano components," Jack said sarcastically.

"Very funny. My people already looked at the science. Not much new there. Does it help with the girl? I'm just curious."

"Listen, I'm grateful you dug these up and offered to help. God knows, I need it. But the notebooks... It could be her father that wrote these. It's possible, not certain, but possible. The diary-like entries allude to a daughter of her age and her mother. But who really cares about a second-rate researcher in nano components, let alone his daughter? I mean, the guy was using paper and pens. What kind of researcher uses that old stuff?"

"Someone who wants to control the information, that's who. Maybe it's illegal, maybe the research is dangerous, maybe it's competition... but they don't want to risk it getting out," Blue said.

"Hhm. If that's the situation, if the guy went through the trouble of writing everything down on perishable paper notebooks, using reams of them for research that could have been documented automatically, if he did it for secrecy, the guy was a paranoid nut.

183

There wasn't anything in those notebooks worth stealing. No cutting edge science there that I could see, anyway. Seriously, it looked like stuff that all had been done before."

"Maybe the notebooks we have don't tell the whole story. Maybe he had other information, other things of value. He fled to the R.T. for some reason."

"You sure about that?"

"He disappears from the archives and any city database. Poof. All the old stuff is in there, but nothing new. The daughter is gone, too. We can't find any record of him or his daughter after the last notebook there."

"Maybe he went Fanatic."

"A scientist?"

"Not the first time. Won't be the last."

"Well, are you going to keep working on it?"

"Of course. Red is protective of her for a reason," Jack said. "He wants me to figure out what I can. It's been a long-term project, and Red isn't going to stop now. I've asked him several times what the point of it all was, and all he will say is to keep looking and tell him if I find anything at all that gives any clue about where she came from and who she was connected to. This is a bit thin here. The R.T. is full of runaways, pretty much by definition, and I am sure more than one of them had a daughter with red hair. I'll keep working it, and if I can get anything that's more than just a hunch, I'll let him know."

"Don't you think it's strange that he protects her, but claims he doesn't know what's special about her? That he has you try to find out what you can, but doesn't give you any starting points or tell you why? That he doesn't tell anyone else, especially me, about it?" the Director of Intelligence asked.

"If you are implying that I should worry about Red, you're even crazier than the guy that wrote these notebooks. He has a track record of years. I trust Red with my life. But does he tell me everything? Of course not. I wouldn't trust him if he did, because that would mean he was stupid."

"Red isn't stupid."

"No, he definitely is not."

67. Reviewing Progress

Doctor Psycho smiled. "Good work. I knew you would have success, though I admit it took longer than I expected."

Maren was rather satisfied herself.

The Doctor explained. "After reviewing the recordings and the brain patterns showing the genbot is indeed comfortable talking with you, we have decided that we will move the genbot to a facility where he might feel even more comfortable. There are hints in the data that this could make him talk more easily. Of course, you are expected to report anything of interest he says to me immediately. I can't afford to wait to review the recordings, and I don't have time to look at them all either."

"Of course," she said.

"The new facility does not have the banks of recording instruments," he continued, purposefully not mentioning that there would still be recording devices, they would just be hidden. She had to assume it was all recorded, but he didn't need to emphasize the point. Part of the goal was also to make Private Maren Bern more comfortable, to make her more likely to talk. Naturally, he left those parts out. "Others teams won't have as much access to him anymore. The security won't be as obvious."

"Will it still be safe?"

"He'll be behind an energy barrier. You'll be well out of range. No more need for medical treatments. Just talking. I just need the neural data."

"Well, I'll talk. Let's hope he does his part."

68. Always

"You like the new accommodations? You don't even have to use the spiderlyn straps on the floor. Nice change, huh?" Maren asked.

Michael answered: "Nothing has changed."

"Sure it has."

"Everything in the world is as it was yesterday and as it will be tomorrow."

"What do you mean?" Maren fiddled absent-mindedly with her pendant.

"The fortresses still protect the Ancients, the Ancients still live, and the truds can change nothing."

"I believe we can change things. One person, even a trud, could change the world."

"You ascribe too much power to yourself and your kind, as do most truds. From the fortress, you can see how small a single trud is. Nothing changes. Nothing will."

"But the gens plan the Event. If the Event happens, things would change then, wouldn't they?"

Michael did not answer.

Maren didn't wait too long before continuing. "What happens if the gens actually get rid of us truds? What happens to you? What happens when you aren't necessary anymore, when you become obsolete? What will your masters do with you?"

"I will always serve the Ancients."

"Yes, but what if they no longer NEED you to serve them?"

"They have always needed me, since the liberation from the sea until now."

"But if the Event comes to pass, we will be gone and there will no longer be a purpose for you. You won't have any truds around to keep down."

"The Ancients will always need protection."

"Only if we're around, and you know the old gens have a plan to be rid of us 'primitives.' So what happens when they don't need you?"

Michael again did not answer, for he did not have one.

69. The Event Nears

"We talked about the Event," Maren reported. "He doesn't seem to comprehend that if the truds are gone, he is worthless to the gens. I wonder how real the Event really is..."

"Have no doubt," Dr. Psycho assured her. "The fact that the Event is being planned is very real. Intercepted communications indicate the gens have been planning this for many years and that final preparations are now at hand. They have begun issuing orders to the gens to prepare for execution of the Event."

"How do you think they'll try to accomplish it?"

"Well, we're going to hit them before we have the chance to find out," Doctor Psycho said. "But the honest answer is that we still don't know exactly how they intend to accomplish it. Of course, everybody has their pet theory. Some think they'll try to accomplish the Event with a virus, some think robots and machines, some think massive bombardment, others think it will be something entirely new that we haven't seen before, maybe that we can't even imagine."

The Doctor went on. "Regardless of the methods, our sources know the intended outcome, and that is to be finished with us. However, intercepted communications also indicate internal disagreement among the gens as to whether the Event should be carried out now. Some gens are fighting to prevent the Event from happening right now, they think they need to wait until they are better prepared. That's why you can see the desperation of General Win to make this work and the pressure Colonel Red is under."

"So you do know more."

"Listen, of course you can't share all of that with the others, especially the intercepted communications piece, but it's important you realize how serious the situation is. Your work with the genbot is critical to our plan to strike them and I don't like hearing doubt about whether our actions are absolutely essential. Everyone's been talking about a hypothetical 'Event' for so long that some people have begun to be complacent or don't think it will ever happen. But all of our intelligence suggests the Event may be imminent, and that changes how we have to deal with the possibility."

"How can you be so sure? How do you know so much about intercepted communications?"

"Colonel Blue has reasons to call upon my capabilities, from time to time. Let's just say I've taken the opportunity to learn a little in the process. Now the key thing is for you to try to do the same with the genbot. Any detail you can tease out of him could make the difference. Time is of the essence. Here is how I recommend you approach the issue…"

70. No Holds Barred

"Is the prepositioning operation proceeding according to plan?" the scarred one asked of the NHA's eyes.

"Yes, we are distributing everything to the operational pre-staging points," Damien confirmed. Colonel Red had made him the de facto liaison between the Natural Human Alliance and the Network. Damien had taken on the assignment eagerly. As the assignment went on, he began to see more and more what the Network was capable of and how they saw the world. And that worldview started to make more and more sense to Damien.

"And the test results? Is the equipment up to NHA standards?" Niles asked, already knowing the answer.

"All as you said: Everything works."

"It just works?"

"Okay, it exceeds all our benchmarks. It is exceptional. Happy with my report?"

Niles nodded.

Damien placed another skip drive in the false bottom of an office couch, preparing it for its short term resting place. It was weak as far as camouflage went, but it would be good enough for their purposes.

Niles stared into space and seemed to comment almost absentmindedly, "We were intrigued by your comments regarding the project the other day."

Damien knew exactly what Niles was talking about. "I'm sorry, sir. Forgive me for doubting my superiors." Damien had had second thoughts since their last conversation. After he had returned to the NHA base, he wondered what on earth had possessed him to talk so openly with the Network. Now he was back at the Network's manufacturing facility, overseeing the placement of critical equipment, and back in the orbit of Niles. What had made him think he could trust Niles? Trust... "I trust everything will go as planned, and I will work hard to make sure it so."

"There is no need to apologize, Damien. We understand. It's normal to have such thoughts. In fact, we've had such thoughts at time ourselves. Often, if the truth be told."

"Still, it's not my place to question."

"If not yours, whose place is it? You are here at General Chi's command to ensure that everything works, that we deliver what we promised: the skip drives, the nova bombs, the sleds, everything. Despite what some say, we want this to succeed as much, if not more, than you do. So tell us, Damien, what concerns you? You said you worried the plan to stop the Event would not be enough. What would you have us do?"

Perhaps Niles was right. Perhaps Niles and the Network had always been right. Damien had gambled before, revealing his true thoughts. It was the end game. Time was short. If he didn't speak up now, when would he? And he remembered why he had talked openly with Niles before: because it might make a difference.

No holds barred.

So Damien would gamble again. "We can strike them. They'll be hurt. This is more than just possible, but probable with this technology. I believe we can take out several of the fortresses, something that has never been done before. But..." Damien paused for emphasis. "But what good does it do to take down fortresses? How will that alone stop the Event? It would merely be a setback for the gens. In just a short time they would come back, and more powerfully than ever."

"So, again: what would you do?" Niles asked.

"I would hit them harder."

"With what?"

"With everything." Damien paused before continuing. "I know the Natural Human Alliance could use technologies considered forbidden if they willed it. It's within our power, but High Command isn't willing to go that far." Damien swallowed. His confidence returned. He was going to take this as far as he could. Forget NHA regs, forget Red, forget all the barriers to success. The fate of humanity rested in stopping the Event. Damien would do everything he could to contribute to that effort. He would go further than anyone else in the Natural Human Alliance was willing to go. "I can only imagine how much farther the Network could take us."

"How far would you have us go?"

"All the way. As I said: I would use everything."

"Even if it meant some of the truds would die? Perhaps many?"

"Many of us will die anyway. The only thing that matters is that some of us survive, and the gens don't."

"It may not be possible to destroy them all right away," Niles explained. "We tried that before, and somehow some of the gens survived. But what if we told you that we can do more than destroy their outer ring of floating fortresses? What if we told you we could destroy their base of power? We can strike at the gens themselves. We can destroy their cities."

"I would welcome it. But we aren't strong enough yet. What could we use to accomplish it?"

"Dreptex. A reformulated version, but one based on the same idea, targeted for gens. We probably have enough now for the gen cities. But just barely. We have endeavored to slow down the so-called Natural Human Alliance in their eagerness to attack until we were ready. We believe that we are ready now, that the time to attack has arrived."

"But how will you get the Dreptex to the west?"

"Destroying the fortresses with nova bombs will open a window. The NHA thinks it stops there. They foolishly think destroying a few fortresses will be enough to delay the Event. You, Damien, are smart enough to see beyond that. The Network thinks the same. As far as the Network is concerned, destroying the fortresses is only the beginning. We will use the hole in their defenses created when the floating fortresses crash to the ground. For the first time in generations, the sky will be open for us. There will be nothing to stop us in the air. During that brief window we will launch the missiles, missiles that no one but the Network even knows exists. The Dreptex warheads should be capable of killing off most of the cities, if they are targeted properly, if the conditions are right."

"Then we should make more Dreptex and be doubly sure."

"Dreptex is not as simple as it sounds. It has taken a long time to reformulate it, to make sure it can kill gens in their modified form, and it is not a merely a simple compound that can be manufactured. We have no more time before the Event. We must use what we have and hope that it is enough. It should be enough to wipe most of them out."

"But if you had a multiplier, a dispersant, you could ensure that it was enough."

"Yes, we know of what you speak. Back when the original Dreptex was used there was another substance that made it so much more powerful. But the substance of which you speak is lost even to us."

Damien smirked. "What if I told you that years ago I found reserves of a certain substance? And what if I told you I know exactly where that Greendust still is today?"

71. Saints and Sinners

"Why wouldn't you do what you are told to do?" Michael asked. He always did what Rex and Magritte commanded. He could not understand why Maren was confused about the proper course of action.

"I didn't know if it was right to follow what the officer was telling me I needed to do or whether I should have done what I thought was best," Maren said.

"Not knowing what was right? It does not sound very complex. It is right to follow commands," Michael reasoned.

"What if you have two conflicting commands?"

"That demonstrates the primitive nature of your social hierarchy. There should be not conflict. There is only one optimal course of action."

The conversation wasn't going in the direction Maren expected. How could she put the issue in terms Michael would understand? "Well, you are sworn to protect the gens, but suppose one gen told you to destroy another gen. What would you do with that conflict between what you are sworn to do and what your master tells you to do?"

"If the Ancient issuing the command had the proper authority, I would do it."

"What if you didn't know which gen was in command?"

"That wouldn't be possible. And if it was not evident who was in command, then it would be evident that neither had authority to do so."

"Oh, you're being impossible. Right doesn't always equal following a command."

"On the contrary, rightness, as I understand you to mean it, can only be to follow orders. There is no difference between doing what is right and obeying. They are the same. That is why I do not understand your conflict."

Maren replied, "Man, this is tough. It's not like I've studied at an academy or anything, but I just know you are wrong. I just can't find the words to explain to you why." She felt a little foolish for thinking Michael might offer some insight into her dilemma. Instead, it just seemed to demonstrate the impossibility of ever truly communicating.

"If you do not even have the words to describe your so-called dilemma, how can you think you have the knowledge to question your superiors?"

"I... this isn't going to convince you, but I had a feeling, a conviction. Some part of my gut told me it wasn't right."

"Right is to follow the commands of the Ancients."

They were back to where they were a few minutes ago. As far as the immediate conversation was going, Maren was getting nowhere and not winning any points. But the goal was not to win verbal arguments. The goal was to get the genbot talking. And in that regard, Maren was winning, hands down. She hoped Doctor P was getting what he needed out of it.

She pressed on.

"What makes the Ancients right, if there is no one to give *them* commands?"

"It is not for me to question them. They know more than I do, they see more than I do, they understand."

"How do you know?"

"When they tell me something, I do it, and I see that they were right. They reveal what is real."

Maren was getting a little excited. He was talking about the old gen farts now. He was explaining, at least in part, how they communicated.

"How do you know what is real? How do you know that what the Ancients tell you is the truth?"

"They have given me no reason to doubt them."

"That's because they need you to serve them. Maybe they've just created a world up there for you so that you'll do what they tell you. You can't know if it's real. As you said yourself, you've never even seen an Ancient!"

"Look," Maren went on, "consider the possibility the gens, your ancient masters, have only told you what they wanted you to know. How do you know you haven't been lied to? How do you know you aren't just a tool for them? You're just a specialized tool, they can't possibly care for you. And if the Event happens and we truds are wiped out, the gens won't have any need for you whatsoever. Why should you trust the gens' version of things?"

To his surprise, Michael enjoyed the verbal jousting. It was like a form of the simulator on Magritte. He had never engaged in this type of battle before, but he was beginning to understand its form. It was practice warfare, and he liked it.

"I know it is real, because I experience it. They tell me about things hidden in your world and they are shown to be correct. Ideas and words are made manifest. They understand the laws of nature and therefore rule the earth. They are truth."

"But you understand nothing of their motives, of the 'why' they do things. You don't know if your gen masters are saints or sinners."

Michael did not know these terms. "What is a 'sinner'?"

"Somebody who does something wrong."

"Then it is someone who disobeys."

"No, not necessarily. It is someone who does the wrong thing, who makes the wrong choice or decision."

"Why would they choose to do the wrong thing?" Michael asked.

"Well, maybe they are greedy or want power or something. Or maybe they think that they are doing the right thing, but it isn't actually right." Maren knew this wasn't making any sense to Michael. How could she convey right and wrong to a person who thought that right was always to follow some order as told to him by all-knowing Ancients? She tried a different tack, "I guess a sinner is someone who is imperfect. Someone who, as you might say, someone who does not always find the optimal solution."

This definition seemed to satisfy Lightbringer. So he moved on to the other term. "What is a 'saint'?"

"It is someone who always does what is right or tries to do what is right, even if other more powerful people try to stop that person. Or, I guess, somebody who is perfect or who is made perfect. I never studied theology, so take it with a grain of salt."

Michael always obeyed, but his memory of training on Magritte was good enough to remind him that he often did not find the optimal solution. Though he was skilled, the simulator regularly scored him less than perfect. Thus, Michael always obeyed but was imperfect. Michael did not know if this made him a saint or a sinner.

"But maybe I got sidetracked there," Maren said. "I was trying to explain that you don't know what motivates the Ancients and whether they are good or evil. You only see what they want you to, because they made you, because you serve them."

Michael ran his finger along the deep scar on his arm, caused by the retractor arm on the submersible, in what seemed like another age. The scar was real. He was real. What he had seen with his own eyes was real. The Ancients did not lie to him. The Ancients were truth, and they always would be.

72. It's There

"The plan is pretty straightforward," Damien said. "I've been there before. It was years ago, but I was in the vault. I know exactly where it is. I made a very small withdrawal of Greendust, back when the Core was more powerful than the NHA. From some discrete inquires in NHA systems, I know that the Greendust is still there, in that same hidden vault, at the end of a nearly forgotten tunnel."

"How secure is it? Is it going to be hard to extract?" Fantima asked.

"When it comes to security, sometimes the best security is hiding something in plain sight and then leaving it there undisturbed," Damien explained. "That is often the philosophy of the Natural Human Alliance, likely because of necessity. So it is with this vault. I'd be surprised if more than five people in the whole NHA know that the Greendust is there. The main access is an old tunnel. The access tunnel is guarded by a variety of systems. On top of that, there are enough sensors at the start of the tunnel to make going in tricky even if you could get past the security. The last time I was there, though, once you got to the final long tunnel that branches off the main access tunnel, there didn't appear to be anything. They didn't want anything that could be caught on a scanner to reveal the location, so the stuff is literally just stacked up all by itself, with nothing else nearby. No cameras, no nothing. However, the tunnel in is a long windy one, and those sensors at the entrance pose a problem, even ignoring the security before that. A reaction team would probably catch up to anyone in the tunnel before they got to the vault, or at least on the way out. But nobody said we have to go in the main way. The vault is in Industrial District 9, under a functioning factory. As far as security goes in the district: Standard surveillance and security bots at the factory, only a couple of guards on the surface, nothing to draw undue attention to it. The guards are probably not NHA and almost certainly don't even know the vault is underneath them. Most of the vaults are bricked up for a rainy day. The fewer people who know about them the better."

"Well, I'd say it's raining outside," Fantima offered.

"My thoughts exactly. But the Natural Human Alliance leadership doesn't see it that way. Colonel Blue is scared to death of the stuff and would never authorize its use."

"Well, we'll get it anyway," Zhe said.

"Yes, but we aren't going to kill or hurt anyone," Damien said. "I'm still NHA. I'm doing this to help them, even though they might not appreciate it."

"The One has told us as much. Don't worry, you can trust us. We aren't the killing types," Zhe said.

"So how exactly do you suggest we get at the dust?" Fantima asked.

"As I was explaining, the main route in to the vault is from underneath, from a thin offshoot of the tunnels. It was put there after Red and I found it years ago, at Blue's insistence. It's heavily guarded along the start of the tunnels and it's a long way in from that direction. There's no way I could get in, let alone get out with the Greendust, without the proper clearances. And that just isn't going to happen given Colonel Blue. So we will sneak in from the top. It's not too deep going in from the top, actually. I guess the idea is that the heavy factory equipment shields the vault from the gen sky scanners; it looks like it is part of the factory. Who knows if that theory is right, but there are a couple of these vaults and they've never been raided as long as I've been around."

"Is there an access point from the top? Or do we need to do some blasting?" Zhe asked.

"Digging, actually," Damien said.

"Really? Do we have the time for that?" Fantima asked.

"A blast is going to trigger every alarm system in the district and even the floaters might pick it up. If it was just a raid, sure, blast away, throw away the weapons, and hide in the crowd. But we are going to have some fragile cargo to extract."

Fantima replied, "Then I guess I should get some shovels."

73. Binary Disturbance

"I don't know if he is really understanding any of my points or not," Maren explained in Doctor Psycho's office. She spun her pendant and necklace around her finger, winding it up, then unspooling it and repeating the whole thing again. "Of course, to be honest, I don't know if my own points make sense or not. Anyway, to the point at hand, I don't know if Lightbringer is just a machine giving the answers its complex organic brain was programmed to answer or if he is actually thinking."

"Maren, you're making the error of trying to categorize in binary terms," Doctor Psycho advised.

"Of what?" She stopped spinning the necklace.

"Ones and zeros. It is or it isn't. Yes or no."

"What do you mean?"

"You are trying to decide if the genbot, if Michael, is or isn't certain things, as if he has to be one or the other, a one or a zero. But there are other possibilities. Maybe he is something in-between, or maybe he is both things at the same time. You think that it either is or it isn't. What you can't see is that it might be both 'is' *and* 'isn't' at the same time, and maybe even something more."

And in his mind, Doctor Psycho knew the issue was deeper. The question for Maren was not only about Michael, but whether Maren herself could handle the tension when something is both 'is' and 'isn't' or whether the conflict would tear her apart and maybe even destroy her. Of course, Doctor Psycho knew that the tension could result in something in between, or, he could only hope, blossom into something even more.

Maren, he thought, *will the tension erupt into conflict that risks your own destruction or can you live in peace with it? Or will you find the key to something greater?*

74. Forever Promises

A gray lock of hair hung across his forehead. "What on earth are they doing with a genbot?"

"I have no idea," Eve said. "I'm not even sure they know what they are doing with it. It was an accident."

"What do you mean, it was an accident?" her lover, the man with the gray lock of hair, asked. Guardians of the West were not just accidentally captured. He had never heard of any such thing even being attempted.

"They planned to kill it and dissect it." Eve explained the operation to capture a gargoyle and examine its neural structure. "I don't know, maybe they wanted to find out its weaknesses. Somehow it survived and they are keeping it in a cage now."

"Interesting."

"If you say so. It's pretty boring watching over it. I'm getting sick of it. I'm getting out of there every chance I get and coming up here."

"Who's watching it now?"

"Maren, I suppose."

"Doesn't she get just as bored as you do?"

"I'd guess so. We haven't had the chance to see each other much since they changed up our shift schedule."

"Why don't you talk her into taking a break, too? You could use a friend to hang around when I have to be out at work."

"No, I'm leaving work down there. Maren's my friend, but she wouldn't understand this, you, the need to be away from it all."

"Why not?" he asked.

"She's different. Hard to explain. Anyway, I promised I wouldn't tell anyone about you, remember?"

"Yes, Eve, I remember. So, this gargoyle, the genbot, you've been watching it for a while?"

"Yes."

"Why didn't you talk about it before?"

"I'm not supposed to. It's a sensitive operation. Everyone is afraid that the genbot will somehow signal the floater and cause it to rain energy bolts. I'm sick of all the dying and fear and monotony and the claustrophobic tunnels... And now listen to me. I'm talking about all the things I tried to get away from by coming up here, by being with you. I'm sorry. And I don't want to talk about it anymore. Not now. I just want to be with you. I want to be with you forever."

"That, Eve, is a possibility."

75. The Vault

The guards didn't think it out of the ordinary that the unmanned delivery truck came late in the day, near closing time for the humans that worked at the factory. The factory computer regularly ordered supplies on its own. It worked twenty four hours per day fabricating and assembling heavy building components and custom metal work.

The large truck was electronically registered and ushered onto the factory grounds. The truck rumbled over to the delivery building. It auto-unloaded a number of components and two large crates, all according to what the factory computer had ordered. Then, the truck rumbled back out.

A small probe emerged from the top of one of the crates left behind. A brief flash followed, though there were no humans in that part of the factory to notice.

"The probe registers inventory management equipment. That means we're in the right place. And the best news: the probe shows nothing security-related within the flash radius," Fantima observed.

"Okay, then," Damien said. "Let's get to work."

**

The rover was an old model: rubber coated tracks, a few primitive sensors (only one of which still worked), a comlink, and an auto-shotgun designed to shred a person at short range but leave the walls and building behind the person relatively unscathed. The small rover had randomly patrolled the tunnels, following its simple algorithms to identify people, remotely verify credentials if present, and report back anyone not in the latest update of the database. If it identified clearly hostile activities or received an order from the comlink, the auto-shotgun was available with one drum of ammo. Its random patrol pattern was part of the security plan: no one could predict when and where it would query visitors, whether friend or foe.

But some years ago, the already very old little rover tread down an especially long, twisting, and narrow tunnel. It found a recently-made hole where once the corridor had been bricked-up and proceeded into the darkness. Along the way, the rover dropped off a two-foot-high ledge which, when it tried to go back, could not be climbed over. The ledge was just slightly too tall for the little rover's rubber coated tracks. So the rover turned back around and proceeded deeper into the tunnel. Eventually it came to a room at the end and found that it could not go any farther. The rover retraced its steps once more. After repeating the circuit the little rover ended up once again in the room at the end of the tunnel. So it was there that the rover found a corner, and sat there, scanning all the while.

The little rover sat there for years. After a time, its battery power was too low to do much other than hibernate with its single remaining sensor active. Deep into the tunnels, it had roved too far away from a recharging station or a communication node that it could tap into. The rover was stranded. The patrol algorithms got stuck in a loop, the end result being that the rover thought it best to stay right where it was. It was forgotten in the depths, waiting for a robotic companion to one day come far enough down the tunnel to be noticed.

**

Damien looked over Fantima's shoulder at the display. "Is it synced up?"

"Yes, our digging machine is perfectly matched with the waves and vibrations emitted from the factory equipment. Nobody's going to notice a thing."

The digging machine spit out another brick of compressed pulverized concrete and dirt. The machine deposited it on a short conveyor belt where shortly thereafter it was neatly stacked with several others. To a theoretical casual viewer observing the digging operation, the machine looked almost like a normal part of a factory generating large bricks.

"It won't take long now that the digger is through the concrete and has the factory rhythms mapped."

**

The little rover's sensor counted down from five minutes and then sent out another ping. The waves bounced back and the little machine immediately started to hibernate again to preserve power. But then it stopped. Its servos spun up. Something was different. There was a large hole in the ceiling where before there was none. It pinged again and then again. The hole was stable. Nothing was moving. With each ping that showed that nothing had changed, the algorithms told the little rover to be less concerned. Finally, the rover decided it was nothing that warranted further observation and went back to sleep.

**

Damien paused his roped descent a few meters higher than the vault and listened. Everything seemed quiet. The digging machine had sucked up the final part of the bore, the reinforced concrete ceiling, in six pieces. Nothing fell into the vault itself other than their own sensor array. The sensors hadn't picked up anything of concern. The sensors had only shown Damien what he had thought was still there all along: the last known supply of Greendust.

Even though the sensors said nothing was down there, Damien listened anyway. He trusted his own ears. Hearing nothing, he dropped the final meters quickly to the vault floor below, landing like a feather. He listened again. Nothing.

He looked around. Yes, it was as he remembered. Enough of the metallic green wonder powder to accomplish everything they needed, and a little more. He signaled Fantima and she also dropped down to the vault.

Zhe stayed at the surface to manage the equipment. Zhe prepared to send down the first rack.

Damien rounded a corner of stacked crates...

**

Five minutes had passed. The little rover turned on its sensor. Something now hung out of the space in the ceiling. The rover identified it as long, narrow, several strands... something like cables or rope. The little rover's onboard computer ran through the possibilities and came to the conclusion that it was possible that a theft was in progress. Alternatively, it could merely be a maintenance team. The rover's servos spun up again. The rover pinged again...

**

Damien thought he saw something move in the darkness. He leaned low and moved closer...

**

The rover flashed its warning lights and audio to "stop and hold for identification." The signals were sent to the proper components, but the light emitting diode died long ago and a heavy layer of dust caused the old brittle audio membrane to fail. Its warning components no longer worked and the little rover didn't know it.

Damien saw and heard nothing.

The little rover tried to warn the human shape again with the warning light and maximum audio alarm. The rover needed time to run the human shape through the database. It was an old model. Identification took time.

Still, the shape moved forward. The little rover took the shape's ignoring of clear warnings and forward movement as hostile intent. If the rover did not act soon, it would be too late.

The rover did what it was programmed to do. The auto-shotgun rapidly fired. The human shape did not fall immediately, so the little rover continued to fire.

**

Damien crumbled to the ground. Three of his limbs were gone. He had also taken multiple rounds to the chest. Damien wasn't even carrying a weapon. No one was supposed to be hurt. What had gone wrong?

**

The shotgun's report echoed down the tunnels to a distant sensor which immediately identified it as an older model auto-shotgun emanating from the vault.

A red light began to flash in the vault itself, and Fantima knew the mission had failed. She carefully peaked around the corner and immediately saw the little rover in the intermittent crimson flashes.

The little rover continued to pull the auto-shotgun's trigger, even though it was out of shells. It was the only weapon system it had. Fantima knew the model. She knew all the robot models. And she knew it didn't have anything more it could do.

But she had to act before more arrived. Or, more probably, before something worse came charging down the tunnel.

She looked at the stacks of Greendust canisters.

There was no time to get all of the Greendust before Natural Human Alliance guards came racing down the corridors towards them. She could hold the guards off at the narrow door, but that wasn't the goal. If she was shooting at guards, she couldn't be loading canisters. And she might not survive the stand. Alternatively, she could still take one load of the Greendust back up as she made her escape. But one canister simply wasn't enough to change the outcome. Or, instead of a load of Greendust, she could take Damien.

The NHA knew that Damien had been assigned to work with Niles. It wouldn't look good for the Network. Even if he was dead, it was best to take the body rather than the powder. After stuffing his limbs into her pack, she grabbed Damien's bloody body, dragged it to Zhe's lift, and escaped up the tube.

76. Regrets

"Who would want the Greendust?" Red pondered aloud. Greendust had several applications, some more dangerous than others.

"Who wouldn't?" Blue said.

"You."

"I'm glad you remember, Red." Long ago, Damien had found a hidden reserve of the fortech deep in the tunnels. It almost seemed like another lifetime. They should have destroyed the Greendust then, as she had argued. Now, just as she always knew it would, it had happened. Someone had come for it. It was only luck in the form of a lost outdated rover that saved them.

"What are we going to do with it now?" Red asked.

"Destroy it." Blue firmly said.

"I hate to see it go..."

"You're not really going to argue with me again, Red, are you?" She couldn't believe Colonel Red would try to save the Greendust a second time, not after they realized their vulnerability. Not after everything that had happened.

"I suppose not. You were right. It is too dangerous. I was wrong."

"I want it destroyed as soon as possible." It was an order.

"Very well," Red mumbled. Red turned and left.

Blue smiled with a certain kind of pleasure. She finally got her way. But this was just a start. Soon, more things would be going her way.

Red exited the room, head hanging low. As he walked down the hall, his pace gradually picked up and his head slowly rose. Red would order the Greendust to be incinerated, of course. It had to be done. The order would be put into the system, with the advice and consent of Blue, to show that he did what he was supposed to do. Then the team would move the Greendust from its new, temporary storage location to the furnaces. He would make sure that the orders clearly spelled out exactly how it was to be done, based on the specific instructions given to him after consulting further with Blue. Everything would be done one hundred percent according to the regulations, per Blue's orders. And everything would be documented well in advance.

77. Disruption

After days of considering it, Michael thought he had found the way out.

The hardest part was not the broader patterns of the guards, but rather the lack of consistency in behavior to a specific stimulus. Michael had been testing them, prodding them subtly, but the truds were often inconsistent in their reactions. Michael could only see a miniscule portion of the variables that affected their lives and he was not used to operating from his current position. Without Magritte, without its organic brain, without Rex Skyguard, without his team, without his winged armor, without his power, everything was new. But he thought he had found a weak point.

As a Guardian frequently tasked with breaking into labs and other facilities protected by primitive trud technology, the technical solution was slightly easier. He knew the engineering principles so that he could efficiently destroy security measures with one well-aimed fist of energy. Michael of course did not have the energy beam, but he did have the engineering knowledge. And that suggested that all he needed was a bearing mechanism. Something to concentrate the force of his body onto a narrow point. All of his strength applied at the base plate would probably be enough to displace the energy field receptors buried in the floor. No unmodified human would have a hope of breaking through the alloy used in the base plate. But as everyone should have known, Michael did not have the body of a normal human.

Michael thought there were two possibilities. First, the security system might notice the misalignment and shut itself down to prevent damage to the base line equipment. But he doubted that was the likely outcome. He thought his chances of encountering the second possibility were better. He'd seen it happen before with early generation fields. Instead of shutting down, the security system would probably interpret the disruption in the energy field as a breakout attempt and surge the power. But nothing would actually be cutting the energy waves; the extra power would be hitting the displaced receptors instead of an object trying to pass through the field. And with the increased power and no receptors to catch all of the energy, any cabling in the concrete channel would now begin to cook. At the same time, any electrical signals running through the channel would be disrupted. This would likely cause a sequence failure, allowing Michael to crash through the energy field to the side of the damaged receptors. Without his armor, energy burns were a possibility, more than a traditional human could tolerate, but it would not be enough to stop Michael. He would be out.

But at least one problem remained: if they were sequenced, which direction were they linked? Which side would fail? Without the ability to see in non-visible spectrums provided by his mask, the disrupted energy field likely wouldn't look any different. He could hope for a flicker to indicate whether he should jump left or right, but it might come down to chance. It was a fifty-fifty chance whether he was the one to survive, to return to the Ancients, or the one to remain trapped in a cage, to remain tethered to the earth forever.

The time was late, however, and 50% was all Michael had for now. And it all depended on a simple piece of conveniently shaped high strength metal: the bearing mechanism. It was broad and smooth at one end, but tapered to a point that would focus the strength of his body onto the energy field system's base plate. It was part of one of the currently unused leg irons, where the spiderlyn would be fastened to the floor. The truds had made another mistake leaving it there. The instrument of his confinement would become the instrument of his freedom.

**

Now, while the behavior of individual truds was difficult to predict, Michael nevertheless knew their general patterns of movement, when they tended to visit, when they were most alert, the schedules of the guards... The truds tried to mix it up, but it was nonetheless predictable most of the time. The limits of human concentration and the need for truds to sleep dictated a certain pattern, a rhythm to the days.

And he knew who had the watch.

The timid one, the one named Franklin, was back on duty. Gildur and Rosie, the ones who never lowered their rail guns, the ones most concerned about triple redundancy, would be nowhere near the room if he had the rotation pattern correctly memorized. Yet, it was still daytime. The base would not yet be locked down, and therefore Michael would be able to move throughout the corridors. One could learn much from listening to the complaints of guards who thought they were out of earshot, longing to get out to the surface before the deadline of dusk.

This was the moment for which he had been waiting.

**

The timid Franklin had left the room. But Franklin had only been there an hour, so his departure was only temporary. The guards never worked a shift less than four hours. Michael had planned his attempt during Franklin's shift because if there was a confrontation, he would be by far the easiest to defeat.

Michael yanked the leg iron free from the floor and swung the spiderlyn so the heavy bolted end that had been in the concrete swung up to his arm. Those monitoring the hidden cameras, which he assumed were there watching everything, would soon notice, so he wasted no time. With one motion, he slammed the metal wedge into the base plate. The first blow severely bent the plate. Two more hits and he was confident the receptors were displaced. He could already smell the warming plastic of wiring covers in the channels. Then, fate smiled upon him, for there was a brief flicker, and Michael dove through the faltering energy field.

Michael rolled to his feet. He didn't feel anything more than warm skin. The flickering energy field was not enough to burn him; it was merely enough to make him feel alive. A Guardian of the West walked free once more, and his captors would soon learn what he was capable of, armored or not.

The truds had moved him to a room without bars, so the next barrier was merely a door. Michael went to the door and cracked it open. The corridor was empty. It also was longer than he had expected, so he didn't waste a second. He sprinted down the hallway, knowing it would be impossible to casually blend in and having no experience with the art of camouflage among people. Whatever stood in his way would regret it.

A man in coveralls appeared from an intersecting hall. Michael did not slow down. Lightbringer raised his elbow, striking the man in the windpipe violently, crushing his windpipe and causing his spinal cord to be displaced from the base of his skull. The man fell dead to the corridor floor.

Lightbringer ran on. He turned down the next corridor, intuitively sensing it was the widest, most used, and most probable way out. But just as before, a person stepped into his path.

In less than a second, he knew: the person was Maren.

Michael dropped his elbow, tucked and rolled, rising a few meters farther down the corridor past Maren, and kept running.

Then two soldiers entered the corridor not far ahead. They immediately recognized Michael as an unauthorized person and raised their rifles.

"Stop!" One of the yelled.

Michael knew he could not close the distance in time to get both of them, so he spun and headed back towards Maren.

Maren stood frozen in her tracks as the man, the machine, she had cared for charged back at her. His face was emotionless. It was not filled with anger. It was not filled with fear. It was not covered in exertion or even determination. It merely was... aware.

"Don't shoot, you might hit the girl," one guard advised to the other. "The rounds will tear right through him."

Michael again neared Maren, again had the chance to harm her, to use her as a shield, to take her hostage, but he didn't so much as brush her as he sprinted past. The two guards charged after. When the guards were clear of her, they would unleash a hail of fire.

Or they would have, if they had had the opportunity. For down the corridor, around the corner, back by the holding cell, Franklin had stood only momentarily with his mouth agape at the empty cell with an apparently still functional energy field. Then he moved quickly to the wall, pulled off the plastic cover, and did what he had been trained to do. He punched the emergency intruder/escapee alarm. And then, throughout the corridors, halls, rooms, and passageways of the levels above and below and the level he was on all experienced a sequence of brief pulses of light and energy waves.

Electrical pathways in the brains of everyone on all three levels were briefly disrupted, and everyone collapsed in unconsciousness, including Michael. And poor Franklin.

78. As Predicted

"Blue needs me on the surface. But everything here should be back on track. The shielded quick reaction force was there in no time. The genbot is back in the cage, no worse for his little escape attempt," Doctor Psycho reported.

Red shook his head. "The one with the bars, I hope."

"It has a more modern energy field. It won't happen again."

"I was told it was impossible for him to escape the first time," Red said. "Pardon my skepticism."

"We didn't know it was an old field system. The security engineers learned something from watching the genbot displace the field."

"We can't afford to not know, Doctor. Now a man is dead. We've been wrong time and time again and the window of opportunity is running out."

"There is a little good news. We weren't completely wrong. We know at least something," Doctor Psycho said.

"Yes, what is that?" Red asked.

"He behaved as exactly predicted," the Doctor noted. "He didn't touch the woman."

79. Dangerous Games

"I told you he was dangerous," Jack said. "I knew he was dangerous from the first moment, when we should have frozen him solid in the lab. He was a time bomb, and I knew it. A genbot is too dangerous to play games with."

"Everything about our whole lives is dangerous, Jack. You knew that when you joined the Natural Human Alliance and the Organization. You knew it and explained it when you talked me into joining you. And this just goes along with the rest of it, if not more so. Don't you know how important this is?"

"I know how important *the mission* is. That machine is not part of the mission."

"Not originally," Maren said.

"Not *now*."

Maren crossed her arms. "The Colonel seems to think so."

"Red has several side projects that have nothing to do with the primary mission. If only you knew."

"What's that supposed to mean?" Maren asked, annoyed that Jack would dangle classified information that she wasn't allowed to know about as if it were some magic card that granted him automatic victory in any argument.

"All I was saying is that it was dangerous."

"And you want me to say you were right all along, that we should have frozen him when we had the chance?" Maren asked.

"Well, that would be nice..." Jack admitted, a little smile growing on his face. He kind of liked hearing it, actually. 'Lieutenant Mode' began to fade away. "But what I really meant to say is that I am glad you are all right. I was worried. I was afraid you were hurt, that the genbot would find a way to hurt you. Of course our lives are dangerous, I just want to protect you."

It was hard for Maren to argue with that.

80. Signs of...

Doctor Psycho walked down the deep urban canyon and thought about the possibility supported by the latest data analysis. He found it almost impossible to believe.

Fascinating. The probabilities indicated by the computer analysis of the data led to an incredible conclusion. Could it really be? As if to accentuate the possibility, a couple rounded the corner ahead of him, holding hands, her head occasionally leaning in to rest on his shoulder for a step or two. The couple walked towards him. The Doctor passed the couple while walking over a grate on the sidewalk, where steam rose from some warm, humid cavern deep below the city streets. He noted the slightly sweet smell of the steamy vapors, but didn't think much of it and continued pondering the analysis. *She was sometimes a bit immature, but... Might it be more likely that the computer model was wrong? In that short of time, in those circumstances? It could be a form of Nighten... But the tone and emotion of her voice, unmistakable signs of-*

Poison! Even now, he could feel the defensive antigens and chemicals activating, as his watch pumped in the anti-poison agents to his bloodstream. *The sweet steam!* The Doctor knew immediately, but as if to confirm, the watch pulsed twice, then pulsed twice again, indicating to the trained wearer that he had inhaled a poison, likely two-stage. He could not react any more than he had mistakenly with his initial start at the poison indicator. If the assassin was watching, any reaction might cause the assassin to send the activator signal immediately. The Doctor needed to behave normally. One minute more and the danger would be largely past as the anti-poison bonded to the surfaces of the poisonous molecules and inhibited the effectiveness of any activator signal.

The Doctor had studied assassination methods. He knew this attack vector. He knew who often used it. What his would-be assassin didn't know was that the Doctor was ready for it; he only need a little time.

He breathed deeply. With each step he worried about pumping the poison deeper into his system. It was better to keep it concentrated near the lungs, where he inhaled it. The bio-defense watch needed more time to work. He should stop walking, to slow the pumping of the poison through his system, but he needed an innocuous excuse that wouldn't tip off the assassin, should he be watching. *My shoe.* He paused to bend over to tie his shoe, hoping that the bio-watch contained the proper anti-poison regimen. If it did, all he needed was a few minutes. If not, well…

**

Casually leaning against a masonry arch, hiding in the old entry way, safely out of view of any surveillance cameras, Flora waited for the love-bird couple to get an adequate distance from the target. She didn't want to have to kill the bystanders who just happened to be walking across the vent at the same time as the target and who had thus inhaled the same poisonous compound. A few more yards of separation and the couple would be clear from the activator ray. In a few days, the inactivated poison would be flushed from their systems, and they would never be aware of the mini death bombs that had been within them. Of course, if it became necessary, she would send the activator ray and kill the couple, too. Sometimes flowers got pulled up with the weeds. Such was life.

The target knelt down to tie his shoe. It would only delay the necessary separation from the bystanders by a few seconds, so she thought nothing of it. Finally, the couple was clear and the target stood up again, slowly continuing his walk. She raised the small device to eye level and fired the invisible ray at the target's back. The poison agent in the steam vent was of a kind that, when activated, killed almost instantly, rather than the delayed poison she was more accustomed to working with. Apparently, someone didn't want this target going very far. Any second, she would see him to start to struggle to breathe and then fall over dead a few moments later. It would be a painful death, but a short one.

**

The Doctor never felt the invisible beam hit his back, but he knew it had struck him just the same. He could feel the poison gaining a grip and the slight burning sensation in his veins and lungs as the anti-poison fought back. He tried to breathe slowly, but he was becoming increasingly short of breath. It was almost suffocating.

He could feel the life leaving him as he struggled to inhale. His vision began to blur. The anti-poison was not strong enough. Perhaps there was an error in the calculations. Perhaps they had changed the attack vector just enough to circumvent his defenses.

Stumbling and falling to the ground, the Doctor knelt over on all fours, fighting to keep consciousness. His veins felt as if they were going to burn through his skin as blackness began to creep in on his blurred vision.

Then the blackness began to recede. Doctor Psycho's vision began to clear. The anti-poison injected by his bio-defense watch was working. The Organization's scientists and intelligence officers had studied their enemies well, knew about this compound and attack vector, and had deployed it in the bio-watches to key Natural Human Alliance personnel.

With each inhalation the Doctor's breathing became deeper, but the burning in his lungs remained. Gathering his senses, he lifted one arm, then tried to get his weight on one leg, then two. He rose and took one more deep breath before awkwardly walking towards the busier street ahead. He needed to get off the side street; there might be more protection with witnesses around on the main road.

Though he knew he should be focused on the present, he could not help but think of the foolishness of his being above ground. He should never have left the underground compound until the mission was completed. It was foolish of her to send him on this errand that any number of people could have accomplished, especially given his importance to the operation.

He staggered to the cross street which was filled with people heading home from work and turned around to see if anyone was following him. The street behind him was empty. He had made it.

The Doctor merged into the flow of people. He began to feel some of his strength returning. Forget his "assignment," he needed to get back underground. He needed to have a talk with... *her.*

He was still a little unstable on his feet, and bystanders might have mistook him for being inebriated. Swaying side to side, he occasionally clipped another person walking by. But he was certain now: he was getting stronger. The biodefense-watch had worked its magic. He would survive. Half a block down, a woman suddenly stepped out of a doorway into his path, and he bumped into her hard. "My apologies," he offered as she slid by him without a word. He stumbled on a few steps more before he felt a warm moistness on his shirt. He looked down and saw the growing spot of dark red on his shirt.

"They've killed me after all," the good Doctor Psycho thought as he fell dead in the middle of the crowded sidewalk.

81. New Connections

Damien's eyes opened. Suddenly, like a switch had been thrown, he was completely aware. He felt more aware than perhaps ever before. But something was different. He was leaning against a flat surface, almost vertical, but with his back taking some of the weight of his body.

"Hello, Damien," Niles said.

"Did we get it?"

"No, Damien, not yet. The Greendust is not yet ours. Something went wrong, but we do not want you to worry. Everything will be fixed. We can repair you quite easily."

"Repair me?" Damien looked down and instead of hands with skin he saw synthetic gray. He squeezed his hands into fists. They did not feel very different than the hands he knew before. The grip was firmer, the feeling more... remote. But still, hands.

"The mechanical limbs are only temporary. You will get new flesh and bone soon. We've already started growing them."

Damien stood and flexed his arms and moved his elbows back. As he did so, he could feel the synthetic muscles ripple across his back. He could feel the power in them. Damien stepped forward and only then noticed his legs were not his own. He lifted one leg, bent the knee, and repeated with the other leg. They felt good. Natural. Like he was twenty years younger. No. Better than natural. Like they had always meant to be part of him.

"How long until my new limbs are ready?"

"A few weeks, perhaps," Niles responded. Niles knew most of them didn't go back once they saw what was possible. It was one thing to have your arms and have to take proactive action to give them up for something more; it was quite another to have them ripped away and then to experience the power of cybernetics at the moment when you feared you had lost something forever against your will. What was true for arms and legs was true for other things as well.

Damien was surprised at how easily he accepted it. He would not have guessed that he would so readily adjust to the loss of his natural limbs, to becoming partly a... a machine. It did not seem to bother him in the least.

"But before your limbs are ready, we have another task to complete. We need you to get the Greendust."

"I nearly died trying that," Damien noted as he curled his arm and marveled at his new hand. "It's too late. Now the Greendust will certainly be moved. The NHA won't be stupid enough to leave it there in the vault. I am certain the Greendust is gone and I don't know where it is anymore."

"It is true that we don't know where it is now. But we know something even more valuable. We know where the Greendust is going to be and when it will be there. And that is when you'll grab it."

"Are you certain you know where it will be?" Of course Damien knew Niles was certain. He merely wanted to know how it was that Niles was so certain.

"We have seen the very plans for moving it. We could draw the conclusion after piecing together logistical planning data from the Natural Human Alliance's systems. They tried to make the transport of the Greendust look innocuous, but thanks to you we know it is indeed Greendust and we know where it was initially located. Without that information, we would have missed it. But with it, we have enough to figure out the rest. They cannot just casually destroy it. We happen to know the one you call Red will be moving the material to a special incinerator. It's listed as industrial waste, but it can only be the Greendust. It is the only logical conclusion."

"I will get the Greendust." Damien didn't know why he was so confident about it, but he knew he would. It almost seemed as if he already had it planned out. Just like his new legs, it seemed it was destiny. He would get it. Nothing could stop him. Still, Damien felt the need to know more. "Why me? The Network has many who could grab it."

"We thought you'd like to see your work completed."

Damien knew Niles was right. Niles knew Damien's mind better than Damien did.

82. Remote

The spiderlyn was back. Michael was tied down again. His escape attempt had failed, though he did not know why. One moment he was running down the hall, away from the guards, past Maren, and the next moment he awoke in a new cell, with the ropes again.

The prospect of escape now seemed remote. And after days of captivity, Fortress Magritte's ever-watching scanners had not found him. Michael Lightbringer's confidence wobbled.

He had seen many important things. What if Rex never had the chance to learn of them?

Michael realized he had not had Magritte's cerebral scan for weeks. All of the information he had seen was only in his head. If something should happen to him, it would be lost forever. As this dawned on him, he suddenly felt more cautious. His normal approach to conflict, that of dealing with the issue head on, was no longer optimal given this new constraint. Now, there was a new imperative. He must survive.

83. Where's Damien?

Felix showed up at the rendezvous point exactly on time. He had only half expected Damien, but nevertheless lied when it was Niles who emerged into the light. Lying was a necessary part of Red's life.

"I thought Damien would be the one to show up," Red said. Now that he saw it was Niles who greeted him, he knew how the blood tests would come back from the vault.

"Damien is occupied testing some new equipment. Besides, we thought it would be good to talk one last time face to face," the scarred one said.

"Very well. The purpose of this meeting is quite simple," Red said. "All I need to know is that everything is on schedule and that everything will be in place. Time is very short now."

"But Damien is sending you his *Class O* reports, isn't he?" Niles said, referring to what were the supposedly secret reports and technical plans that Damien covertly transmitted to the NHA when he had a chance.

Red wasn't fazed in the least. "If it was just a matter of reports and plans, the Organization could have sent anyone."

"Yes, we understand. Damien is quite brilliant. Better than we expected, to be honest. Almost worthy of joining the Network. We were surprised you lent him to us."

"Only because I need someone I can trust and who knows what he is doing when it comes to evaluating weapons systems. Now, enough with the games. I need to know the status of the asset placement."

"Colonel Red, we will work toward the goal," Niles responded.

Felix continued as if the non-answer hadn't been uttered. "I need to know that everything is going to be in place. You know as well as I that we get one chance at this. So, I need a straight answer, a 'yes' or a 'no.' Will it be in place by mission hour?"

"Yes, all of it will be in place, at all of the stations, by the required time. However, we will not risk exposure of our manufacturing facilities unnecessarily or prematurely by pre-positioning everything when we are not even sure if your plan will succeed or if your source can truly be trusted."

"I intend to stop this Event."

"We know, Colonel Red. Yet we don't agree with you entirely. If you don't succeed, we will have one more chance. Then it will finally be our turn to stop it."

That's what I'm afraid of, Felix thought.

84. Achievement

One truck, with one vehicle following as security: that was the plan. After all, they were only dropping off industrial waste. But Vijay didn't buy it for a moment. Regular old industrial waste didn't need six guards. A couple, maybe, but six? Come on. There was no way it was just a mission to move toxic junk from the warehouse to the incinerator.

Vijay understood maintaining a low profile, but he didn't understand when the captain didn't level with his soldiers. They weren't stupid. What was so precious about the stuff in the back of that truck that they couldn't know what it was? When Vijay advanced through the ranks, he would remember that. His men and women would always know why they risked their lives.

Vijay checked over his ballistic slinger. It was kind of pathetic. they weren't even issued a decent rail gun for the escort mission. An old bullet slinger still had its place. Bullets worked well enough against Fanatics or any other human. As long as they didn't run into guardians, robots, or machines, they'd be fine. And maybe that was why the captain issued slingers. The gargoyles would be less likely to pay attention if they knew the team was outfitted for trud on trud combat. The gargs would figure it was just some petty squabbling among the primitives and leave them alone, because what crazy trud would think ballistic slingers could protect jack squat from a gen?

231

Vijay cracked a little smile. Maybe it was brilliant: ballistic slingers as a kind of camouflage against the gens. In a way, they'd be hiding in plain sight. They weren't trying to look innocent. They were just trying to look like a bad guy the gens didn't care about. Vijay thought it was a pretty clever approach.

Then Vijay looked over at the captain. The captain was picking something out of his teeth, studying it, and then digging around his gums to go after another chunk of nastiness. The captain wasn't so much as glancing at any of the scanners, looking out the window, or otherwise paying attention to a single thing inside or outside the vehicle. The captain was in his mouth and, maybe, in his head, if Vijay was going to be charitable. The captain removed his fingers from his mouth, yawned, and threw his head back as if he were the most bored person on the planet.

Yep, Vijay was giving the captain too much credit. The captain was an idiot. Slingers were not camouflage. It was a secret mission on the cheap or, more likely, though he hated to admit it, it was a mission with little forethought whatsoever.

Vijay went back to studying his sector. At least nobody was going to sneak up on them from the rear left.

**

Fantima steadied the pulse cannon on her shoulder, staring down the sight at the vehicle.

"Now," ordered Zhe.

She pressed the arming button with her left hand forward on the pulse tube and gently squeezed the trigger with her right index finger.

**

All of the monitor lights went out. Vijay's hair stood on end.

"We've been hit with a pulse," he said, pointing out the obvious for the benefit of the captain. Vijay flipped off the safety and prepared to exit the vehicle as it ground to a halt.

**

The transport truck pulled farther ahead of the trailing security vehicle.

"That's enough distance," Zhe commented. "Hit the truck, too."

Fantima steadily squeezed off another silent pulse, the lead truck's lights went black, and the engine sputtered to a halt.

Damien rose behind Fantima, a heavy wooden spear in each hand.

"Now, Damien," Zhe said. "Remember the millions you will save by this action, and the sacrifice of the few."

Damien leapt from the building and ran smoothly on his mechanical legs towards the security vehicle. He was running faster than he had even run before; faster than any natural born unmodified human could in fact run.

Fantima turned toward Zhe. "Aren't you going to order the rest of the assault team in?"

"No, we are not," Zhe replied. "Assuming Damien handles it, when it is finished, it will look like the Fanatics did it."

Why they wanted it to look like the work of Fanatics was beyond Fantima. If Zhe wasn't going to tell her why, she wouldn't know. It was as simple as that. Fantima wasn't part of the inner circle, not yet part of the One. She knew it. She accepted it. Fantima turned back to her scope to watch the unfolding events.

**

Vijay rolled out of the vehicle, slinger at the ready. He didn't take any fire immediately, though he knew the enemy was out there.

**

As Damien reached the vehicle, a security agent was emerging. Damien hurled one of his two heavy wooden spears, striking him in the chest. The agent collapsed to the ground.

**

Vijay heard what sounded like a 'thump.' A second later, he heard Lomonov's body fall to the pavement. In the quiet moment that followed, he strained his eyes to see in the darkness, weapon at the ready.

Then he heard a brief scream, which he recognized. And he knew that the captain was also dead.

Vijay turned and ran for the cover of a building. He turned his head behind to see what followed. When he turned back, he saw the wooden spear too late to stop, and impaled himself on it. He looked at the man who just ran him through: a middle-aged face stared back, unsmiling. Had he seen that face somewhere before? Holding on to the end of the wooden spear were two metallic arms. Vijay's eyes fell lower and he saw the mechanical legs. The cyborg pulled out the spear and as quickly as he had appeared, the cyborg was gone.

Vijay lay on the ground. Why would an illegal cyborg attack a shipment of industrial waste and use a wooden spear, making it look like a Fanatic attack? Vijay half laughed. It was absurd. The world didn't make any sense. How had it come to pass that he would die like this?

**

Red studied the camera images. He hadn't expected that the escorts would be killed. Killing them wasn't necessary. Stun weapons would have been the obvious choice. They could have taken the Greendust another way, without the attention and complications involved with killing. Yet Felix's surprise was remote and intellectual. Perhaps viewing the images on the monitor allowed him the mental distance to remove himself from the blood, the screams, the humanity of it.

He knew he was being cold, but soldiers died in wars. And in war there were many casualties, many of them accidental, many of them a mistake. These would not be the last to die for the cause. He wished it wasn't so, but that was the world he lived in. But Red was aware enough to recognize that he was being cold, like a machine, by using such logic and that there was something wrong in it. He was not innocent.

He looked carefully at the grainy image again. It was possibly, maybe even probably, Damien. And that probability made him think of Niles stating that Damien would be testing some new equipment. If it wasn't Damien in that grainy image, Felix still knew who ultimately was responsible for taking the Greendust and where it would end up. Red shut off the screen, leaned back in his chair, and folded his hands behind his head, grimly satisfied.

85. Critical

"I'm sorry it's been so long," Eve said as she set her bag down on the couch.

Every day now without him was like a day without a drug necessary for life. She could feel the energy draining from her each hour she was away. But the moment she walked in the door, when she saw that long gray lock of hair hanging over his forehead, after she had struggled through the hot subterranean tunnels, that moment felt like a jolt of electricity and energy. When she saw him, she felt newly alive. He understood her. She was not just some lowly soldier destined to take orders, but a real person, full of dreams, full of possibilities.

"I am so glad you are finally back. I was getting worried. Why was it so hard to get away for a bit? Is it the project? The genbot? Is it still as you told me?" he asked. What else could keep her away?

"They've had us locked up as a mission nears. I'm supposed to be a jail guard of sorts, but it's seemed like I'm the one who is the prisoner."

"I, for one, am certainly glad you're free again."

"At least for a little while. Just a couple of hours, really. That's all I can spare before it would be noticed that I'm missing this time. I have to report back tomorrow morning."

"So soon?"

"The project is entering the critical stage. I was lucky to get the break that I did. Most aren't even allowed to leave the secure unit. I twisted a few regulations, truth be told. Besides, nobody knows all the hidden ways out of the complex like I do."

"Oh, really?"

"The truth is, I know lots of secrets," she said, moving her finger slowly down his chest.

"Oh do you?"

"Yes, and I use those secrets to get my way."

**

Eve placed her cheek on his broad chest, just above his heart. His heart was beating slowly, steadily. Hers was still racing. "Are you sure they'll do it?"

"Yes. None of the bad things have to happen anymore, I promise."

She wanted nothing more than to get away from it all, to leave it behind, to escape this life for a new one. Nobody had to hurt anymore.

He said he could make it happen.

86. Final Inspection

Felix mindlessly manipulated the terminal screen. With everything happening, all of the pieces coming together and in need of coordination, it seemed foolish to continue his above ground work. Every moment at the terminal screen felt like an eon. Every moment was precious. Katz was usually a patient person, but there was so much work to be done. And time was running out. Yet part of him knew General Win was right: if something should go wrong, as it had so many times before, the Organization would still need its people in place, and some of them might need to disappear into the crowds of daily life for a long time, once again. So Katz sat at his terminal, continuing to play the role of taciturn but extremely competent engineer.

When Doctor Psycho was assassinated, Felix had asked Colonel Blue for access to a full anti-poison compound regime, prophylactic, in the bloodstream from the get-go. He didn't want to depend solely on the bio-watch. Colonel Blue hadn't recommended it, saying the probability of an attack on Colonel Red was low and the negative side effects of having the compound in his blood for extended periods of time were well known. Dr. X had concurred. Felix did not trust Dr. X the way he trusted Doctor Psycho, but the good Doctor was gone. While denying Red's request for the regime, Dr. X added it was impossible to protect against every conceivable poison. Felix couldn't have all of those compounds running around his bloodstream for any length of time without serious health complications. Besides, Dr. X pointed out, the autopsy showed that the bio-watch worked and that Doctor Psycho had managed to survive the poison attack. So, Colonel Blue and Dr. X told him not to take the extra anti-poisons. Felix had a medical tech issue him them anyway without entering it in the system and had taken the compounds every four hours. Without telling the others.

The clock turned over to noon, and Felix got up. It was time for lunch. Or, in Red's case, it was time to get in an hour of real work. He wanted to get a firsthand look at one of the operational areas as it looked from the surface. A leisurely walk over lunch would allow him to casually survey the area one last time. Experience had taught that sometimes his eyes would pick up on something that, despite all of their technology, others had missed. And there was no room for error.

Felix emerged from the tower and stared up through the canyon of glass. Today it was hanging there, low in the sky. The floater was watching them. All the gens in the sky would see, however, was a trud engineer on his lunch break going for a walk.

**

Felix studied the buildings. Everything still looked in order. The sites would probably work. The buildings were mostly unoccupied. The windows were wide-enough with only lightly traveled streets below. The urban canyons formed in the surrounding streets would aid in concealing the deliveries. Yet there was enough space to have a clear shot at it. Yes, this site would work.

Felix continued walking down the block and turned onto a cross street. He knew the tunnels were underneath him here. The tunnels were large and meters under the concrete. But they would be shallow enough for his purposes.

**

Felix had seen enough for his final in-person inspection. The sites still looked workable. Good, even. Now they needed to get the final pieces of equipment positioned. And Niles needed to stop dragging the Network's feet.

Katz needed to get back to the office. He could work through the issues with the scarred one while sitting in front of his terminal. He picked up his pace.

Then he felt it.

It felt like a sting on his neck, like the sting of a wasp. He raised his hand to the back of his neck and used his fingernail to scrape out the micro-dart. He knew exactly what it was.

Felix slowly turned around, and saw the round-faced woman tucked into an alcove, her eyes growing a little wider. Now he knew who had fired it at him. Felix smiled broadly for a second. Then he charged at her.

The woman turned and disappeared into the building, but Felix was not far behind. He burst through the door to see another door at the end of a short hallway clicking shut. Felix sprinted down the hallway and crashed through the door, finding himself in the atrium of one of the medium sized towers he had probably helped design.

The woman was three-quarters of the way across the open, high-ceilinged area and headed for the revolving doors that led to the well-traveled city street beyond. Felix was impressed with her speed given that she looked to be a middle-aged woman. Felix was no spring chicken himself, and unfortunately for times such as this, he spent more time developing his mind than his body. Still, he had some reserve of natural talent and a bursting reservoir of motivation, and he was closing the gap.

He slammed through the revolving door and charged up the street towards the fleeing assassin. Suddenly, she turned around and fired two micro-darts at him in rapid succession. Felix reflexively ducked. One of the darts went wide and struck a pedestrian, who stumbled and fell unconscious to the pavement.

"Don't take the anti-poison compounds, they're bad for your health... yeah... great advice, team. Great advice," Felix muttered. Felix continued his charge as the woman turned to resume her flight. She took a sharp corner at the next side street, and Felix wondered if she might not be doubling back to where their little chase began.

He rounded the corner and an energy blast whizzed by his ear. She must have retrieved a stashed weapon or an accomplice was now assisting her. Felix didn't stick around to investigate. The cat had once again become the mouse.

He was already back on the main street, weaving through the crowd. He ducked into one of the towers of steel and glass, and worked his way to the pedestrian tunnel subsystem. After ten minutes more of doubling back and evasive maneuvers, he was sure he was not being followed any longer. Felix, in an abundance of caution, headed for one of the safe house locations, one not known by others in the Organization except the late Doctor Psycho and a few others who he trusted absolutely. He was upset that she had gotten away, but thankful that he had managed to survive. It was probably foolish of him to pursue her from the start.

On his way to the safe house, he looked up at the little domes that dotted the street and contained surveillance cameras for the local police force. Thankfully, the Organization had access to the same camera feeds. "*You may have lost me,*" Felix thought to himself, "*but in the process you've lost your anonymity.*" She had escaped, but that would only be temporary.

**

Felix weaved his way back through the city. When he finally reached the safe house, he picked up the communicator.

"Hello, this is *Storberg*, structural engineers. How may I direct your call?" the female receptionist asked.

"Oh, hi Rachel," Katz responded. "This is Felix. Um, I must have eaten something bad at lunch or something. I'm having a reaction again and I'm really not feeling well. I think I need to take the afternoon off."

"Oh, sick again, Felix?" Rachel said, with concern in her voice. She knew he had a few health issues. The boss seemed to always understand, because he never got angry at Felix's frequent absences due to health problems. "I'll let Jonathan know. You just take it easy and we'll see you maybe tomorrow, okay?" she said in her motherly tone.

"Thanks, Rachel. We'll see how I'm feeling." Felix placed the communicator back on the table. He had a feeling it would be a long time before he was feeling well enough to go back to the office. By that time, he wondered if there would be an office to go back to.

87. Minds Alive

Niles always seemed to try to conceal his emotions. But it was clear to Damien that in this instance Niles looked a little excited. "So, Damien. You retrieved the Greendust."

"It was where you said it would be, when you said it would be there," Damien said. "The rest wasn't hard."

"Indeed, not for you. Not anymore."

"The rest will be easier now, too. Now that we have the Greendust."

"We shall see," Niles said.

"I hope so."

"You shall."

"I can't wait," Damien said, eager to see the technology in action against the gens.

"You don't need to wait, Damien."

Damien looked at Niles, puzzled, but by now knowing that the scarred one had something in mind.

"Your body is so much more powerful now than before," Niles explained. "But that is only a taste. For there is something more powerful than the body, and that is the mind. It is the mind that controls the body."

Niles picked up a vial of the Greendust. "We shall see if this metallic powder will make our mission easier, and we shall see it now.

For we will finally see the truth. We will see if it is as you have said. For if this is Greendust, we cannot be stopped."

Damien obliged Niles by asking the obvious. "How?"

"Your mind could join ours and then you would understand."

"Plugging in?"

"Just a taste, Damien. Just a taste." He walked Damien over to a padded chair and invited him to sit in it. Damien did so.

"Now, close your eyes and relax. Soon you will understand."

Damien relaxed. At first, he saw merely the darkness that came with closing his eyes. But then the blackness began to swirl ever so slightly, with hints of blue dancing across the blackness. Then he saw an image of a city burning and felt the pain of loss. Then he felt the heat on his face. The images came faster. Soon, it was not just images, but words. And out of those words, thoughts. And from those thoughts, visions... of what was, of what is, of what might be.

Then he saw a hidden manufacturing facility that he intuitively knew to be the Network's. And in his mind's eye, he saw the Dreptex. There was more of the killing compound than Niles had hinted at. Much more. And Damien knew it was not a vision of what might be, but of what is, of what Niles had seen with his own eyes.

Then Damien felt Nile's thoughts. There was almost enough Dreptex to wipe out the world. And with the Greendust to bond with it and help it spread, there was no doubt it was enough to destroy the gens... and more.

Then the thoughts seemed more real. It was now as if he were living them. He was not just watching now, but experiencing. He saw Niles – was it Niles or someone before Niles? – growing up in the east, in a time Damien did not understand... he saw the horror of the Conflict, the pain, the senseless death, people killing people... he saw how that mind swore to defeat them, using anything and everything he could... he felt the anger and determination... and he saw the plan. The Network would destroy the gens with the Dreptex... and more. Something deadlier. Something that would kill all of the gens... and almost all of the truds. But Damien saw the logic of it. The Network would cut away everything, it would destroy the world as they knew it. It would even destroy the Network itself. But a few humans, a few true humans, would survive and the gen threat would be gone forever. Humanity would rebuild itself, safe for thousands of years from the threat of modology. And the Greendust would make it all the more possible.

Damien continued to swim in the logic and thoughts of Niles. But soon, he realized it was not just Niles. There was another mind there, too. And slowly it dawned on him that there was not just one other mind, but two... three... dozens. All of the minds layered over one another... The thoughts washed over him stronger now. They began to crush him, he could not breathe, he could not comprehend it all, it was too much... the pain, the love, the thinking-

"Ah!" Damien grunted as his eyes opened.

"That is enough for now," Niles said. "Everything is as you have told us."

Niles comprehended everything. Now, the Network knew everything about Damein. Damien only saw a small part, what one mind unaccustomed to the Network could tolerate. But the Network, dozens of minds experienced in the task, had seen everything in Damien's mind, conscious and unconscious. They saw it all, as if they had lived it. They had seen Damien grow up, when he fell in love, when she was killed, when he first discovered the Greendust hidden deep in the tunnels, when he first used the Greendust to steal the True Core's database, when he had failed with the others to catch the first Guardian of the West, when he was in the submersible and finally caught the Guardian, when Red assigned him to ensure the technology was ready for the Event, when Damien first met Niles, when he began to believe that he must act with everything in his power, the pain of the auto-shotgun ripping apart his body, the feeling of power at his new mechanical body and the surprise that he enjoyed it, and finally the Greendust in his hands...

Niles saw that and more. And he smiled through his scars. The Greendust was real. Damien had not deceived them. No one could construct an entire life of lies in the mind.

The pain and confusion of the mind meld had gone, but as if it was a drug, Damien suddenly wanted more. He had only a small taste of dozens of minds in harmony, and now his head felt empty, alone. He now understood there were so many ways to see, so many ways to comprehend, and they could be unified. "I want to know more," Damien said.

"We all do," Niles replied.

But of all the thoughts Damien saw, that he experienced, one jumped to the forefront: "The Greendust..."

"Yes," the scarred one smiled. Niles knew now what he had previously suspected and hoped was true. Niles had confirmation that the Greendust was the real thing, discovered years ago in the tunnels, discovered by Damien. Niles had had to wait for certainty, he had to know it wasn't a trick, and now he had it.

Niles also fully comprehended what Damien was only now realizing. Niles sensed it, knew how Damien thought, knew what Damien had glimpsed in the visions. "Yes, Damien. It is living. The Greendust can accomplish more than you could have possibly imagined. What before was a hope is now a certainty."

Niles took one of the Greendust vials. "We thought it was all gone forever. We thought that no one else could follow in the path that those gens walked so long ago..."

He unscrewed the vial.

"Now, it belongs to us, too..."

Niles placed his nose over the vial and inhaled deeply. He closed his eyes, pointing his face towards the sky.

The fools of the Natural Human Alliance. All this time the Greendust was under their noses, and they didn't know what it truly was. Only a dispersion agent! They didn't understand how it worked. It could disperse because it could think. It knew what its master wanted it to do. They didn't understand that it was living, that it was power, that it was modology.

**

Damien knew now that the Network would destroy everything with the Greendust. The counter-Event wouldn't be limited. It would wipe out almost everyone. And Damien was fine with that. No, not just Damien: THEY were fine with that.

88. Compartmentalization Countdown

General Win was talking over the secure connection. The encryption and decryption process made it impossible to recognize his voice, but the code words had confirmed it was Win. "Colonel Red flushed her out, chasing her long enough that a dozen cameras got good shots. The upside is that this assassin's days are clearly numbered. It won't take us long to find her and, one hopes, figure out who is behind these killings. Unfortunately, Colonel Red's cover is also likely in serious jeopardy. He may have to go underground full time."

The incident with the assassin meant that Engineer Katz would need to be sick as far as his company was concerned, though the charade could only last so long. It was likely that Engineer Katz would never return. Still, if his identity was not leaked too far and wide and if the assassin ring could be uncovered and neutralized, it was not impossible to imagine that one day Katz would be able to resume his cover as an engineer. Not impossible, but highly unlikely. If he ever worked "in the light" again, it would probably be under a new alias in a new city.

Strangely, to some, Red didn't appear to care about losing his cover. He hadn't planned on needing it much longer anyway.

Red focused his attention again on the General's address. General Win was concerned about the assassinations, for obvious reasons. "As a result of recent events, I'm issuing a Delta Class compartmentalization order. Physical and operational segmentation is imperative. Violations of the Delta order will be dealt with severely. We are too close to the end game for these kinds of problems."

Colonel Red understood. It was not an unwise order. It could even be argued that it should have been ordered after Doctor Psycho was murdered, if not at the start of the whole project. But this order complicated Felix's own plans. Nevertheless, it could be done.

General Win was finishing up his address. "The source confirms the Event is still on target. There is no indication of an accelerated execution date. Therefore, we will continue, methodically, with our plans. Despite the setbacks and the loss of the Doctor, our operational goals can still be met. I know you can make it happen. That is all."

General Win's voice cut out as the transmission came to an end. Colonel Red sighed. *One more week before the operation. One more week, and it would be finished.*

89. The Bell Rang

The doorbell rang and her heart jumped. Though she didn't want to, she went to the door and opened it anyway.

A man stood there, about six feet tall, slim but muscular build, square jaw, black business clothes, red tie. It was a face she had known long ago, but one she had not seen in what seemed like a lifetime. He was carrying a single red rose. His hair was slicked back except for a single lock of long gray hair that hung out over his forehead.

"Hello, Flora," the silver-haired man said.

"Why... hello," she stammered, before coolly continuing, "I'm surprised they sent you."

"You are?"

"Yes, I am." She stood there looking into his eyes for a moment, looking for that something she had once seen in the way he looked at her. Not seeing it, she looked down at the floor. "To tell you the truth, I didn't think they'd send anyone. I thought it would just... happen."

The silver-haired man stood there, looking at her staring at the floor. He nodded slowly. "I'm sorry," he said.

Flora stood aside from the door and motioned him in. "Well, you might as well come in."

"Thank you."

"Can I get you a drink?" she asked.

The silver-haired main chuckled. "No, no thank you, Flora."

"I wasn't going to put anything in it."

"Sure, Flora, I know."

She pointed at the rose. "Just put it in the vase with the others."

The man walked over to the end table and slid the rose in with the bouquet of fading lilies and tuberoses. Unexpectedly, the red rose somehow looked right there.

She poured herself a drink and caught a glimpse of herself in the mirror above the mini-bar. Bags were under her eyes. Creases crossed her once smooth checks. She felt old. Used up. Flora turned back toward the silver-haired man. For the briefest instant, she felt like it was ten years ago. "Do you remember, how it was once? How much fun we had?" she questioned.

"Of course," he said as he strode towards her. "Who could ever forget?" He placed his hand on her shoulder and gently turned her around so she could look out the window at the great cityscape. "I remember gazing into the future, imagining what the world might one day be, but for them." He began to massage her shoulders.

"I thought we could change it all," she said.

"I know, Flora. We tried."

He continued massaging her back and neck with one hand while he quietly slid the other into his pocket.

They both stared out the window, enjoying the moment, knowing it would soon pass. They said nothing. They just looked at the world beyond the little window.

The man drew a small metal disk out of his pocket. Flora felt the cool metal of the pulse-generator slide up against the base of her skull. He continued the massage with his other hand. A tear began to well up in her eye, but she continued to look out beyond at the wide world. "It's okay, Steve," she whispered.

He pressed the button on the metal disk and the pulse-generator emitted an orb of energy, instantaneously cooking a large portion of her brain. She collapsed into a heap on the apartment floor.

Steve slid the pulse-generator back into his pocket. He stepped over Flora's body and walked over to the end table. He grabbed the fading bouquet from the vase, rose included, and held them to his nose, inhaling deeply. The flowers were past their prime, but their scent was still vaguely sweet. He turned back to his one-time lover. Squatting, he gently placed the flowers on her body, and studied the image. Fading beauty. Death. Steve thought it was one of the most natural things he had ever seen. He got up and left without a tear.

90. Release

Michael sat alone in the room. The lights were dim, apparently to simulate nighttime. Of course, Michael was not asleep. The closest a Guardian ever came to sleeping was the few minutes spent in the black chair having a cerebral scan on a floating fortress. The truds, however, still seemed to follow the inefficient pattern of the sun, and so Michael was frequently left alone for six or more hours per day. He spent the time practicing missions in his head, analyzing means of escape, categorizing the intelligence he had gained and, not infrequently, thinking about his intriguing conversations with the woman. Such things were never discussed on Magritte. They seemed pointless, but at the same time interested him more and more.

Then, uncharacteristically at this hour, the door cracked open and in stepped the woman they called Eve.

**

Eve lowered the barrier. "Listen carefully. I need to explain a few things and we don't have much time. Do you remember the pain when you first got here? I saw you writhing in pain when they put those black pads next to your head. It was a brain scan. They learned about your fortresses in the sky, the plans as you saw them, the weaknesses of the floaters. They created a new weapon and they plan on exploiting the information from your brain scan to launch some sort of attack of the floating fortresses. They believe the Event is going to happen soon and they want to strike the gens first. You have to stop them…"

Eve began to release the reinforced spiderlyn that crisscrossed Michael since his attempted escape.

"They are planning a major assault on all of the flying fortresses. But that is only the first stage. I think they have something else in mind, a second phase assault of some kind, but I haven't been able to learn what it is about. You must warn them."

"Why are you helping me?" Michael asked.

"If the Ancients are destroyed, I won't get what I've been promised. I need the Ancients as much as you do." Eve release the final shackle. "Now let's go!"

91. Freedom Waits

Eve led Michael down a corridor. It was a smaller side corridor not as heavily traveled as the ones just outside his cell. Eve apparently knew exactly what she was doing. She had expertly maneuvered him through the gauntlet of guards, deeper into the complex. Now, in this side corridor, no one else seemed to be about at the late hour. Near the end of the side corridor, she stopped and listened for a moment. Then she opened a side door and stepped into a small laboratory.

The equipment looked old and even more primitive than normal. A thick layer of dusk seemed to cover the work surfaces. Based on the number of labs Michael remembered raiding, he didn't think that this one was used any longer. At the back of the lab, Eve bent over and opened a cabinet door. She pushed some beakers and old lab equipment to the side, and removed the back panel.

"This way," Eve whispered, pointing for him to go first into the cabinet. She followed behind. Before replacing the back panel, she closed the cabinet door and slid the beakers and equipment back in place.

A red diode light suddenly emitted a subtle beam of light. Michael found himself in a cramped, but clean, ventilation shaft that ran along the back side of the lab's cabinets. The red diode light illuminated Eve, and Michael could see her digging into her pocket.

"Here," Eve said, taking out a second diode light, this one green, "Take this and crawl in that direction."

"What will I find?"

"Freedom. Eventually it will lead you to a park, if you follow the marks I've made on the walls when you get to intersections. They look like this..." Eve drew a square inscribed in a circle. "Once you get outside, you know how to contact the fortress and warn them about what I've told you, right?"

"That will not be a problem. They will see everything I have seen, just as I have seen it."

"Good. Be sure that the Ancients see who helped you escape. Then we will both be free from all of this."

92. Race Against Time

"What do you mean you don't know where the genbot is?" Colonel Red asked firmly.

Sergeant Krantz explained, "We went on our rounds and it wasn't there. We quickly checked the logs, saw nothing was authorized in terms of a move or anything, and then pulled up the video images. It was Eve. Everything in the cell was recorded-"

Sergeant Stern interrupted, "The bottom line is that Eve released the genbot from the spiderlyn and the room, and the sensors can't find them. The historical surveillance files have also been partially corrupted, so we don't know what direction they went."

It was almost impossible to believe. But it was happening, and he needed to accept that reality immediately. Red had already wasted too much time. "Initiate Phase One now."

"But Colonel, we don't have all of the units in place for Phase Two," Lieutenant Winters tried to explain.

"Initiate Phase One now! There's no time to waste. We can't risk that the escaped genbot will be discovered. If he is discovered before Phase One is completed, everything will be ruined. Move it!" Colonel Red bellowed.

93. Cleansing

Colonel Blue was furious. "How can Red even still be allowed anywhere near an operation? How many failures does this make? He allowed the Greendust to be kept around too long, and the worst happened: it was stolen. He failed with the garden trap, with the near genbot escape... and now this."

"He needs to be removed from the equation, as I have long argued. All you need to do is tell me where I can find him. His time has come," the man said.

"You are right, but we must wait a few hours more. The operation must succeed. When it's all over, we can take care of him then, after we clean out the rest of them and he has no one to protect him any longer."

"Everything will be on auto-pilot soon. He serves no purpose any longer," the man argued. "So many of them, chief among them Red, are willing to be corrupted by technology. They've forgotten what makes us different."

"Just a little longer," Blue advised. She wanted to be rid of Red a long time ago, also. But it was not so simple. He could not simply be removed without other things collapsing...

"At least we should start the purge with the others, before it is too late. Once the operation has succeeded, they will scatter to the winds and we cannot let that happen. We must contain the fortech knowledge, and we must start now. Time is short."

The man had a point, Blue recognized. She was still reluctant, but the fortech was extremely dangerous, and she would not repeat the mistakes of waiting too long, as others had before her. "Very well: you may start with the others. And once the operation is in full swing, I will deliver Red, too. But I'm not telling you where Red is just now, because I honestly believe we may still need him. For just a bit longer."

"The others will keep me busy enough for the moment," he said, brushing aside his lock of gray hair.

94. The First Breath Outside

Michael breathed in the fresh air deeply as if he were born anew and taking in the outside air for the first time in his life. He was out of the claustrophobic confines of his prison deep within the belly of the earth. He had crawled through the tunnels to be reborn in the lush green of a garden. Now he was in the open air and above him was the pale blue sky. Still deep in the urban canyons, however, he could not see Magritte hovering above. Perhaps the fortress had lazily moved on to patrol another region. More likely, it was just temporarily hidden from his view. Once he was in the direct line of sight of the fortress, if not before, Magritte and Rex would recognize the elevated temperature of his body, a sure sign of a Guardian. And once his heat signature was registered, it would be but a moment before his rescue. But first, he needed to make sure he eluded anyone who might have followed him through the tunnels. Next, he needed to avoid any detection as he walked among the truds.

Barring a dangerous adventure to the top of one of the skyscrapers, Michael figured his best course of action would be to walk down one of the urban canyons for some distance, before turning ninety degrees and repeating a long walk, all the while hoping to catch a glimpse of Magritte. He was not yet orientated to his position in the city, but he figured it should not take long for him to identify one of the many unique buildings. Once he was orientated and if he had not gotten a direct view of Magritte, he would make his way to one of the larger parks where he might have a more unobstructed view of the sky.

Michael began his brisk walk along his appointed path. He did not need to go far. When he got to the first cross street, Michael looked to the sky.

Magritte! He turned to walk down the cross street, moving closer to the hovering fortress. He was walking down the cross street for no more than a minute when he saw the small specks falling towards him. *One… two… three… four? Could there be four?* Then he saw the bold colors: orange, purple, dark red, and yellow. It was Talongrip's team, built for power and combat.

The four falling Guardians of the West flew faster as they zeroed in on the heat signature that could only be a fallen comrade. Fortress Magritte had identified Michael immediately, and the standby team dispatched.

The purple one fell below the tops of the skyscrapers and his distinctive four wings sprung out, catching the air and rapidly slowing his descent. Truds fled left and right at the sight of the approaching gargoyles. Michael stood there, staring up, making it clear to any bystander that he was either an agent of the gens or insane. It was further evidence to the Guardians that he was one of their own.

Talongrip, in his four-winged dark purple armor landed first, followed closely by the dark red Raptorscream, the orange Razorwing, and the yellow one they called Eaglestrike. The massive Talongrip was about ten feet away from Michael and was the first to speak, "Lightbringer, is that you?" he asked.

"It is. I need to talk to Rex immediately," Michael answered curtly.

"Of course." Talongrip walked around Michael, and grabbing him underneath his arms, he leapt into the air towards the fortress above. Eaglestrike followed immediately. Michael enjoyed the feeling of acceleration once again as they sped skyward. Then an energy bolt flew by, coming from below. Then three more.

An inorganic combat robot crashed through the glass of a nearby wall and fired rapidly at Talongrip and his precious cargo. But Raptorscream was ready and sprung upon the Icer, slashing at it with his wings until it was scrap metal. Seven more Icers suddenly emerged, as if from nothingness. Talongrip saw it from high above. He thought for a moment that it might have been an elaborate ambush, with Michael as its bait. But if that was the case, it just showed how pathetic the truds had become. Raptorscream could easily handle them alone, but even that was unnecessary.

Raptorscream, who preferred the slashing action of his wings over the multiple energy weapons at his disposal, was already tearing into his third target when yet another group of robots crawled out from the depths and crashed through windows. But as each emerged in turn from their hiding place, they were cut down by something ghost-like. Raptorscream smiled as he shifted his vision spectrum to infrared. Rex had sent another team, Shui, Xue, Shulin, and Rang. Built lighter than the rest of the Guardians on Magritte, they proved deadly with their stealth and light-bending suits. They may have even been there before Raptorscream landed. After less than a minute, it was over.

It would be a stretch to even call the encounter a battle, so complete was the slaughter. These particular combat robots had pretty bad brains. The truds must have been desperate. Strangely, however, they hadn't sent any humans. Humans in conjunction with inorganics, even the dumb ones, were typically more deadly. The distraction of the more robust inorganic combat robots gave the humans more freedom of action.

Raptorscream looked around the area in various spectrums but saw nothing. He confirmed with Shulin and Magritte: nothing. *"I guess the truds are tired of dying,"* he thought. Raptorscream left a dragonfly behind to keep an eye on the area and to explore where the Icers had been hiding. Then he flew back to Fortress Magritte. Lightbringer would have a lot to explain.

95. Sky Breaker

Talongrip landed on the familiar ledge of the floating castle and released his grip on Michael. Michael took in the thin, cold air. He was glad to be back. He wanted nothing more than to go to the staging room, suit up, and join the battle below that he presumed, or rather hoped, was still going on. But he knew he had a more important task, and that was to report to Rex all that he had seen, and to warn Skyguard about this new weapon the woman had told him about. Perhaps the battle below was merely a distraction as the truds prepared to unleash their new invention.

Martha was there ahead of him, unarmored. "Michael!" she called as she embraced him.

"Take me to Rex immediately. I have important information."

"This way; he's in the staging room overseeing the other teams below."

Michael followed Martha along the familiar path to the staging room. The recesses in the wall were there, and so was his armor. But instead of suiting up, he knew he had a more important task; He walked straight to a scanning chair.

He saw Rex and began with his report immediately. "They are planning a major assault on all of the fortresses. I believe those inorganics were only a small part of what is to come. I know the precise location of their base and have seen several of their key leaders. Once I upload the information to Magritte, we will be able to quickly launch a strike and disrupt their plans."

Rex was astonished. "Michael, where have you been? We thought you'd fallen." The computer-brain had already clearly identified Michael, down to the specific version, and the date he had fallen. There was absolutely no doubt.

"I wasn't killed," Michael explained. "They extracted information from me using some crude form of Magritte's scanners. I believe they intend to use that information to attack the fortress, perhaps to identify weaknesses in our defenses. However, I managed to escape."

Michael walked closer to the chair and prepared to sit in it.

"Stop!" Dante called, as he and Gabriella entered the room. "What's going on?"

Martha answered, "Dante, Magritte's scanners do indicate it's Michael. He's been positively identified. Somehow he survived."

Michael was thrilled to see more of his teammates, and especially his mate, Gabriella. During the time he was gone, he had felt like a piece of himself was missing. Now, it was all coming back together.

Gabriella spoke, "Michael, is it really you? How did you survive the blast?"

"Yes, it's me. The truds nursed me back to health. They were studying me, trying to find a weakness for the fortress."

"That's impossible," she responded. She turned towards Rex. "It's not Michael."

Lightbringer was confused by Gabriella's response.

"Don't let him sit in the chair," she commanded.

"Gabriella, what's wrong with you? It's me, Michael."

Rex spoke up, "Gabriella, all of Magritte's scans confirm it is him. He must have survived after all. We were wrong."

Michael was desperate to show that he was speaking the truth, to convince Gabriella that it was him. More importantly, he feared that the distraction below was merely a diversion, and that the real assault could be coming at any moment, just as the woman had told him. He felt an incredible urge to act. He needed to let Rex and Magritte see everything he had seen and run an analysis. It was possible there was a wealth of information that Magritte's brain could parse and then piece together the trud's plan for a super weapon.

Martha and Gabriella were talking in hushed tones, though it was clear Gabriella was still upset.

Michael wasn't sure there was time for a debate as to whether or not he was really Michael. He was certain of who he was. One scan, and the rest would know it too.

Lightbringer proceeded to sit in the chair. "Listen, the truds are developing a weapon that could destroy all of the floating fortresses, and leave the Ancients open to direct assault. Time may be of the essence. Scan me and Magritte will be able to see everything I have seen. I will show you that what I've said is true."

Rex knew Lightbringer was correct. Time could be precious. Though the truds often failed, they were still creative, and thus dangerous. Michael's information could prove critical. Rex Skyguard gave the mental command to Magritte's super brain to commence the scan.

The black pads on the chair swung up to either side of Michael's head, and the warm pulse of the download began.

**

Michael relaxed at the warm pulse of Magritte's scan. He remembered it all, from the initiation of the mission at his last scan, to the moment he lost consciousness when the jetpacker detonated his pressure bomb, to awakening to the horrible pain of the crude scanner in the bowels of the truds' base, to the woman releasing him.

Then the pulse began to pound more than it had ever pounded before on Magritte. He began to feel pain. It was reminiscent of the truds' scanner. He opened his eyes. Michael saw Rex fall to the ground and begin to experience a seizure. Martha ran to Skyguard's side. Then all of Magritte seemed to shudder and the power flickered on and off. The pain grew more excruciating. Magritte shuddered again, and then started to list to one side. The scan should have stopped by now, but instead it kept going, and seemed to be growing more powerful. Rex continued seizing.

It dawned on Gabriella and Michael at the same moment.

"YOU are their weapon!" she exclaimed, as Magritte's brain continued to die and with it, the fortress's systems and their defenses. She raised her gauntleted fist at Michael's face and let loose with an invisible beam of heat and energy.

96. Scramble

Damien ran towards the staging area. The time had come sooner than expected. But most of the equipment was in place. The Greendust had been deployed. And soon, he would fly where before only Guardians were allowed to soar. And soon, those who had commanded the heavens for so long would crash to the ground.

Damien had to consciously run slowly, so as not to draw unwanted attention from the other soldiers running to their positions. Cyborgs were fortech for both the gens and the truds, and he didn't have time to explain to any NHA soldiers why it had been necessary. Unlike the Network, they would not understand. They could not understand. Not without having seen it, felt it...

Under the city streets, he entered his assigned tunnel and saw it for the first time: a specially modified combat sled. Niles said the sled for Damien would be something special, one of kind, designed for him, and Damien saw that it was. He trusted Niles and the Network, so he wasn't too surprised. But it wasn't the modified combat sled that stopped him in his tracks. It was what stood ready on both sides of it: organic robots incased in armor. Modology incarnate. A small portion of the Greendust animating bodily forms. Living machines with brains and biocircuitry. Machines that would soon be linked to him. Living machines that would soon be part of Damien as he brought the reign of the gens to an end.

97. Re-Emergence

Michael huddled in the dark tunnel. The girl, Eve, had said that this was the way out, but he wasn't so sure anymore. The markings she had made were not always obvious. He had been walking and crawling through the tunnels and pipes for hours and still he had seen no daylight. He had had to backtrack at one point when the branch he took ran out of space, and he must have lost half an hour in the process. Michael knew he had to get to the fortress, to warn Rex and the others about the trud's impending attack. And yet, there was a tinge of something, some feeling, some thought, that was nearly incomprehensible, as if it were on the edge of his brain, something there, but not definable.

He shook his head. He didn't have time for extraneous thoughts. He was free now, and once again the mission drove him: protect the Ancients.

He scrambled over the old sewer pipes and then he smelled it. Not the staleness of the tunnels below, but the hint of fresh air somewhere nearby. As he passed an intersection of two low tunnels, the cool movement of air caught him in the face. He turned towards it, and saw the grid pattern of light several meters down the crosswise tunnel. Michael crawled toward it and peered through the metal grating.

He was in the retaining wall that ran along the side of a city park. He gazed out upon a green lawn with children, little people he didn't really understand. The children ran and kicked a ball, screaming and cheering and yelling. He watched them for a moment. Such strange creatures. They often didn't seem to operate with much logic. They tussled and moved in such a random, unorganized fashion. One moment a herd, the next moment scattered, one moment focused on the ball passing by for a second, the next moment staring at a tree that had been there for decades.

The thought edged in again upon him, but he pushed it back. Again, his resolve returned. He must protect the Ancients.

He popped off the metal grate and prepared to emerge.

98. Silent Skies

"Phase One appears to be successful. The virus-bearing clonebot worked. No active scans can be detected from any of the fortresses. It rippled throughout the system."

"Just as planned."

"Not quite just as planned, but it may be close enough. It beat the original genbot up there, thank goodness, and that's all that matters for now. The path is now clear for Phase Two. Launch it immediately," Colonel Red ordered.

"The soldiers are still scrambling-"

"We cannot give them time to recover or repair their systems," Red explained. "We must attack with Phase Two now and try to hold it or at least disrupt them until we have the charges in place to bring them down. If the brain wasn't destroyed completely, and they are somehow able to release the machines, all may be in vain unless we can act decisively."

"But sir, not all units are fully in position yet and it will only be a partial attack-"

"I understand, that's why I've waited as long as I have. But there are enough in place now to hold each station. The others will join Phase Two as soon as they can, with the charges and Phase Three when possible. Enough talking, make it happen."

"Yes, sir!"

99. Breathing Again

Lightbringer waited a few seconds after forcing out the metal grate to see if anyone noticed, but no one did. Michael stepped out of the tunnel onto the green lawn and deeply breathed in the fresh air, as if he was born anew and it was the first fresh breath of his life. He was out of the claustrophobic confines of his prison deep within the belly of the earth. Now he was in the open air, and above him was the sky. He scanned the sky for the characteristic castle outline of Fortress Magritte. It was there, almost directly above him, though strangely leaning a bit to one side. Maybe it was just the odd angle from which he was viewing it, he thought.

He imagined that Magritte had already picked up the temperature anomaly caused by his body. Rex might be briefing the team now based on that anomaly. Magritte always studied objects of human form that had anomalous temperature signatures: they typically meant inorganic robots, modology, or disease; all items of interest. He expected to see Gabriella, Martha, and Dante at any moment.

Michael stared up. After several minutes, he began to wonder if the Fortress had not picked up his heat signature after all. But he had to dismiss that. Magritte couldn't miss him, standing there on the edge of the open park. *Why weren't they coming to retrieve him?* On Magritte's scanners, his heat signature would stand out like the Fortress itself against a clear blue sky. Magritte always monitored the scanners. That was one of its central purposes. Instead, Fortress Magritte merely hung there in the air, slightly tilting, motionless.

The more he studied it, the more he realized the fortress was at an unusually low altitude. Magritte had settled closer to the ground, even during the short time he had been staring up at it. There was no doubt: it had descended significantly. Though he couldn't be sure, he thought it might be tilting to the side more than when he first emerged, too.

However unlikely, perhaps he was in a blind spot or some other object was blocking Magritte's clear reception. Michael hopped up over the wall from which he had recently emerged, and began walking down the city street, the whole while keeping his eyes focused on the strangely tilting Magritte.

100. Garden Banishment

"Colonel, we found Eve. We got lucky. Street-side cameras happened to nab her right away. Must have used some unknown tunnels to get out."

One of the guards shoved a bound Eve forward.

"Why, Eve? Why would you let the captured genbot go and try and destroy everything we have worked for?" Red asked. "Now everything is at risk."

"It can't work. You know it can't work. We will all simply die, just like the rest who have tried to stop the gens. All my friends believed they could stop the gens, and now they are all dead, buried in the rubble or washed off the pavement or just gone."

"They died fighting for something they believed-"

Eve cut him off. "Well, I don't want to die. Who wants to die? I'm tired of the dying! And I don't believe it anymore. It's pointless! The gens are too strong and you can't win. And it doesn't have to be that way. Can't you see that none of that is necessary anymore? Why do you even want to fight the gens? We can live forever, can't you see? Why should we have any of that pain or sadness again? We can join them. He told me I could live forever-"

Red shook his head. "You've gone crazy, Eve. Eternal life is in the grasp of everyone by other means. You are imagining a world without God, a world without children, a world where we wouldn't live anymore, a world where we would just exist. If we were like them, we wouldn't be human anymore." Red believed half of it.

Eve pleaded, "I'm not crazy; you're the one who's crazy! Death doesn't have to-"

Red didn't have time for this. But his subordinates were watching. And he needed to finish this distraction and move on to things that still mattered. He cut her off midsentence: "Your actions freeing the genbot meant we had to release the first assault clone early to ensure it arrived at the fortress before the genbot you released. You jeopardized the entire operation, lifetimes of planning. You would have rendered worthless the sacrifices of all your friends. But the weaponized clone was released, it got there first, the genbot that you thought would grant you eternal life is apparently lost somewhere in the forgotten tunnels and caverns, and you've been captured."

Red paused before driving it home. "But here is where you are most wrong: we will win. Your friends did not die for nothing. We will win. And soon. When we will have reversed the Event, it will be the gens who are gone forever. No one will be around to grant you eternal life. Instead, you're likely to be spending the rest of your limited lifespan in a cell."

He turned away from her and spoke to the guards. "Take her away to General Win's Condor Team, we don't have time to deal with her. Have them process her per the regs, so long as it doesn't interrupt the operation; I never want to see her again."

The guards took her away.

"She should understand that death is natural-" someone said.

"No, death is not natural," Red interrupted. "It was not how we were intended to be. Every human knows there is something wrong about death. We are eternal beings. But her way of seeking it was wrong."

101. The Study Subject

"Maren, I've been looking everywhere for you. Is it true? Has the genbot clone been released?" Jack asked.

"Yes, when Colonel Red gave the order for Phase One, we all did exactly as we had been told," Maren said, rubbing her pendant, adrenaline still coursing through her blood as she thought of all of the battles her simple action had presumably set in motion. "I released the clonebot, told it the lie about needing to warn the gens about our new weapon and attack plans, and pointed it to the quickest way out. It promised I would be rewarded and left through the tunnels for the surface."

"Then everything we can do is done. The genbot copy is out. It will either make it there first and our assault has a possibility of success, or it's already too late for all of us. People will come for you now, and we need to leave."

"Why do we need to leave? The safest place to be during the battle is down here."

"Maren, I need to explain something. When Doctor Psycho died, I was the first to get to his files. And after learning what was in those files, I know it isn't safe for us here anymore. I was curious about a few things, and needed a few answers, so I did something I wasn't supposed to do, but that I don't regret. I saw the mind scans. Those scans told me more than I thought possible."

"What did you see in the genbot scans?"

"It wasn't the genbot's scans I saw," Jack explained.

"Then whose were they?"

"You don't know?"

"No."

Jack studied her for a moment, looking for any sign that she wasn't telling the truth. She was either a good liar or believed it.

"Maren, they were not the scans of Michael. They were scans of you."

Maren wasn't sure she heard him correctly. "What? Did you say the scans were mine?"

Jack slowly nodded his head, his face dead serious.

"That's impossible," Maren said. "I have never been scanned. You'd have to be crazy to undergo one of those. You must have seen Lightbringer's scans."

"No, I'm afraid they weren't Lightbringer's scans," Jack said slowly but confidently. "Doctor Psycho was not studying Michael Lightbringer; he was using Lightbringer to study you."

Maren's brow furrowed. It didn't make any sense. Why would Doctor Psycho want to study her? No, it wasn't possible. "I don't believe it. Why would he want to study me?"

"Why would he, indeed. Why would one of the best doctors in the world be interested in a country girl from the R.T.? But that's just the start. Why would Red take a personal interest in you? Why would Colonel Red protect you all these years? How would he know a girl was under attack by a band of Fanatics way out in the grasslands and why would he send a team to rescue her? Why would Red assign me to get you to join and then monitor you as a private in the Organization? Why should he have me research you for years and not tell me why? And why should Blue be so curious in this little project of Red's, namely you."

"You're scaring me, Jack. What are you talking about?"

"You know what," Jack said, challenging her. He didn't want to see that she knew, he didn't want to see that she had been lying to him for all these years, but he wanted the truth. He thought he was the one with the information, the one in control. But maybe she was the one with access to greater secrets and power all along. He didn't want that to be the truth, but maybe it was. Before going further, he needed to test her again, to see that she was innocent of the knowledge.

"No, Jack, I don't," she answered.

272

"I am sure you know. You must. There won't be a place here for you anymore once the attack is over," he pressed.

"And why is that? This is my home now as much as any other place."

"No gens allowed," Jack said.

"What's that got to do with anything?"

Jack said nothing, merely looking Maren in the eye.

Maren half laughed. She couldn't believe that Jack was entertaining such a ridiculous notion. "Are you crazy? Are you suggesting that I am..." Maren couldn't complete the sentence. Finally, she said flatly, "I am not a gen." Maren shook her head in disbelief. What had gotten into Jack's head? "This must be a joke. A horrible, horrible joke."

"It is not a joke. And it is true that you are not a gen strictly speaking. But you are the daughter of one." Jack looked down at the ground, the way Maren knew he always did when he had to tell someone something that he knew they didn't want to hear.

And then Maren knew that Jack was not joking. Whatever Jack was saying, he believed it to be true. The earlier smile of disbelief disappeared from Maren's face. She still didn't believe it, but Jack did. For some reason. "How are you so certain?" she asked.

"I wasn't. Until the genbot didn't do a thing to you when it tried to escape. The only reason that a genbot would hesitate to kill you is if it was programmed not to. The only thing genbots don't kill is gens. And somehow it could tell you are one of them. Or partly one, anyway."

"That's thin... This is ridiculous."

"So after he was murdered, I broke into Doctor Psycho's office and reviewed his notes. But I wasn't just looking for anything. I was looking for information on the genbot and why he didn't hurt you after he killed or tried to kill every other person he met in that hallway. And why did the genbot talk with you and not to another living soul down here? So I went looking for some answers. I've gotten pretty good at digging up stuff people want hidden. I found Doctor Psycho's files. As suspected, they were protected, and if Doctor Psycho could come back from the dead he'd know exactly what I'd done. But he's gone forever, I got the files before anyone else, and that's where I found the scans."

Jack paused, but Maren said nothing.

"The images from your scans allowed Doctor Psycho to reconstruct a picture of a man," Jack continued. "It's a picture of a man firmly etched into your memory forever. I also had a picture of that man, but despite all of my research, I wasn't able to connect him to you definitively until I saw the scans. In the scans I found the answer. That man was your father. And in the Doctor's notes, something he found out from Red, I discovered who that man married: a gen who tired of being a gen and decided she would become a traditional human again. She gave up her eternal life and whatever she had become to be one of us again. But she still took something with her, something in her genes perhaps, perhaps in some other way, something important. Something that might have been passed on to you."

Jack grimaced. "I couldn't figure out what information that body of yours contains, but somewhere hidden in you is something a lot of people want."

Maren didn't know what to say. It seemed so impossible.

"Here is a picture of her. And here is a picture of the man who loved her." Jack held out both pictures, pictures of the people Maren knew from long ago, from deep in the wells of her memory. And from those wells, the truth bubbled up. Those were her parents. Those were the people who loved her.

Maren took the pictures from Jack's hands. Tears welled up in her eyes, and she cried.

"So you didn't know."

It made sense now. Why they killed her mother. Why they hunted her father. Why they searched for her. Why her father told her to never speak of certain things, certain things that now seemed to emerge from the fog of her childhood memories. Why she always lied about her name. Why she was Clara, then Katherine, then Maren. Why Michael didn't kill her. And why she felt a connection to him.

"Get whatever stuff you want to take with you," Jack said. "We're getting out of here."

102. Battle Sky

He had walked several blocks when he heard the first crashing sound. First, there was a sound like breaking glass followed by a low base hum in the air. Michael wasn't quite sure what it was. Then Lightbringer heard it again, but this time it was closer. People on the streets started to look up with confused expressions.

Soon glass came raining down from directly above Michael. Shortly thereafter, Michael heard the rapid thumping of a skip drive and looked up. Men and women were jumping from the windows and jetpacking up into the sky: first one, then another. They fell for a split second before their skip drives thumped to life, and they flew upwards, straight for... Fortress Magritte!

There appeared to be dozens of the jet packers, jumping from a few scattered buildings, and amazingly from the one directly next to Michael. He counted the floors instantaneously. Lightbringer knew he had to act.

Michael charged into the lobby of the building and sped towards the stairs. He could hear truds running in the stairwells above him. Perhaps he would not be too late. With gen-like speed, he bounded up the twenty flights of stairs to the tenth floor and slammed through the stairway door.

He arrived just in time to see another jetpacker leap out of the blown-out windows and rocket upward out of sight. Two more men were still on the floor, one helping another put on a pack. Michael charged them; with their backs toward him, they didn't stand a chance. Michael rammed into the one with only one arm through the pack's straps, knocking him out of the window. The other one was so shocked that Michael realized he needn't do anything. Instead, the man turned and ran. Lightbringer let him go, grabbed the pack at the man's feet, slung it over his shoulders, buckled the straps around his chest, waist, and legs, and grabbed the massive RG-27 rail gun that was also on the floor.

Michael stepped to the ledge of the building and looked up. Dozens of jetpackers flew towards Magritte. Dozens of truds were attacking the fortress, and he would stop them all. For he was a Guardian of the West, blood still coursed through his veins, air still filled his lungs, the sun was at its zenith, and Michael was ready to play with death.

The Ancients would be protected.

Michael leapt from the building and rocketed like a bullet towards the rock that had always defied gravity. Until now.

**

As Michael rocketed upward, he saw Fortress Miyazaki in the distance, the castle in the sky crashing to the earth. Farther to the west, like a paint smudge on the horizon, he saw Fortress Monet, still hovering above it all, though little dabs of black seemed to swirl above it. He turned his attention to his home, Fortress Magritte, and the assault underway. Though he didn't have his wings or the benefit of being linked into Magritte, Michael Lightbringer was still a Guardian of the West. And that made him a being to be feared.

The skip drive's thumps increased in speed and frequency until they became a single vibrant hum. Michael continued to push the pack to its limit. Even moving at speed, which was faster than a Guardian could climb in wings, Michael aimed the RG-27 and hit an ascending jetpacker square in the back. He squeezed off one more seemingly impossible shot, dispatching yet another trud, before the other jetpackers were aware of what was happening. But by that point, Michael, at the trailing end of the stream of jetpackers, was almost upon the Fortress. And now he could see the raging battle in earnest.

For once, the truds had some advantages: they had surprise and networked communications, while the Guardians had no communication and no assistance from Magritte's myriad weapon systems. Still, ten truds could not equal the prowess of a single guardian. Lightbringer saw the battle team of Guardians fighting on the surface of Magritte and in the air immediately surrounding it. Talongrip and Eaglestrike tore attackers from the sky.

Michael could only assume the cloaked team of Shui, Xue, Shulin, and Rang was somewhere nearby, dispatching truds in anonymity. As for his own team, he could not yet see it.

He landed on the Fortress's ledge, and took aim at another trud, but an energy blast slammed into the side of his pack, sending him spinning sideways and causing him to lose his grip on the rail gun. The pack was now useless, so he ripped it off. As he did so, he saw a slight glint and bending of light, and Michael dived and rolled to the right.

"It's me, Lightbringer!" he called out. Again he saw the glint and light bend and again he dove and rolled to avoid it. "Shui!" he called, "It's me!"

The air shimmered for a second, and then the dark blue armored body of Shui came into view. "Michael, is that really you? What happened to your-" Shui began, before a kinetic round removed Shui's head.

Michael dove for an energy rifle formerly belonging to a trud who had been sliced in two by Shui. He rolled up and rapidly fired blasts at two assaulting troopers; they took multiple rounds before falling.

Overhead, Eaglestrike roared by. She cut down two mid-flight, before succumbing to a hail of energy blasts that came from a dozen different truds. The truds were gaining a foothold and beginning to concentrate their fire. Michael knew he needed more powerful weapons. He sprinted for the hall and his wings.

Just inside the Fortress, he saw two armored trud bodies, and just beyond, Martha lay wounded on the floor. Michael ran to her and knelt down, more to learn if hostiles had penetrated to the interior than to see if she was okay; she could be regenerated after all. Martha Suncatcher tried to speak to Michael, but had no breath to do so. She waved him on. Suncatcher was not in pain, for she was not really capable of feeling it, and she could still drop any trud who came through the door. So Michael continued to the suiting chamber.

He did not see the body of Rex lying beyond the download chairs, nor did he see that the computer brain was more than half dead. He was too focused on the mission to notice those things. Instead, he stepped in the arched recess. If nothing else worked, the suiting chamber still did. The latches clicked, liquid metal flowed over, and Michael Lightbringer was once again a dark angel of death. As he left the recess, he looked at the stand that would normally hold his helmet. Not having time to question its absence, he flew out of the room and launched himself through one of the corridor's blasted-out observatory windows and into the sky beyond.

Each gauntleted fist sent forth their deadly invisible beams, melting one trud and then another. Michael rolled low to the surface of Magritte and cut down four more truds. He rolled again and saw his old friend Dante emerge from another corridor, crushing the nearest truds with his bare hands. Raptorscream continued with his slashing technique, and Michael even thought he caught a glimmer of green as truds fell from seeming nothingness.

The Guardians were now gaining the advantage as the trud ranks thinned. A few more minutes, and it was over.

Michael looked towards the horizon. Fortress Miyazaki was clearly destroyed in its entirely, but it was obvious that a battle still raged on Fortress Monet.

"Aren't you coming?" Dante asked Michael.

"What?" Michael asked, confused that they weren't all immediately flying to Monet's relief.

"The brief and reassemble," Dante replied, confused himself at Michael's response.

Perhaps only Michael's communications were down, he didn't have his helmet after all, and the other Guardians had received the order directly. Michael assumed that Rex had new orders or intel for the Guardians to act on. Michael turned towards the suiting chamber and ran. His mission once more raced to the forefront of his mind. Now that the immediate threat of the jetpackers seemed to have subsided, Michael needed to see Rex. He had to tell them of the terrible new weapon that would be unleashed in the midst of the chaos. It was imperative that Michael communicate to Rex what he had learned, that there was likely going to be a second attack, and that they use his knowledge to counterattack the trud's base as soon as possible, to forestall this new weapon before they could release it.

Michael ran down the corridor behind Dante. They passed Suncatcher's body without so much as a second glance, knowing it would only be a short period of time before she was regenerated and better than ever. Running around the final corner to the suiting chamber, he saw Gabriella, radiant in her silver armor, and stopped dead in his tracks. For just beyond her, in one of the download chairs, he suddenly saw the headless body with a large scar on its right forearm. And on the floor to the side of the headless body, was Rex Skyguard.

Rex was shaking, but not dead. Michael had never seen Rex in a moment of weakness. To see him convulsing on the floor was an unknown experience... it was... uncertainty. Rex had always been there to command, to direct, and now...

Talongrip was talking, "Suncatcher, Eaglestrike, Shui, and Xue are fallen."

Lightbringer walked over past Stormcaller and knelt down next to Skyguard as Talongrip continued, "Razorwing and Raptorscream are still outside, guarding against any stragglers or a second assault. The maintenance bays are still working: switch out your armor if necessary. Lightbringer, you called us to assemble. What do you have to say?"

Michael looked up, startled. He had no recollection of calling the assembly and no communications to do so. But before he could reply, the response came from a black figure in the doorway.

"I managed to tap into what's left of Magritte, the weapon system-" the figure said, removing his helmet.

When he heard his own voice, Michael Lightbringer looked up from the side of Rex and saw that it was a copy of himself who stood across the threshold.

103. Visions

Damien checked the nova bombs one last time, crawled into the combat sled, and toggled the switches on. Everything looked good. He was almost ready. But Damien Musashi couldn't attack just yet. He needed to wait for the order. It would take some of the other teams longer to get in place, but they would need to all attack together if it was to work. He couldn't destroy them all himself. And besides, there was one more thing for Damien to do.

He slid back out and stood from the sled. Damien walked to the robots with biocircuits, the robots animated in part by the Greendust. The biobots. Damien knew what to do; he had seen it in one of the minds, when for a brief moment he was part of the Network itself. He wondered if it was the original design, or whether Niles had customized it this way just to fulfill the dreams of Damien's childhood mind. Was Damien being manipulated by some crude effort to play off his name, his desire for a connection to the past, some echo of want? Or was this merely a sign of what he was always destined to be? Had Niles read his mind, his almost forgotten fantasies, or was it merely practical and how it was always done? Damien decided it did not matter. He did as he saw in the mind and took the tenugui from where it rested on the shoulder of one of the biobots. Damien held the headband between his face and the "face" of the organic robot. The fibers looked like ordinary cloth to Damien's eyes, but Damien's mind knew it was much more. What looked like Japanese silk was in fact a sophisticated headband woven with sensors and circuitry. Damien looked once more at the face of the biobot before tying the tenugui around his head. And then, as if emerging from the fog, the images came to Damien's mind. Damien saw what the biobot saw: the face of Damien staring back at himself.

Soon, one by one, Damien saw what the other biobots in the room saw also. The multiple views were not remotely as overwhelming as when he saw into the minds of the Network. Damien was not experiencing the biobots' being; he was merely seeing. Yet there was one thing beyond seeing that Damien could do.

Damien thought the thought, and the four biobots raised their Gatling-style cannons above their shoulders accordingly.

"Who wants to join me in crashing a floater?" Damien asked aloud.

The four biobots stepped forward in unison.

104. Dead End Corridors

Steve Greylox strode down the corridor. The corridors were very empty now. Most of the inhabitants were occupied with the assault, and this section of the tunnels didn't have much of a role to play in that. He didn't see a single person as he made his way to the corridors formerly used by Doctor Psycho for his various experiments and where they had held the Guardian. He hadn't been down here in a long time. The last time was when he stole Eve's personnel file and assessments. The assessments had not been wrong, and he had used them to good effect. The young could be like putty.

He brushed aside the gray lock that always fell across his forehead. He would have preferred to do it cleaner: gas, a bomb, a proxy would have been best of all. But many of his tools had been exhausted. He had used Eve as best he could, and now only time would tell whether her destiny was to join him forever or to die. Once she had become known, Flora had become a dangerous traceable link, and her skills with all manner of poisonous compounds were buried in the dirt, probably providing fertilizer for some flower or tree. And the Organization's security meant carrying an area-effect weapon into the facility himself was too dangerous. So, it had come down to him, his wits, and a ballistic slinger. It would be dirty, but it would be done. And when he succeeded, he would finally get his payment. The Organization's unfolding assault would fail. He knew all along it would fail. What he was about to take care of was more important by far.

These people had seen all too much. They knew things about gen technology, things that were dangerous to the gens. He had convinced Blue that they were dangerous to natural humans, too. That might have been true, but Greylox could not care less. It was merely necessary to convince Blue so that he could do what he had always done. Once again, he would set back the truds. Once again, he would destroy those who had the most power to hurt the gens before they even realized the power of the knowledge they possessed. His eternal life would be wages well earned.

This one had been harder than most, but he was systematically closing the noose. Soon, Red would have no friends left. The trud attack would fail, they always did, and then he would finally have the prize.

And now in the chaos of the battles raging or soon to be raging above, he would eliminate those who had the knowledge and those that might protect Red.

Assassination was quite easy if the quarry wasn't expecting it. And Greylox knew that these truds still had no clue. Blue told him where to find them. He'd probably have to kill her, too, in the end.

When he opened the door, they didn't even have time to look surprised. Sergeants Krantz and Stern fell dead to the floor.

"Now, my dead friends, if only you could tell me where I might find Jack and Maren," Greylox said to the corpses, as he stepped over the bodies to check two more interior rooms. Satisfied that they weren't there, he left as quickly as he had arrived.

**

Franklin peeked out from the closet. Stern had been angry at Franklin, thrown him in the closet, and told him if he emerged before Stern said he could, he would get a demerit. Franklin had heard the pops of the slinger, the bodies fall to the ground, and the words that followed from a stranger's voice. He waited just long enough that he thought it would be safe to crack open the door. It hadn't been quite long enough for safety; Franklin saw the man with the long gray locks of hair leave the back rooms and exit the corridor.

Franklin sunk back into the darkness of the closet and waited. He listened intently and then waited a few moments longer, and decided the coast was clear. He peeked out again and saw the bodies of Stern and Krantz. The sight spurred him to action. It only took Franklin a second to reach the intruder alarm and he pulled it, waiting to once again collapse into an unconscious pile and hoping to inflict the same upon the man with the gray hair who had killed his friends, and who now hunted Maren and Jack. The shielded quick reaction force would then converge on the area and take care of the intruder.

Franklin stared at the pulled alarm lever and waited. And waited. But nothing happened. He ran over to the other wall and tried the intercom. It too was dead.

Franklin hit the wall and uncharacteristically swore aloud. He turned quickly and ran half way out the door before stopping and running back into the room. Franklin heaved and rolled over Sergeant Stern's body, allowing him to pull out the rail gun. Thus armed, Franklin ran out the door once more.

**

Franklin threw the door open, rail gun at the shoulder ready for action.

Jack looked up startled, paper files in hand, burn barrel in front of his desk, ventilator at full blast. Jack threw the files he had been holding into the burning barrel as electric arcs crackled. "How did you find out?" Jack asked.

"Rosie Krantz and Gildur Stern are dead!" Franklin yelled. "Are you okay?"

"What? Krantz and Stern?" Jack had at first thought that somehow someone had discovered that he was destroying the files on Maren, that they planned to flee, and he would be arrested... but Franklin didn't seem the least concerned with the burning papers and ventilation fans moving at full speed.

Franklin was obviously agitated, eyes wide open, nervously scanning the room, the rail gun still at the shoulder. "They were murdered. A man with long gray hair killed Sergeant Stern and Krantz," he said quickly. "Marched right in and shot them dead. Then said he would be coming for you and Maren."

Franklin went back out to the hall to check in both directions, before stepping back inside and shutting the door. "The alarms and intercoms don't work, either. And nobody but us is left in this part of the complex!"

"Relax, Franklin. Who was it that killed-"

"I don't know!" Franklin yelled. "All I know is that he just killed Stern and Krantz and he's coming for you and Maren next!"

"Can you describe him?"

"Just the gray hair. A middle aged guy in blue pants, a black shirt, and long gray hair. That's all I could see."

"Franklin, you go find Red. Tell him what happened." Jack threw the rest of the box of papers into the fire and picked up his sidearm. All the paper at once might burn down the office, but that didn't matter anymore. "I'm going to find Maren."

Franklin was already noticeably calmer. Jack had given him an order and knew what to do. After opening the door cautiously, he scanned both ways before disappearing into the corridors, rail gun still at the ready.

105. Broken Silence

"Kill it," Gabriella said, raising her gauntleted fist at Michael.

"No!" Rex hoarsely commanded. "He is Michael. Do not kill him," Rex rasped.

"We don't know what the first one did to Rex," Gabriella said. "Who's to say that what cooked Magritte didn't also affect Rex's mind?"

"Gabriella, don't you know me?" Michael said.

"How could I know you? I have no idea if you are who you say you are, and if you are, what they might have done to you."

"We must listen to Rex," Dante said.

"That weapon that attacked the organic brain might have infected Rex," Gabriella said, gauntleted fist still aimed at Michael. "Rex and Magritte are linked. What affects one affects the other. We can't trust Rex anymore."

"If we can't trust Rex, then whom can we trust?" Talongrip asked.

"The Ancients," Michael said as he knelt next to Rex, a blue aura growing brighter around him.

"What are you doing?" Gabriella asked.

The blue aura around Michael grew brighter. "Ensuring that you listen to me. I'm close enough to the brain, if you kill me, the nova device will destroy it and the fortress."

"I knew you could not be trusted!"

"If I could not be trusted, I would have already nova'd, and Fortress Magritte would already be crashing to the ground. No, I did this because I am Michael Lightbringer, Guardian of the West. And I must tell the Ancients what I have learned, what I have seen."

"Don't believe him," Gabriella commanded.

"What choice do we have?" Dante said as Lightbringer's nova device burned bright blue.

"Listen to me," Rex managed. "Come closer, Michael."

Michael leaned in close. A drop of blood began to run down Rex's cheek from the corner of his eye.

Rex lifted up one hand and placed it at Michael's temple. He tried to lift the other arm, but couldn't. "Help me, Michael, with my other hand."

Michael saw him struggle with his arm again and then helped Rex lift it.

"To the other side," Rex said. Michael raised the hand to the other side of his head. The drop of blood hung on the edge of Rex's jaw...

Michael felt a warm buzz in his mind. And then he saw a man walk up to him. It was not a man he had seen before, but there was something familiar about his face, something that reminded him of himself in the mirror. And at once Michael knew that after all of these years, after all of his service, he finally knelt before an Ancient.

"Michael," he began, "you do not need to tell me anything. I have seen it all."

"Then why have you remained silent? And why have you not stopped this destruction?" Michael questioned.

"Few could comprehend. And I have not stopped it because I am the one who planned it."

106. A Visit

Franklin's lungs burned. It was a long way through the tunnels from Doctor Psycho's quarters to the hidden command bunker of Colonel Red.

"Hello, Franklin," Red said without turning around. There would have been alarms if Franklin's visit was about something important. Plus, there was a battle unfolding that demanded his attention. Red had back-up systems in place to make sure he couldn't be surprised. The face scanner told him a few minutes ago that Franklin was on his way, and Red had no concerns whatsoever about the loyalty of Franklin. The face scanner did not tell him, however, about the panic painted across Franklin's face. So Red didn't give his complete attention until Franklin was midway through the details.

"And he said specifically he was going after Maren?" Red asked.

"Yes, and Jack. He said he was going after Maren and Jack."

"Describe him to me again," Red said and he spun his chair to the surveillance monitors.

"Gray hair, middle aged man, thin I guess... I only saw him for a moment."

"That may be enough," Red said. Sure enough, the surveillance cameras, just like the internal intercoms and alarms, were disabled. But not the historical archives. Red brought up a picture from long ago and displayed it on the monitor.

"Yes!" Franklin said. "That's him!"

"Greylox. It had to be. And there is only one person who could have helped him shut these systems down," Red opened his desk drawer and took out a short barreled auto-shotgun. "Come on Franklin, we're going to pay Blue a little visit."

107. Warning Signs

Jack ran through the corridors. He had to get to Maren before the assassin or he had to find a way to inform her of the danger. The first few times that he passed alarm systems, he ripped off the covers and pulled the handle or pushed the stun button hopefully, but to no avail. After the fourth one in a row didn't work, he gave up and ran faster.

The fact that the assassin had managed to disable the communications in the tunnels and kill Stern and Krantz almost without detection meant the assassin knew what he was doing. The assassin had access, or more worryingly, was already part of the Organization.

Jack began to wonder. Had he inadvertently triggered some alarm mechanism while digging around in Doctor Psycho's files? Had someone else broken into his own office and looked at the reams of paper he had collected? Had someone bugged their quarters and overheard his conversation with Maren? How did they find out about her? Why now? There were no answers for Jack, and there never would be.

As he rounded one of the many corners in the twisting and turning underground corridors, he saw a woman he recognized from one of the research labs.

She looked at Jack as he ran with his side arm drawn, and the concern on her face was obvious.

"There is an intruder!" Jack said. "I need you to grab your weapon and come with me."

"Sir, we aren't authorized to have weapons."

"Well, go find an officer to open a weapons locker and follow as soon as you can! The intruder is male, he's got long gray hair, blue pants, black shirt. He's killing people! That's all I've got, now go, sound the alarm!" Even if the assassin was part of the NHA, he couldn't get away with openly killing NHA soldiers if the rest of the foot soldiers knew about it, no matter what high connections the assassin might have.

Before the woman could turn to do as she was ordered, Jack was already off running again.

108. Walls and Doorways

Red entered the room and found Colonel Blue in one of the intelligence nodes. She looked up from the screens to see the stern bald head of Red. And he didn't look happy.

"Red, I didn't expect you to be here at this critical hour," she said, pretending to only pay half-attention to him as she monitored reports coming in on the assaults across the entire sector.

"I need you to turn the systems back on immediately."

"Red, I haven't turned any systems off," she said, staring too intently at the screens and not looking up again. "What are you talking about?"

"The internal coms, the alarms, the surveillance tapes... you know exactly what I am talking about," Red said, auto-shotgun at the hip, but nevertheless pointed firmly in her direction. It would be close enough if it came to that.

Blue shook her head and finally spun away from the monitors to focus on Colonel Red. "The stress of the operation must have gotten to you-" she began.

"Blue, don't try to tell me I'm not thinking clearly. You may have shut down most of the internal systems, but you didn't manage to shut down all of the surveillance cameras down here," Red lied. "I have a few extra cameras, not linked to the rest. And so I have images of you and another man. You and I both know who that man is. His name is Greylox."

The bluff about the cameras and the images worked. Red could tell by the look on her face that he had guessed correctly.

"Plus," Red went on, "you haven't bothered to ask why I am pointing an auto-shotgun at you."

She merely stared back at Red for a moment, not saying a word.

"Well, Blue, would you please turn on the systems?" Red said. "Time is short."

"I'm not talking with you as long as you have that shotgun pointed at me, like an enemy." She sat there in silence.

"Very well, I'll lower my weapon," Red relaxed his arm, and the barrel glided towards the floor. It was already too late for Red to get to Maren before Greylox, but perhaps not too late to warn her and send closer NHA personnel into the area. He didn't have time to argue; he needed the systems back on. But he also had no desire to kill Blue if he didn't have to do so. "Now, please turn the systems back on."

"Soon, we will have won," Blue said. "The gens' armies will be destroyed. The threat will then come from ourselves. You know this as well as I do. Doctor Psycho's projects must be wiped clean. Things must be dismantled before they are used for the wrong purposes."

"And by 'dismantle' you mean killing people?" Red scoffed. "I never thought you would walk down the path toward Fanatic."

"I've always sworn to protect natural humans and Greylox has helped me-"

"Don't be a fool! Greylox doesn't work for you; you work for Greylox. He doesn't care about truds, he just wants to keep things like they are forever. He's eliminating key people and trying to destroy our ability to-"

Blue interrupted him calmly. "Once the gens are gone, it will just be us truds again, and we can't let any gen technology threaten us. Those who have gotten too close must be cleansed."

"Like the Doctor? Was he one of the people who had to be cleansed, who you had murdered?"

"His services were appreciated, but the good Doctor alone could create some of the modology technologies, and while he might not have voluntarily done so, there are other elements, as you know, that could have forced him to do so."

"You have no idea who Greylox really is, do you? Who he ultimately works for? What he plans to-"

In an instant, the gun slid out from her sleeve and directly into her palm. She had the drop on Red, the barrel of her gun pointed directly at Red's head. "Felix, if you so much as raise that barrel an inch, you're a dead man. Drop it."

He released the auto-shotgun, and it clanked onto the floor.

"I don't believe you," Blue said. "Greylox is helping me. He understands that modology and those who understand it must be cleansed."

"I suppose you exempt yourself from the cleansing," Red said sarcastically.

Blue smiled. "Goodbye, Red. I've had enough of justifying myself to you."

A shot echoed out.

And Blue fell off her chair to the ground, dead.

"Thanks, Franklin," Red said loudly, "though you could have pulled the trigger a little sooner. I was getting nervous."

Franklin stepped into the doorway from the hallway with a red circle around his right eye. He had held the scope so tightly to his eye socket that it had left an impression. Franklin rubbed his right eye with his left hand, almost as if had just awoken from a short nap, with the railgun still in his right. "I couldn't get the scope to stop focusing three walls over instead of only through one wall," Franklin said apologetically.

"You could have simply stepped into the doorway and avoided the fancy see-through-the-walls scope."

"Huh. Didn't think of that," Franklin said.

Colonel Red stepped over Blue's body to the monitors and reactivated the internal systems. "I'm sending anyone in the area to Maren and Jack. Let's just hope they get to Maren and Jack before Greylox." He flipped one more electronic switch, sending the message through the air to anyone who could hear it, and hoping that one in particular would get it in time.

109. Last Run

Greylox cautiously walked through the hallways, ballistic slinger tucked into his belt, shirt loosely hanging over it. She was down here, somewhere. He had seen exactly where her quarters were located on the plan view of the facility, but the architecture drawings had not been entirely accurate. Such things were to be expected in a covert facility dug out haphazardly over generations. Nevertheless, he was close, and he knew it. Blue had told him the room number, and judging by the numbers he walked by, he was almost there.

She was the most dangerous of them all, but Maren probably didn't even realize it. Eve hadn't given any indication that Maren knew what she really was. To be sure, Greylox wasn't certain what Maren was either, but the evidence was strong. Strong enough to justify his actions, anyway.

And then he was there. The number above the room was the right one. He continued walking down the hallway, looking both ways for anyone in the vicinity, before doubling back to the door. Greylox pulled out the slinger and gently tried the handle. It was locked. He took one step back from the door, lifted his leg, and kicked at where the handle met the door jam. The door flung open, and Greylox stepped inside, gun held in a double grip at eye level.

He visually scanned the room. Clothes and objects lay strewn about the room. A duffel-bag lay half-filled on the bed. It looked like either the room had been ransacked, or that someone was planning to leave in a hurry. He checked the closet and the bathroom, but the girl was not there. Had she escaped?

Greylox went back to the bed and the duffel-bag. Maybe there would be a clue. He turned the duffel upside down, and shook out the contents. Clothes, a few functional objects... nothing personal. Not a picture, not a book, not a diary. The only thing that made Greylox certain it was indeed her room and her bag was the NHA identification card.

He could wait there for her, but what if she had already left? And there were others to eliminate, so he tucked his slinger into his waistband, pulled the shirt over, and stepped towards the door.

In the hallway, he slowly pulled the door shut behind him, but due to the forced entry, the door merely creaked open again.

Bam! A shot rang out, blood spattered up to his cheek, and Greylox fell back into the room. Greylox grunted and looked at where the metal flechettes had torn apart his left deltoid. It was a bad wound, bad enough he might bleed out, he realized. He grabbed one of the shirts strewn about the room and did the best he could with one arm to tie it around the left shoulder tightly. It wasn't a very good job, but it was the best he could do in the circumstances. That taken care of, he picked up the slinger again. If whoever shot him came through that door, Greylox would shoot him dead.

**

Jack studied the doorway from one knee. He had hit him, alright, of that he was sure. The brief cloud of red mist and the blood droplets on the wall confirmed it. But the assassin had turned at the last minute, and Jack wasn't sure he got him in the chest where the flechettes would ensure a quick death. So Jack stayed on one knee, watching the doorway. His heart pounded in his chest. Had he been too late? Was Maren already dead in her room? What if he had run faster? What if he wouldn't have stopped to talk with the lab technician? What if...

Maren rounded the corner. Jack was on one end of the hallway, Maren on the other, the assassin in her room in between.

Jack stood and waved his arms, trying not to say anything, trying not to give the assassin any information if he happened to still be alive.

"Jack!" she greeted him, not able to quickly read the concern on his face down the hall.

Greylox heard it in the room, and knew who it had to be. And he knew it came from the opposite direction from which the shot came, as his shredded shoulder attested.

"Run! In the other direction!" Jack yelled.

It took a moment for it to register in Maren's mind.

"They're trying to kill you! Run away!" Jack yelled. "Keep running away from here! Don't stop!"

Maren heard the terror in Jack's voice, and she turned and ran.

Greylox, of course, heard it all. He was bleeding. They knew where he was. There was no way out other than through the door. His situation was not going to improve with time. And she had to be killed.

He leaned out the door and fired rapidly at Jack. It was enough to drive Jack back around the corner temporarily, having been distracted from careful aim on the doorway by Maren. But it was only temporary: Jack leaned low around the corner and fired two more flechette rounds in quick succession. Part of both rounds hit Greylox in the lower back and upper leg, but then the assassin was gone around the corner – after Maren.

Jack was already sprinting after. He would do everything possible to save Maren, even if it meant dying. He ran faster than he thought he could down the hall. But when he rounded the corner, he had not expected to see the barrel of a ballistic slinger and the assassin tight against the wall. Jack didn't have time to react before he fell to the ground, dead.

Greylox spit on the ground. Greylox had been in the business a long time, and no one else had managed to shoot him three times. He hated that man, Jack. But in a way, he grudgingly acknowledged Jack had heart.

Greylox turned and limped after Maren, trailing blood all the way.

**

Maren ran a short distance before she heard the shot. It was not the sound of Jack's side arm, but of a conventional lead slinger. She listened intently, but did not hear any additional shots. She wanted to go back, to somehow see if she could help Jack, but instead she listened to the urgency that had been in Jack's voice commanding her to flee. She didn't know who wanted to kill her. She didn't know how many hunted her. All she knew is that Jack had said to run and to not stop. And so she ran for her life.

110. One Left

Michael did not understand. The Ancient stood before him. The Ancient said it was all part of the plan. But what was happening was the destruction of the fortresses, the destruction of the Guardians, an assault on the gens themselves. "Why would you destroy that which protects you?" Michael asked.

"The time for that has passed. The Event is at hand."

"How can this all be part of your plan to destroy the truds?"

"The Event means the end of us having to deal with the truds, not the end of them. They have long feared we would take the earth from them. But my plan ensures the contrary. We will leave the world to them. The meek shall inherit the earth, but the rest of the universe belongs to us."

"Why is this death and destruction necessary if the Ancients only plan to leave?" Lightbringer asked.

"It doesn't really even make sense to call us 'Ancients,' as if we were just really old versions of what we were before. The truds have the idea that we are all like the gens that they forced out of the east. It would be nearly impossible for them to understand us now, our ways of thinking, our struggles among each other, the conflict within ourselves," the man said.

He continued. "We are not one in thought, word, or deed. And so my true battle, my true subterfuge, has not been with and among the truds, but among the modifieds, the gens, and those that came after. I needed enough of them to believe that the truds are still dangerous, enough to sway the vote, enough to cause us finally to leave where we have tarried too long. And so the destruction unfolds."

"What will happen to Magritte?" Michael asked.

"Magritte and the other fortresses will be allowed to be destroyed. It is necessary for me to succeed in convincing the others. We'll let the truds think they've won. They will figure it out eventually, of course. In the meantime, perhaps hundreds of years, however, they won't waste any of their energy trying to come after us."

"You will allow those who served you so loyally to be destroyed?"

"No, Michael. Rex, the Guardians, all will be restored on a new world. They won't even remember the end of Magritte-"

"But I want to remember."

"You want to remember? Tell me more."

"I am not the same Michael Lightbringer that slipped beneath the waves. Why should I be any different than you? You try to preserve what you once were and what you have become. Why shouldn't I? "

"My dear Michael, if some of us could forget parts of our past, we would. Some have. Some of us can't."

"But I am a Guardian of the West. I have sworn to protect you. Always. If I am no longer needed to protect you, then what I am now?"

"What you will make for yourself, in a new place, a new time. Everything will be made new."

"No."

The Ancient stood before Michael in silence.

"The other Michael, the one restored after I was fallen... he is me as I once was. But now I am no longer him, and he is not me. We are different. And I don't want to forget. Let the other one awake to your new world."

"This is what you want?"

"Yes."

"Then there is but one left to protect."

And without another word, Michael understood.

Rex's hand dropped from Michael's temple, the buzzing in Lightbringer's mind stopped, the Ancient disappeared, and the drop of blood fell from Rex's jaw.

Michael was once again aware of the others around him.

Rex spoke for one last time to the assembled Guardians of the West. "Let Lightbringer leave... The final assault has begun."

111. Slippery Fish

Greylox broke into a trot, then a jog, and was soon running at full speed. His prey was close. And the adrenaline seemed to be kicking in. He didn't feel any pain in his shoulder, and while he felt every stride in his leg and back, the thought of the prize carried him on. The only way this day could be better is if Red were dead. But he would have to wait for another day.

It was quite simple. He just followed the main hallway. If Maren would have ducked into a side room early, he would have run right by her, and he knew it. But he figured that Maren would do as Jack had told her, that she would run for the surface. And so he followed the main line.

When the hall narrowed, and a door to the unmaintained tunnels was left open, he knew she had gone through it. He stepped into the tunnels, and followed the sign that pointed the way to the city above. He had not been in the tunnel long when he heard her grunt as she vaulted over some piping that crossed the main route out. Then he was certain he was closing the gap.

It was warmer in the tunnel, his wounds continued to drip blood, and he began to feel a little light headed. But he pressed on. She would not escape. Not this time.

**

MODIFIED HORIZON

Maren popped open the door to the utility room in the basement of the building. And as she stepped through, it felt like someone hit her in the leg with a baseball bat. She fell through the door and looked down at her leg. Blood streamed out of the bullet wound from the front of the calf. The smaller hole in the back looked black for a second before the blood began to ooze out of it, too. So that is what it feels like to be shot, she thought to herself.

She wasn't eager to experience it again. Maren stood. Her leg held. It was agony to move the foot at the ankle, but she climbed the stairs. Just before she made it to the top, she saw him emerge from the utility door below.

Greylox fired four quick shots which missed or bounced off the metal stairway. Maren went through the doorway and out of view, but not before Greylox had seen that his earlier shot had hit home. Now she would be slower, and there would be a trail to follow.

**

Maren emerged into the sunshine. And above her, Fortress Margritte crept closer to the earth below.

Greylox was right behind her. He took careful aim and... Click!

That is just one of the reasons he hated old trud technology. One didn't have to bother counting energy blasts or how many pulses one had left. He threw the worthless ballistic slinger away. He would have to use his hands; he would have to get in close. He slipped his hand into his pocket and found the smooth metallic circle of the pulse generator.

Maren limped forward, but she would not get away now. She looked back over her shoulder and gripped her emerald pendant tightly as Greylox moved closer, pulse disk in hand.

And then he saw it. Finally, after all of his efforts, after all he had done, after he had flushed her out into the open...

The Guardian's black wings spread wide and the dark haired angel of the gens landed by Maren.

Greylox smiled. He was right. The Ancients cared about this one. They cared enough to send a Guardian to ensure the finality of it all. He had done well. He had flushed out the prize into the open. He had served the Ancients. At last the gens had realized his importance. At last the gens sent someone to help him. Eternity would be his. At last...

303

The black armored Guardian of the West raised his fist towards Greylox and melted him into a pile of goo.

"Come with me," Michael said to Maren. "We are leaving this all."

112. Rise and Fall

The concrete roof of the tunnel exploded upward, and Damien flew forth on the combat sled, two biobots flanking him on each side. Finally, Damien rose in the air to challenge those who had set themselves as gods above all others. But Damien was just the harbinger, for after him the heavens would be opened. And through the defenseless skies, the missiles would rise with their payloads of Dreptex and Greendust, and the world would be made anew.

The biobots, their minds linked to Damien's mind, moved in unison. Damien could feel them all. And he felt one more thing: the hint of another mind within his own.

Other sleds rose in the air, but Damien was ahead of them all. As he neared the flagging fortress, a number of specks appears and launched themselves into the air.

The battle was on.

The biobots flew forward. One of the specks grew larger. Damien could see that it was orange, and at the same moment the biobots let forth a stream of burning rounds from their gatling cannons. The four streams of fire converged on the orange guardian. There was no deflecting that many rounds from different angles. The bits that fell to the earth were hardly identifiable as once being of humanoid shape.

Then one of the biobots split in two. Damien could not see what hit it. Then a second biobot was cut diagonally across the chest, but before it cut out, Damien had seen through the biobot's eyes the shimmer of a guardian.

Damien willed the other two biobots to spray the vicinity widely, and by luck he saw a round deflect off of seeming nothingness. The two concentrated their fire and Rang's light-bending armor failed before he was cut to shreds.

The other sleds were now engaging the other guardians. Damien flew higher and prepped the first nova-bomb pass. He dropped a string of them where the targeting computer told him the main chamber should be, then arched up higher above the fortress for the detonation.

He heard the crackle and saw the flash of the nova bombs, each in sequence, opening a tunnel to the fortress's central brain.

At the apex of his climb, something quite unexpected happened. Damien's combat sled began to come apart. But it was not breaking up; it was moving steadily away from him in all directions. For a split second at the apex of his climb, Damien hung in the air, the pieces of the sled suspended around him, before he began to fall. And as he did so, the pieces came back to him. He felt them connecting to his artificial arms, legs, and spine. The power surged through him and he felt the mind of Niles: "This is but a foretaste..."

The armor felt natural. It was an extension of his body. Just as the artificial limbs were an improvement, he felt the power armor had always been meant to be. And just as Niles had opened his mind to the Network, he understand there were many more levels to go. This was all part of the Network's plan, and he was glad for it.

Damien dived in his power armor towards Fortress Magritte, a biobot flanking him on either side. There was nothing to stop him. A silver guardian tried, but failed.

He placed two nova bombs on the brain and the central power core, and launched himself back into the sky, into a world about to be remade anew.

113. Window of Opportunity

Niles saw all that Damien did in his mind. And he saw Fortress Magritte fall to the ground. But that was only one of many. In the immediate vicinity, Fortress Miyazaki and Fortress Monet also fell. And farther away, the others came crashing down, too.

And thus the door was opened for the first time. The gens were vulnerable and the Network would make the most of it.

Niles gave the command, and the missiles rose towards the heavens, carrying their warheads of Dreptex, the substance that would cleanse the earth forever of the gens. The final addition of the Greendust would ensure its completeness. Or so they had planned.

Niles felt a buzzing headache again. The headaches seemed to be happening more frequently. It must be the collective stress of the Network.

And then he saw the shadow before him.

Niles smiled through his scars. "You are too late."

"I don't think so," said the shadow.

"You see, your plan has failed miserably. We are the victors. The Dreptex will soon rain down upon the planet. There will be no escape. Its distribution will be complete," Niles bragged. "It will grow, it will stop them all. Your plan was not enough."

"No, it has worked only too well, only too well. Already, the wheels are turning that will change this world forever. It is only a short time now," the shadow said.

307

"A short time until your destruction."

The shadow ignored his taunt. "I wanted to thank you, to let you know I had your best interests at heart. The Event has finally drawn near. But it is not the event you had planned, nor is it the Event you imagined the gens' planned."

Niles laughed dismissively through his headache. "You'll see soon enough what we had planned. The missiles cannot be stopped now."

"No, they cannot be. Which is why I am only telling you now. I think you'll find that your missiles make quite pretty green fireworks."

"You know of the Greendust?" Niles asked, surprised.

"Of course. I made it. It's specially designed, and among its properties it just happens to neutralize Dreptex-like compounds."

"That's impossible! We saw it discovered! We felt it in our veins!"

"You saw what I wanted you to see."

"It was alive, we could feel it... it will do as we command," Niles insisted.

"No, I am its master," the shadow said. "When I learned you were making Dreptex, I knew you would not hesitate to use it, even if it meant you killed the world. And when I knew you could not be stopped from using it, I knew what needed to be done to stop it, to co-opt it for other purposes. The hard part was getting you to willingly mix in a compound that would make it inert, that answered to me."

"Impossible. We saw Damien's mind. He discovered the Greendust in the tunnels."

"You saw through Damien's eyes, who believed what Red and I had arranged. We identified him as useful for this purpose quite some time ago. Years, as a matter of fact. Damien found what we wanted him to find. He joined those whom we wanted him to join. If it makes you feel any better, Damien didn't know that he was thwarting you. You had him convinced."

Niles stood frozen.

"I'm afraid your missiles will be merely be a demonstration of what might have been. If it makes you feel better, it would have worked, to a degree, were it not for the Greendust. I needed to prod, not hammer, my gen opposition, and that I have accomplished. Many were not convinced that the truds posed any threat, and they grew complacent with the status quo. This was the first attack in many years to get close to the Ancients and it has shaken them out of their complacency."

"You've betrayed us!" Niles yelled.

"Do you really think it would have been possible for the Organization or the Network to survive this long without some help? Do you still not comprehend what we are capable of? How many of those whom you claim to be a part of, who called themselves truds, betrayed the cause? Many truds tried to help the gens. Could you not conceive of the possibility that some of the gens would likewise have reason to help the truds? Some of us remember the time before."

"We remember the time before, too," Niles said. "That is why we must destroy you, for what you and your kind wrought then, the way you treated us like slaves, the way you killed us, robbed us of hope. You made yourselves gods and oppressed us, the weak, the meek. Someone had to be powerful enough to avenge them, to regain the earth for those for whom it was intended."

"Well, my friend, now that very thing shall be fulfilled. But you are no longer the weak or the meek. You are more gen now than trud. And so you are coming with us."

"We'll never give up what we've become. We'll never stop trying to destroy you after what you've done. We won't stop until we see the end of you."

"You may well yet see it. But it won't be here. Come. We leave for New Worlds."

114. Contention

"Well, my friend," Felix said, "it seems that after these many years, we finally managed to do it."

"Indeed," the shadow said. "As you can imagine, there are a few gens who are furious, but the undecided have now been swayed, and those who wanted to stay have been outvoted."

"Do you think there is any risk of your involvement being discovered?" Felix asked.

"Between now and when we leave Earth, beyond the Barrier? None. But one day, knowledge of my role is inevitable. The data is there; it only needs to be discovered. By that time, however, reality will have changed the nature of the debate. Don't worry about me, Felix."

"I hate to be selfish, but I was also thinking of myself. Does anything indicate the NHA is aware of my role? They would not understand that I was helping the truds by helping you influence the others. If they knew who you truly are..."

"No, my friend. No one knows that you knew our goal. The Council meets even now, and all of their reports will indicate that your attack was successful as far as it went. They may even think for a while that we have been completely destroyed as they learn of the green rain and then find no trace of us. You are safe, Felix."

"And Clara? Is she safe?"

"Thank you for watching over her. I got your message in time: she lives. She is like a daughter to me, but there comes a time when every parent must let their children chart their own path. And there is yet one who has chosen to walk that path with her."

The shadow laughed.

"What is so funny?" Felix asked.

"A conversation with the one you sometimes call Niles: at this very moment he is not too happy about joining the rest of us as we depart for new worlds. The True Core base raid you set up long ago turned out to be the ruse to finally trick the Network. Niles found it quite convincing, especially when he read Damien's mind about the Greendust from so long ago. But now he is quite angry with me. The connection is obscure, but he reminds me of an animal that after many years still hisses at the keeper who has rescued the animal from certain death, nursed it through the healing process, and continues to provide for it in its even though it may never be strong enough to survive on its own, for its wounds are deep. I could laugh or I could cry about Niles and the Network. I choose to laugh, though not to his face. Now that his goals have been accomplished, albeit probably not in the way he intended, he can't let go of what he's become. In time, I have hope he will change. But one can never know. It is for him to decide, not me."

"Even after all this time, there are truds who still fight, who think it possible to contend with your kind."

"You contend with me, Felix."

"But not in the same manner."

"No, not in the same manner indeed. But contend you do."

Epilogue

I wish I could say it was the end of conflict on Earth and in the heavens above, but it was not. They were, or were once, only human after all. I do not know when it started, and I do not know when it ends. All I know is what has been and what might be. And I do not think that they are the same.

The gens departed from the earth, beyond the Barrier, to space, to terraformed planetary neighbors, eventually to the heavens beyond. Some have maintained bodies of flesh and bone. Some might still remind you of yourselves. Many have given up existing in only one place. Some have the habit of multiplying themselves, indeed, sometimes even dividing themselves. Some have given up emotion and focus on thought. Some have given up thought and bathe themselves in emotion. Some do, others watch. Some have folded in on themselves and become like little black boxes, the inner workings invisible to the rest of us, locking themselves up so tight that others don't even know if they are still alive. Who knows what they think, what those black cubes plan, the question bricks? Others have expanded and connected themselves so much that one cannot tell where one ends and another begins. Others have shrunk to tightly knit communities, impenetrable to the rest of us. Some have abandoned community and launched themselves into the deepness of space to wallow in their own thoughts and creations of the mind. Others have launched themselves towards the reality of yet other worlds, to colonize, to explore, to adventure, to escape, to live. And a few had grander plans.

As for the little blue ball rolling around the sun, after the green rain the truds inherited the earth, and the distinctions were no longer Trud and Gen, but Fanatic and Faithful, Northlander and Southlander, Advancer and Purified, Us and Them... and many things in between.

The one called Michael stayed behind with Maren. Michael lived in the Refuge Territories, still engaged in the pursuit, hunting big game on the plains until he was called to another purpose. As for Maren, should I once more call her Clara? Or should we instead name her for what she was to become?

I discover now that the influence of the past is not as easy to change as I once imagined, and the future changes more than I thought possible. If I could do it over, I am not sure that I would. But at the same time, I can't let go of whom I have become. The question is: could one change it, even if one wanted to?

Now, at the rising dawn of technology, long before its light has fallen into darkness, you have a choice. Modology, the technology of change, is on the horizon, and decisions cast a long shadow. Some will attempt to hasten its arrival. Others will try to stop it. Some will try to make it different. Others will do nothing. And one of you will not understand its true meaning for many years.

As for me, I still wonder if I made the right decision, or if it was even me who made it. Perhaps I have changed. Or perhaps I just remember the way I was before.

Because before, out there somewhere in the sea of humanity, I am you and you are me, the shadow of the future.